Howard Waldrop

DOUG POTTER

Heart of Whitenesse

Heart of Whitenesse

Howard Waldrop

SUBTERRANEAN PRESS • 2005

ISBN
1-59606-018-2

Subterranean Press
P. O. Box 190106
Burton, MI 48519

e-mail:
info@subterraneanpress.com

website:
www.subterraneanpress.com

Contents

In Mississippi long ago, Jiggs and Frissie and Ben; and in Texas these years, Butch and Rat and Watson and Clash and Peaches: *Here, doggies, doggies.*

Introduction:
The Perpetual Halloween

Last time (*Going Home Again,* Eidolon 1997/St. Martins 1998) I said, "see you 'long 'bout the Millenium."

At my age, three or four years off ain't bad.

And now, after 7½ years in the Pacific NW, I find myself, after a short detour to Cowtown, back where I was for more than two decades, Austin TX.

All the stories in here (except the original) were done while I lived in Oso, WA (even though one was written in Perth, Australia on a blazing hot January day) between 1995 and 2002.

I think they're just about the most varied bunch of stories I've ever done. There are the usual accouterments you'll find in all my collections; the stories, an Afterword to each one telling you something about the writing of them; there's even an explication that was printed *with* one of them...

And they seem to be coming (with a few exceptions) harder every time out. Is it me? Have I slowed down that much? Or is it that I'm having to go further ("more stenuous marches on the liver" in Norman Mailer's phrase) every time in an effort not to repeat myself, ever?

As I tell students at the various Clarion SF Workshops: Writing Is Hard. I've been doing this for 3½ decades now: As Gary Larson *(The Far Side)* said, If I knew I had to keep it up this long I would have paced myself. But you never know what it's going to look like *backwards,* which is what we call a career, when you're starting out.

Howard Waldrop

I hope there are some surprises in here for you (besides the original, I mean.) Some of them surprised me, while I was writing them. I'm proud of them, with good reason.
If you keep reading them, I'll keep writing them.

—Howard Waldrop
Deepinahearta, TX

The Dynasters

Vol. I
On the Downs

Ug and his friends stood in front of the hillock, wondering how to get the bear out of the good cave. It was getting colder, and the other cave leaked.

Meanwhile the women and children were doing something useful like finding stuff to eat.

The men looked at the cave.

"Stick holes in same time?" asked Ab.

"You *seen* thing?" asked Nu.

"No," said Ab.

Ug spread his arms wide, hairs fluttering in the cold wind. Then his son Nu jumped up on his shoulders and held his hand up as high as he could.

"*That* big?" asked Ab, and looked at the cave again.

Mo was chewing one of the last leaves. They turned to him.

"Stick fire in face," he said.

They ran around gathering up stuff.

Afterwards, he was known as Mo the Smart.

∞∞∞∞

They stood at the water's edge, in the snow, under the high white cliffs.

From the top of them you could see more land way way off, across the Big Water. Only now, where the bottoms of the cliffs used to be covered, there was much sand and rock. It went far out before the water began there.

"Bad feeling," said Ug.

"What happening?" asked Ab.

"No know," said Ug. "Will ask Mo."

On the way back to the cave, on the path, they threw their pointy sticks into one of the Big Head-horn things that was browsing in the crusted snow. It took them half the day to drag it back to the other people.

∞∞∞∞

"Uh-oh," said Nunu.

She ran back to the cave as fast as she could through the thick snow, putting her feet in the holes she'd made coming out.

"Quick!" she said. "Stoop-shouldered guys big jaws coming!"

They grabbed their clubs and pointy sticks and all ran to the top of the cliffs.

Out a ways on the mud and sand ramp that divided the two parts of the Big Water, which stretched out toward the land far away you could almost see when it was clear, men were coming. They could see their big jaws this far away, and their skins flapped around them, dark in the breeze.

Mo counted.

"We more," he said.

"Get 'em," said Ug.

ᴏᴏᴏᴏᴏ

Afterwards, they found that the big jaws belonged to the men themselves, and admired them. They were large and were out in front of the mouth. Some of the children wobbled those of the dead ones—yaga yaga yaga. Their teeth were all different too, the front ones not as sharp.

But the skins, which had flapped and fluttered around them while they were fighting, were not theirs at all. They belonged to dead animals. They could be taken off the stoop-shouldered men.

Ug wrapped one around himself. After a while he said, "Hey! This warm!"

They rushed to grab them.

Mo was looking at the sandy causeway.

"Next time, bring more," he said, pointing toward the far land. "They tough. Take long time die."

Ug had two skins wrapped around him. He danced.

"Hey!" he said. "What have supper?"

ᴏᴏᴏᴏᴏ

Nu looked for the bug crawling in the fur of his leg, found it, pinched it to pieces.

It was his time to watch from the top of the tall cliffs as he had done many many times before in his youth and early manhood. Now he had children of his own. The stoop-shouldered guys big jaws never had come back. It had gotten colder, though there had been a few golden summers in there.

He sighed, and watched, and waited, and hummed the song about the big animal with the horn in the middle of its nose.

∞∞∞

Mo the tenth Smart sat at the edge of the cliff on a cool summer night and looked at the quarter moon. His grandson little Nu lay beside him, looking up at the summer stars and the pictures they made—the Big Thing, the other Big Thing, the Ugly Thing, the Little Boy with the Snake.

"Which that?" he asked.

"That Woman with Stick," said Mo the tenth Smart.

"Over there?"

There was a long pale light across the sky with a bright dot at the front.

"That Girl Look for Husband," said Mo. He poked little Nu in the ribs. "Maybe marry you. She come round long time between. Mo the fourth Smart saw; told Mo seventh Smart who saw, Mo tell me."

Little Nu rolled over and looked at the moon.

"Will Moon get eaten tonight?" he asked. It had happened when he was very little and it had scared him.

Mo pointed. "Remember words Mo fifth Smart: 'Quick bites come out Moon only full.'"

"Forget."

"Learn not forget," said Mo the tenth Smart.

He looked over at the big strip of land that went between the two shallow Big Waters. As usual there was just dirt and the bushes that grew there.

Little Nu propped himself up on his elbows.

"Where come from, Grandad Mo?"

"From cave," said Mo, and laughed.

"No! Where come from? All us?"

"We always here," said Mo the tenth Smart.

ooooo

Weena and Oola lashed together the summer hut with tendons from one of the big red deer. The breeze was warm. They were setting up the hut near the break in the cliffs where the stream came through.

Mo the many Smart stood looking at the mouth of the stream. Some of the men and boys floated on logs, sticking things in small fish, or falling off into the water beyond its mouth. There was once more Big Water all across in front of the cliffs though it was not very deep.

"Something bother?" Oola asked him.

"Yummy fish not back."

Every year big fish had shown up at the mouth of the stream, which was up the coast from where the land used to divide the Big Water. They came up in the stream. You could stick things in them, or hit them with rocks, or pick them up with your hands. They ignored you, only continuing to make eggs and sticky stuff and flopping around. They did that for most of a moon, and everybody ate and ate until they made fish puddles from their mouths.

"Next moon," said Oola.

"No," said Mo the many Smart. "Next moon when come while land *there.*" He pointed. "Land not there. They come this moon when used come before land there. All Mo's know when that was. Now should come this moon."

"Me see day before day," said Oola.

"Is where?"

"There." She pointed down the coast where the Big Water curved around into the Big Big Water. "Them come. Them swim round. Then go that way." She waved her hand, indicating the Big Big Water. "Go round all land-world. Here next moon."

"Why them do that?" asked Mo. "Them right here!"

Oola lifted her shoulders and raised her hands.

"Hmmm," said Mo the many Smart.

∞∞∞

A moon later, in the middle of the night, they heard flopping in the creek. They all ran down there with sticks with pointy deer horns on them and clubs and rocks. For most of that moon they ate and ate and ate.

Mo the many Smart lay between two big broken chalk boulders. His stomach was stretched tight under his fur. He could barely move.

Oola walked up to him.

"Told so," she said.

"Not forget," said Mo. Then he made another fish puddle from his mouth.

∞∞∞

After a storm, Nu the many-many ran into his hut.

"Stop dinner!" he said.

"Make leg-of-wolf roasted tubers," said A-la the many.

"Change plans," said Nu the many-many. "Blue painted guy some jaw wash up, log thing. Jabber a lot. Ug the many-many poke him, no feel ribs. Big feast coming, yum yum eatem up. Have wolf day-add-day."

"Blue paint some jaw?" asked A-la. "Not pictured up guy some jaw?"

"No. That one-back-one. This blue all over. Paint come off. White as cliff."

A-la sighed. *Men!*

∞∞∞

Ab the many-many had troubled eyes, yellow and far-seeing.

He was on the cliff, looking toward the land you could barely make out.

He came up to look at it often. He did his work in the village on the downs, but his mind was not in it.

He came down to where the men and boys were making log-boats that would hold man-add-man for fishing.

"What there?" he asked Mo the lot Smart.

"Big Trouble," said Mo.

"How know? Every time man come we eat," said Ab the many-many.

"Goes back long way land here," said Mo. "Land come. Stoop-shouldered guys big jaw come. More try come before land go way. Then grandfather time pictured up guys some jaw and blue painted guys some jaw wash up. No be too careful."

"What we know them?" asked Ab.

"Them trouble," said Mo.

"Me find out!" said Ab, jerking his thumb toward his chest fur.

"Smart of ages, Ab," said Mo. "No look trouble. Trouble find anyway."

"Me find out," said Ab.

∞∞∞

They had watched him build a boat-log that would hold man-add-man-add-man. It had taken him day-add-day-add-day. Then he put his pointy stick, his club, hide cloak, and food into it. Then he launched it, pushed out, lined up on the big white cliff and began to paddle hard.

They sang him the song of safe journey, Ug the lot himself beating on the big singing log. Then they went up to the top of the cliff and watched until he was lost from sight.

∞∞∞

It was almost a moon later that one of the fishermen called them all from their huts in the village on the downs, and they went to the shore beneath the cliffs.

It was late afternoon and there was a dot on the water. It got bigger but very slowly.

"It Ab," called down the watchman from the cliffs.

He came to shore slowly. He paddled with only one arm. When he was close enough they saw one of his eyes was missing and his head was swollen up on that side. His right arm flopped at his side. He beached the log and hopped out, bracing himself with his left arm. (Some things a person has to do themselves.) His right foot was missing toe-add-toe-add-toe.

"Hello, Ab," said Mo the lot Smart.

He was looking back across the water with his good eye. "No understand, Mo," he said. "They kill each other over there *all* the time."

"*All* the time?"

"All the time. Every day."

"Come. Me fix up," said Mo.

"Something do first," said Ab. He leaned down in the log-boat and made a big fire, and they all watched it burn.

"Mo?" asked Ab, as cinders drifted over them on the beach.

"What, Ab?"

"Mo. Me ever want go somewhere again, kill me with club."

"Can do," said Mo.

Then they led him back toward the village huts.

ⲟⲟⲟⲟⲟ

Then came big nosed guys some jaw, and they brought with them the Great Big Things with Long Noses and Two Big Curved Teeth. They came in big log-boats with big square hides on trees and many many paddlers.

Ug the lot-many-lot said, "Get all people up down coast, jump on them."

The big nosed guys some jaw lined up all together in one place with shiny pointy sticks all sticking out in one place. In front of them they put the Great Big Things with the Long Noses and the Two Big Curved Teeth.

"They just like old ones great-great-many-many grand-fathers hunted. Only they no have hair," said Mo, the lot-many Smart.

"We know how do *them*," said Ug the lot-many-lot. "Get 'em."

ⲟⲟⲟⲟⲟ

The fattest big nosed guy some jaw they chose for signal honors.

They whacked up the Great Big Things with the Long Noses and the Two Big Curved Teeth, the people of the other villages carrying off as much as they could.

They found that the one-add-one-add-one big log-boats were filled with men who were fastened where they sat. They jabbered, afraid. The people broke up the things that held them down with some of the useful hard implements they found. They herded all the loosened men onto one big log-boat.

Ug the lot-many-lot made a shooing motion with his hands.

"Go way," he said. "Go way."

The men looked at him a moment. Then they began yelling and making noise and running up and down and below into the log-boat, and the big hide flopped down and they waved and yelled and ran out of sight and the paddles all started working. And the big log-boat went out of sight toward where the Big Big Water started.

They wrapped the fattest big nosed guy some jaw with the things which had held the paddlers to the log-boats.

He jabbered, but he stood straight and tall.

Ug the lot-many-lot leaned in very close.

"Yum yum eatem up," he said.

∞∞∞∞

Nu the lot-many-many stood on the cliff, looking back over the downs and the village. He could see a herd of the red deer browsing not very far away, and further up a flock of birds drank at the mouth of the creek. He could see women gathering seeds at the weed fields, and a couple of men were out killing hares up near the boggy place.

Down in the village, the gray shapes of the old boat-logs from many-lot-great-grandfather time, which had been made into a meeting place where the people from all up and down the coast came every twelve moons to make Ug All-Boss, stood out from the other hide and mud huts. Here and there was smoke from a cooking fire. He raised his eyes and could just see smoke from the next village far up the coast.

He turned his eyes back to the Big Water, still dull in the early morning sun, and the far smudge of the land you could barely make out. It was going to be a warm fine day, and Mo the lot-lot-many Smart said it was just one more moon until the yummy fish came up the creek again, and there were signs of a mild winter.

Later he would go down, he thought, and join the boys poking sticks into the little fish that were always in the Big Water. They would have to do until the yummy fish came in.

∞∞∞

Girl Look For Husband was in the sky. Even in the late afternoon, a swatch of white with a glowing head stretched halfway across the heavens. "She *really* looking this time," the people said.

All-Boss Ug the lot-many-lot was fixing his hut, pounding wooden pegs in with a big rock.

"Grandfather! Grandfather!" yelled little Nu the lot-many-lot, running in from the cliffs.

"Not have time everyone come in flaring sagittal crest," said Ug. "What now?"

"Ab many-lot-lot say big logs come again. Come quick bring clubs pointy sticks."

Ug dropped the rock and began to yell everyone out of their huts and send ones running to the other villages.

∞∞∞

All the people stood on the big white cliffs. It would have been dark had not Girl Look For Husband been blazing bright as a full Moon. Everything was a sort of silver-gray twilight.

They looked down where lot-many boat-logs were drawn up on the beach and saw (what Ab who had seen them before dark had said were) weasel-eyed guys some jaw there. Many-many-lot. They all had long pointy sticks with shiny ends and shiny flat things on their hip-clothes, and some had curvy things on their backs and bags full of little sticks.

Ug poked Mo the lot-many-many Smart.

"More them than us," said Mo.

"Not wait day," said Ug. "Go get 'em!"

Yelling and waving their clubs and pointy sticks, they charged down the hills.

Afterword to "The Dynasters"

As far as I know, in the whole history of this terraqueous globe, I'm the only person ever to write a story about Piltdown Man (and Woman).

∞∞∞∞∞

In case you're not hep to the jive, here's the short version: Early 1900s, amateur archaeologist in England finds fossil skull on the downs; big human skull brain-case, big ape-looking jaw, stained from the ferruginous soils of the local gravel beds. Science goes wild—after initial skepticism; for instance, place where primitive jaw-process meets human skull is conveniently missing—this is *just the thing* the theories of the time were looking for—brain developed before rest of the body left the ape-like (as opposed to current theories that everything developed together—better eyesight, upright posture, omnivorous eating habits). "The First Englishman" they called him (although there were no fossil greater apes in Britain), *eoanthropus dawsonii*, "Dawson's Dawn Man". Tielhard du Chardin—still a seminary student at the time—was in on some later finds at a quarry a couple of miles away. The British Museum got involved; all the books were rewritten to shoehorn Piltdown Man into the evolutionary ladder leading to *us* (the Whig Theory of History).

By and by radiocarbon dating comes along in the late 1940s as a byproduct of the Atomic Age, and they slap ol' P. Man's skull down and *voila!*—it's an old human skull and a recent orangutan's jaw. The orang teeth have been filed down to look more human, and the whole thing was probably buried a couple of years in wet gravel to get the uniform staining, then "found" later.

In other words, Science Had Been Had.

There've now been five or six books on the hoax, blaming this or that person—all of whom were dead by the time the carbon-dating had been done, except du Chardin. Most likely suspect: the amateur archaeologist, everyone else was duped—but persons ranging from du Chardin—dead by the time the charge was made against *him*—to Sir Arthur Conan Doyle, who lived a few miles away, but the finds were made long before he went over to Spiritualism and had an axe to grind with science…

∞∞∞

I got to thinking, why not Piltdown Man? How about a world where there were Piltdown People? What would that be like? Well, they'd have to remain isolated somehow, at least till up toward the Middle Ages—the exact opposite history of the British Isles, which is nothing but wave after wave of peoples looking for more chow, tin, and a longer growing season.

You'd have to talk about the land bridge that used to exist between southern France, Spain and Britain (which is the reason the "yummy fish"—Atlantic Salmon—still go *all the way around Scotland* to get to the Thames and other southern rivers.) You'd have to make the Piltdown People pretty tough and at the same time not breed themselves out of food.

You'd have to deal with their increasing intelligence and show it to be folly of a different kind: they were just right at the time for the conditions they lived under. It's the conditions that changed on them—the rise of other species with more organization, and more, in a way, ruthless.

So I did all that. With a nod to Thomas Hardy and the Little Rascals' short "The Kid from Borneo." Someone said, if you want to make money, write a generation-spanning saga of a family down hundreds of years.

So I said, okay, and did it in 3000-something words or so in a day.

This was published in the 50th Anniversary Issue of *The Magazine of Fantasy and Science Fiction*. I was as pleased as butter to be in there.

I'm the *only* guy in there without his name on the cover…

Mr. Goober's Show

You know how it is:

There's a bar on the corner, where hardly anybody knows your name, and you like it that way. Live bands play there two or three nights a week. Before they start up it's nice, and on the nights they don't play—there's a good jukebox, the big TV's on low on ESPN all the time. At his prices the owner should be a millionaire but he's given his friends so many free drinks they've forgotten they should pay for more than every third or fourth one. Not that you know the owner, but you've watched.

You go there when your life's good, you go there when your life's bad; mostly you go there instead of having a good or bad life.

And one night, fairly crowded, you're on the stools so the couples and the happy people can have the booths and tables. Someone's put $12 in the jukebox (and they have some taste), the TV's on the Australian Thumb-Wrestling Finals, the neon beer signs are on, and the place looks like the inside of the Ferris Wheel on opening night at the state fair.

You start talking to the guy next to you, early fifties, your age, and you get off on TV (you can talk to any American, except a Pentecostal, about television) and you're talking the classic stuff; the last *Newhart* episode, *Northern Exposure;* the episode where Lucy stomps the grapes; the coast-to-coast bigmouth *Dick Van Dyke; Howdy-Doody* (every eight-year-old boy in America had a jones for Princess Summer-Fall-Winter-Spring.)

And the guy, whose name you know is Eldon (maybe he told you, maybe you were born knowing it) starts asking you about some sci-fi show from the early fifties, maybe you didn't get it, maybe it was only on local upstate New York, sort of, it sounds like, a travelogue, like the old *Seven League Boots*, only about space, stars and such, planets...

"Well, no," you say, "there was *Tom Corbett, Space Cadet; Space Patrol; Captain Video* (which you never got but knew about), *Rod Brown of the Rocket Rangers; Captain Midnight* (or *Jet Jackson, Flying Commando*, depending on whether you saw it before or after Ovaltine quit sponsoring it, and in reruns people's lips flapped around saying *'Captain Midnight'* but what came out was *'Jet Jackson'*...)

"Or maybe one of the anthology shows, *Twilight Zone* or *Tales of—*"

"No," he says, "not them. See, there was this TV..."

"Oh," you say, "a TV. Well, the only one I know of was this one where a guy at a grocery store (one season) invents this TV that contacts..."

"No," he says, looking at you (Gee, this guy can be intense!). "I don't mean *Johnny Jupiter*, which is what you were going to say. Jimmy Duckweather invents TV. Contacts Jupiter, which is inhabited by puppets when they're inside the TV, and by guys in robot suits when they come down to Earth, and almost cause Duckweather to lose his job and not get a date with the boss's daughter, episode after episode, two seasons."

"Maybe you mean *Red Planet Mars*, a movie. Peter Graves—"

"...Andrea King, guy invents hydrogen tube; Nazis; Commies; Eisenhower president, Jesus speaks from Mars."

"Well, *The Twonky*. Horrible movie, about a TV from the future?"

"Hans Conreid. Nah, that's not it."

And so it goes. The conversation turns to other stuff *(you're* not the one with The Answer) and mostly it's conversation you forget because, if all the crap we carry around in our heads were real, and it was flushed, the continents would drown, and you forget it, and mostly get drunk and a little maudlin, slightly depressed and mildly horny, and eventually you go home.

But it doesn't matter, because this isn't your story, it's Eldon's.

ooooo

When he was eight years old, city-kid Eldon and his seven-year-old sister Irene were sent off for two weeks in the summer of 1953, to Aunt Joanie's house in upstate New York while, not known to them, their mother had a hysterectomy.

Aunt Joanie was not their favorite aunt; that was Aunt Nonie, who would as soon whip out a Monopoly board, or Game of Life, or checkers as look at you, and always took them off on picnics or fishing or whatever it was she thought they'd like to do. But Aunt Nonie (their *mom's* youngest sister) was off in Egypt on a cruise she'd won in a slogan contest for pitted dates, so it fell to Aunt Joanie (their *father's* oldest sister) to keep them the two weeks.

Their father's side of the family wasn't the fun one. If an adult unbent toward a child a little, some other family member would be around to remind them they were just children. Their cousins on that side of the family (not that Aunt Joanie or Uncle Arthridge had any) were like mice; they had to take off their shoes and put on house slippers when they got home from school; they could never go into the family room; they had to be in bed by 8:30 PM, even when the sun was still up in the summer.

Uncle Arthridge was off in California, so it was just them and Aunt Joanie, who, through no fault of her own, looked just like the Queen in *Snow White and the Seven Dwarves*, which they had seen with Aunt Nonie the summer before.

They arrived by train, white tags stuck to them like turkeys in a raffle, and a porter had made sure they were comfortable. When Irene had been upset, realizing she would be away from home, and was going to be at Aunt Joanie's for two weeks, and had begun to sniffle, Eldon held her hand. He was still at the age where he could hold his sister's hand against the world and think nothing of it.

Aunt Joanie was waiting for them in the depot on the platform, and handed the porter a $1.00 tip, which made him smile.

And then Aunt Joanie drove them, allowing them to sit in the front seat of her Plymouth, to her house, and there they were.

ooooo

At first, he thought it might be a radio.

It was up on legs, the bottom of them looking like eagle claws holding a wooden ball. It wasn't a sewing machine cabinet, or a table. It might be a liquor cabinet, but there wasn't a keyhole.

It was the second day at Aunt Joanie's and he was already cranky. Irene had had a crying jag the night before and their aunt had given them some ice cream.

He was exploring. He already knew every room; there was a basement *and* an attic. The real radio was in the front room; this was in the sitting room at the back.

One of the reasons they hadn't wanted to come to Aunt Joanie's was that she had no television, like their downstairs neighbors, the Stevenses did, back in the city. They'd spent the first part of summer vacation downstairs in front of it, every chance they got. Two weeks at Aunt Nonie's without television would have been great, because she wouldn't have given them time to think, and would have them exhausted by bedtime anyway.

But two weeks at Aunt Joanie's and Uncle Arthridge's without television was going to be murder. She had let them listen to radio, but not the scary shows, or anything good. And *Johnny Dollar* and *Suspense* weren't on out here, she was sure.

So he was looking at the cabinet in the sitting room. It had the eagle-claw legs. It was about three feet wide, and the part that was solid started a foot and a half off the floor. There was two feet of cabinet above that. At the back was a rounded part, with air holes in it, like a Lincoln Continental spare tire holder. He ran his hand over it—it was made out of that same stuff as the backs of radios and televisions.

There were two little knobs on the front of the cabinet though he couldn't see a door. He pulled on them. Then he turned and pulled on them.

They opened, revealing three or four other knobs, and a metal toggle switch down at the right front corner. They didn't look like radio controls. It didn't look like a television either. There was no screen.

There was no big lightning-bolt moving dial like on their radio at home in the city.

Then he noticed a double-line of wood across the top front of it, like on the old icebox at his grandfather's. He pushed on it from the floor. Something gave, but he couldn't make it go farther.

Eldon pulled a stool up to the front of it.

"What are you doing?" asked Irene.

"This must be another radio," he said. "This part lifts up."

He climbed atop the stool. He had a hard time getting his fingers under the ridge. He pushed.

The whole top of the thing lifted up a few inches. He could see glass. Then it was too heavy. He lifted at it again after it dropped down, and this time it came up halfway open.

There was glass on the under-lid. It was a mirror. He saw the reflection of part of the room. Something else moved below the mirror, inside the cabinet.

"Aunt Joanie's coming!" said Irene.

He dropped the lid and pushed the stool away and closed the doors.

"What are you two little cautions doing?" asked Aunt Joanie from the other room.

∞∞∞

The next morning, when Aunt Joanie went to the store on the corner, he opened the top while Irene watched.

The inner lid was a mirror that stopped halfway up, at an angle. Once he got it to a certain point, it clicked into place. There was a noise from inside and another click. He looked down into it. There was a big dark glass screen. "It's a *television!*" he said.

"Can we get *Howdy-Doody?*"

"I don't know," he said.

"You better ask Aunt Joanie, or you'll get in trouble."

He clicked the toggle switch. Nothing happened.

"It doesn't work," he said.

"Maybe it's not plugged in," said Irene.

Eldon lay down on the bare floor at the edge of the area rug, saw the prongs of a big electric plug sticking out underneath. He pulled on it. The cord uncoiled from behind. He looked around for the outlet. The nearest one was on the far wall.

"What are you two doing?" asked Aunt Joanie, stepping into the room with a small grocery bag in her arms.

"Is...is this a television set?" asked Eldon.

"Can we get *Howdy-Doody?*" asked Irene.

Aunt Joanie put down the sack. "It is a television. But it won't work any more. There's no need to plug it in. It's an old-style one, from before the war. They don't work like that anymore. Your uncle Arthridge and I bought it in 1938. There were no broadcasts out here then, but we thought there would be soon."

As she was saying this, she stepped forward, took the cord from Eldon's hands, rewound it and placed it behind the cabinet again.

"Then came the war, and everything changed. These kind won't work anymore. So we shan't be playing with it, shall we? It's probably dangerous by now."

"Can't we try it, just once?" said Eldon.

"I do not think so," said Aunt Joanie. "Please put it out of your mind. Go wash up now, we'll have lunch soon."

∞∞∞

Three days before they left, they found themselves alone in the house again, in the early evening. It had rained that afternoon, and was cool for summer.

Irene heard scraping in the sitting room. She went there and found Eldon pushing the television cabinet down the bare part of the floor toward the electrical outlet on the far wall.

He plugged it in. Irene sat down in front of it, made herself comfortable. "You're going to get in trouble," she said. "What if it explodes?"

He opened the lid. They saw the reflection of the television screen in it from the end of the couch.

He flipped the toggle. Something hummed, there was a glow in the back, and they heard something spinning. Eldon put his hand near the round part and felt pulses of air, like from a weak fan. He could see lights through the holes in the cabinet, and something was moving.

He twisted a small knob, and light sprang up in the picture-tube part, enlarged and reflected in the mirror on the lid. Lines of bright static moved up the screen and disappeared in a repeating pattern.

He turned another knob, the larger one, and the bright went dark and then bright again.

Then a picture came in.

∞∞∞

They watched those last three days, every time Aunt Joanie left; afraid at first, watching only a few minutes, then

34

turning it off, unplugging it, and closing it up and pushing it back into its place, careful not to scratch the floor.

Then they watched more, and more, and there was an excitement each time they went through the ritual, a tense expectation.

Since no sound came in, what they saw they referred to as "Mr. Goober's Show," from his shape, and his motions, and what went on around him. He was on anytime they turned the TV on.

ooooo

They left Aunt Joanie's reluctantly. She had never caught them watching it. They took the train home.

Eldon was in a kind of anxiety. He talked to all his friends, who knew nothing about anything like that, and some of them had been as far away as San Francisco during the summer. The only person he could talk to about it was his little sister, Irene.

He did not know what the jumpiness in him was.

ooooo

They rushed into Aunt Joanie's house the first time they visited at Christmas, and ran to the sitting room.

The wall was blank.

They looked at each other, then ran back into the living room.

"Aunt Joanie," said Eldon, interrupting her, Uncle Arthridge and his father. "Aunt Joanie, where's the television?"

"Television…? Oh, that thing. I sold it to a used furniture man at the end of the summer. He bought it for the cabinetry, he said, and was going to make an aquarium out of it. I suppose he sold the insides for scrap."

∞∞∞

They grew up, talking to each other, late at nights about what they had seen. When their family got TV, they spent their time trying to find it again.

Then high school, then college, the '60s. Eldon went to Nam, came back about the same.

Irene got a job in television, and sent him letters, while he taught bookkeeping at a junior college.

∞∞∞

April 11, 1971

Dear Bro'—

I ran down what kind of set Aunt Joanie had.

It was a *mechanical* television, with a Nipkov disk scanner. It was a model made between 1927 and 1929.

Mechanical: yes. You light a person, place, thing, very very brightly. On one side of the studio's photoelectric cells that turn light to current. Between the subject and the cells, you drop in a disk that spins 300 times a minute. Starting at the edge of the disk, and spiraling inward all the way around to the center are holes. You have a slit-scan shutter. As the light leaves the subject it's broken into a series of lines by the holes passing across the slit. The photoelectric cells pick up the pulses of light.

(An orthicon tube does exactly the same thing, except electronically, in a camera, and your modern TV is just a big orthicon tube on the other end.) Since it was a mechanical signal, your disk in the cabinet at home had to spin at exactly the same rate. So they had to send out a regulating signal at the same time.

Not swell, not good definition, but workable.

But Aunt Joanie (rest her soul) was right— nothing in 1953 was broadcasting that it could receive, because all early prewar televisions were made with the picture-portion going out on FM, and the sound going out on shortwave. (So her set had receivers for both) *and* neither of them are where TV is *now* on the wavelengths (where they've been since 1946.)

Mr. Goober could not have come from an FCC licensed broadcaster in 1953. I'll check Canada and Mexico, but I'm pretty sure everything was moved off those bands by then, even experimental stations. Since we never got sound, either there was none, or maybe it was coming in with the picture (like *now*) and her set couldn't separate four pieces of information (one-half each of two signals, which is why we use FM for TV.)

It shouldn't have happened, I don't think. There are weird stories (the ghost signals of a Midwest station people saw the test patterns of more than a year after they quit broadcasting. The famous 2.8 second delay in radio transmissions all over the world on shortwave in 1927 and early 1928.)

Am going to the NAB meeting in three weeks. Will talk to everybody there, especially the old guys, and find out if any of them knows about Mr. Goober's Show. Stay sweet.

Your sis,
Irene

OOOOO

Eldon began the search on his own; at parties, at bars, at ball games. During the next few years, he wrote his sister with bits of fugitive matter he'd picked up. And he got quite a specialized knowledge of local TV shows, kid's show clowns, *Shock Theater* hosts, and eclectic local programming of the early 1950s, throughout these United States.

OOOOO

June 25, 1979

Dear Eldon—

Sorry it took so long to get this letter off to you, but I've been busy at work, and helping with the Fund Drive, and I also think I'm on to something. I've just run across stuff that indicates there was some kind of medical outfit that used radio in the late '40s and early '50s.

Hope you can come home for Christmas *this* time. Mom's getting along in years, you know. I know you had your troubles with her (*I'm* the one to talk) but she really misses you. As Bill Cosby says, she's an old person trying to get into Heaven now. She's trying to be good the *second* thirty years of her life…

Will write you again as soon as I find out more about these quacks.

Your little sister,
Irene

∞∞∞

August 14, 1979

Dear Big Brother:

Well, it's depressing here. The lead I had turned out to be a bust, and I could just about cry, since I thought this might be it, since they broadcast on *both* shortwave and FM (like Aunt Joanie's set received) but this probably wasn't it, either.

It was called Drown Radio Therapy (there's something poetic about the name, but not the operation). It was named for Dr. Ruth Drown; she was an osteopath. Sometime before the War, she and a technocrat started work-. ing with a low-power broadcast device. By War's end, she was claiming she could treat disease at a distance, and set up a small broadcast station behind her suburban Los Angeles office. Patients came in, were diagnosed, and given a schedule of broadcast times when they were supposed to tune in. (The broadcasts were directed to each patient, supposedly, two or three times a day.) By the late '40s, she'd also gone into TV, which is of course FM (the radio stuff being shortwave.) That's where I'd hoped I'd found someone broadcasting at the same time on both bands.

But probably no go. She franchised the machines out to other doctors, mostly naturopaths and cancer quacks. It's possible that one was operating near Aunt Joanie's somewhere, but probably not, and anyway, a committee of docs investigated her stuff. What they found was that the equipment was so low-powered it could only broadcast a dozen miles (not counting random skipping, bouncing off the Heaviside layer, which it wouldn't have been able to reach.) Essentially they ruled the equipment worthless.

And, the thing that got to me, there was *no* picture transmission on the FM (TV) portion; just the same type of random signals that went out on shortwave, on the same schedule, every day. Even if you had a rogue cancer specialist, the FCC said the stuff couldn't broadcast a visual signal, not with the technology of the time. (The engineer at the station here looked at the specs and said 'even if they had access to video orthicon tubes, the signal wouldn't have gotten across the room, unless it was on cable, which it wasn't.')

I've gone on too long. It's not it.

Sorry to disappoint you (again). But I'm still going through back files of *Variety* and *BNJ* and everything put out by the networks in those years. And, maybe a mother lode, a friend's got a friend who knows where all the Dumont records (except Gleason's) are stored.

We'll find out yet, brother. I've heard stories of people waiting twenty, thirty, forty years to clear things like this up. There was a guy who kept insisting he'd read a serialized novel in a newspaper, about the fall of civilization, in the early 1920s. Pre-bomb, pre-almost everything. He was only a kid when he read it. Ten years ago he mentioned it to someone who had a friend who recognized it, not from a newspaper, but as a book called *Darkness and the Dawn*. It was in three parts, and serial rights were sold, on the first part only, to like, *three* newspapers in the whole U.S. And the man, now in his sixties, had read it in one of them.

Things like that do happen, kiddo.

Write me when you can.

Love,
Irene

oooooo

Sept. 12, 1982

El—

I'm ready to give up on this. It's running me crazy—not crazy, but to distraction, if I had anything else to be distracted *from*.

I can't see any way out of this except to join the Welcome Space Brothers Club, which I refuse to do.

That would be the easy way out, give up, go over to the Cheesy Side of the Force. You and me saw a travelogue, a *See It Now* of the planets, hosted by an interstellar Walter Cronkite on a Nipkov disk TV in 1953. We're the only people in the world who did. *No one else.*

But that's why CE3K and the others have made so many millions of dollars. People want to believe, but they want to believe *for other people*, not themselves. *They* don't want to be *the ones*. They want someone else to be the one. And then they want everybody to believe. But it's not *their* ass out there saying, "the Space Brothers are here; I can't prove it, take my word for it, it's real. Believe me as a person."

I'm not that person, and neither are you; OR there has to be some other answer. One, or the other, but not both; and not neither.

I don't know what to do anymore; whatever it is, it's not this. It's quit being fun. It's quit being something I do aside from life as we know it. It is my life, and yours, and it's all I've got.

I know what Mr. Goober was trying to tell us, and there was more, but the sound was off.

I'm tired. I'll write you next week when I can call my life my own again.

Your Sis

ooooo

Cops called from Irene's town the next week.

After the funeral, and the stay at his mother's, and the inevitable fights, with his stepfather trying to stay out of it, he came home and found one more letter, postmarked the same day as the police had called him.

Dear Eldon—

Remember this, and don't think less of me: what we saw was real.

Evidently, too real for me.
Find out what we saw.

Love always,
Irene

∞∞∞

So you'll be sitting in the bar, there'll be the low hum and thump of noise as the band sets up, and over in the corner, two people will be talking. You'll hear the word "Lucy" which could be many things—a girlfriend, a TV show, a late President's daughter, a 2-million year old ape-child. Then you'll hear "M-Squad" or "Untouchables" and there'll be more talk, and you'll hear distinctly, during a noise-level drop, "...and I don't mean *Johnny*-fucking-*Jupiter* either..."

And in a few minutes he'll leave, because the band will have started, and conversation, except at the 100-decibel level, is over for the night.

But he'll be back tomorrow night. And the night after. And all the star-filled nights that follow that one.

Afterword to "Mr. Goober's Show"

Written, as I said elsewhere, on a blazing hot January day when the temperature was in the high 30s…

I'm talking Perth, Western Australia. I'm talking Centigrade.

∞∞∞

They had me down for Swancon, and for the Eidolon Press publication of *Going Home Again*. On Friday night I'd read "Scientifiction," the original for *that* collection. Now, I had to read another story at 5 pm Saturday.

I got up at 5 am Saturday, and began to write and write and write. At 12:40 pm I took a shower etc. and was on a panel at 1 pm, where, in the middle of it, the *whole convention* came into the room and sang "Waltzing Matilda" to me (the words to which I've had in *every* billfold I've owned since I cut them out of a *Life* magazine article about *On the Beach* in 1959…) It was Australia Day Weekend—their Fourth of July—and I was moved beyond tears.

But I'm a pro. As soon as the panel was over, I ran back up to the room and wrote till about 4:49 pm, brushed my teeth, went down to the main room, delivered a short approving rant on Joe Dante's *Matinee,* and then read the story.

∞∞∞

After I got back to Oso, and started rewriting this, I realized I needed a piece of information on Drown Radio Therapy I didn't have (I knew enough to fudge it in the first Australian draft) and wrote Andrew P. ("call me Andy") Hooper down in

Howard Waldrop

Seattle. Off goes Andy on a rainy-ass 38° (F.) day to the Fremont Library; the third day after I mailed my letter to him, his answer chock full of cogent details and insights comes back to me. Thanks Andy, for service way above the call of friendship to this story…

So I rewrote and tightened things up, and in general did all the writer-stuff you do in second drafts, and sent it off.

There's way more coming about this one *after* it was finished.

∞∞∞

I've written about the non-linear history of mass communications before ("Hoover's Men," "The Sawing Boys")—that history of lone cranks and corporate dreamers who came up with radio, television, the copy machine—that could have led to *lots* of other places and things than what we have now (We *should* have had movies on disc before we had videotape—both RCA and CBS were working on them in the late 1960s—RCA was ready to go but with a *stylus* system, like a phonograph, and while everyone was waiting for CBS to make one with a laser, along came Sony with the Betamax….)

It was like that *all along* (later, in "Major Spacer…" I talk about the FCC Freeze of 1948-52, when *no* new TV stations were licensed, because they were fighting over color TV—RCA's system compatible with black and white sets already made; CBS going *back* to a mechanical system—as in this story—and all sets made before 1948 would have to be scrapped—as all sets made before 1941 *had been scrapped* by the postwar systems—that would have made 3 obsolete formats in 11 years…This has *always* been going on—it ain't just the Betamax/VHS/vinyl/cassette/CD/Laserdisc/DVD of *your* lifetime. This stuff started with your great-grandfather, kid, and just wait for HDTV, son….

I'd always wanted to write a story wherein the obsolete technology picked up something nobody else could *possibly* have seen or heard. And what would happen if it were *you* that had seen it?...

ᴏᴏᴏᴏᴏ

I sent this to Ellen Datlow, then at *Omni Online*. She of course bought it. *Omni* was going through one of its periodic upheavals—magazine to online. Months go by, payments taking longer—the usual. *Not* Ellen's fault. *Omni Online* puts "Mr. Goober's Show" up on March 30, 1998.

And pulls the plug on *the whole operation* on April 1, 1998.

ᴏᴏᴏᴏᴏ

On about April 3, two days after Ellen got the news and called the store and told me (All *I've* got is a story nobody's seen: *she's* out of a job...) I get a letter from Gordon van Gelder at *F&SF:* he's heard the news and wants to buy NA serial rights to the story...

So I sell those to *F&SF,* and the story comes out *again.*

Andy Hooper reads it and says "It would have made a great original *Twilight Zone* or *One Step Beyond* episode." He's probably right. (Sorry I didn't write it thirty years earlier, Andrew...)

ᴏᴏᴏᴏᴏ

But wait! There's more!

Last year a book came out on local kids' shows of early television, the late 40s to the early 60s.

There *was* a Mr. Goober's Show. Some yankee place like Pittsburgh or Cleveland. He was a doofus hayseed type and hosted cartoons. *Nothing* like my guy (who I envisioned as something like a legume with tentacles coming out the bottom, like something from George Metzger's "Master Tyme and Mobius Tripp" underground comic strip from circa 1967...)

I *swear:* I made my story *all up.* I never *heard* of that other Mr. Goober. *Really.*

∞∞∞∞∞

"There used to be this TV show. And I don't mean *Johnny Jupiter…*"

Heart of Whitenesse

For John Clute:
the hum of pleroma

Doctor Faustus?—He's dead."

∞∞∞

Down these mean cobbled lanes a man must go, methinks, especially when out before larkrise, if larks there still be within a thousand mile of this bonebreaking cold. From the Rus to Spain the world is locked in snow and ice, a sheet of blue glass. There was no summer to speak of; bread is dear, and in France we hear they are eating each other up, like the Cannibals of the Western Indies.

It's bad enow I rehearse a play at the Rose, that I work away on the poem of the celebrated Hero and Leander, that life seems more like a jakes each day. Then some unseen toady comes knocking on the door and slips a note through the latchhole this early, the pounding fist matching that in my head.

I'd come up from the covers and poured myself a cup of malmsey you could have drowned a pygmy in, then dressed as best I could, and made my way out into this cold world.

Shoreditch was dismal in the best of times, and this wasn't it.

And what do I see on gaining the lane but a man making steaming water into the street-ditch from a great bull pizzle of an accouterment.

He sees me and winks.

I winks back.

His wink said I see you're interested.

My wink back says I'm usually interested but not at this instant but keep me in mind if you see me again.

He immediately smiles, then turns his picauventure beard toward the cold row of houses to his left.

Winking is the silent language full of nuance and detail: we are after all talking about the overtures to a capital offense.

∞∞∞∞∞

I come to the shop on the note, I go in; though I've never been there before I know I can ignore the fellows working there (it is a dyer's, full of boiling vats and acrid smells and steam; at least it is *warm*) and go through a door up some rude steps, to go through another plated with strips of iron, and into the presence of a High Lord of the Realm.

He is signing something, he sees me and slides the paper under another; it is probably the names of people soon to decorate a bridge or fence. This social interaction is, too, full of nuance; one of them is that we two pretend not to know who the other is. Sometimes *their* names are Cecil, Stansfield, Salisbury, sometimes not. Sometimes my name is Christopher, or Chris, familiar Kit, or The Poet, or plain Marlowe. We do pretend, though, we have no names, that we are the impersonal representatives of great ideas and forces, moved by large motives like the clockwork Heavens themselves.

"A certain person needs enquired about," said the man behind the small table. "Earlier enquiries have proved…ineffectual. It has been thought best the next devolved to yourself. This person is beyond Oxford; make arrangements, go there quietly. Once in Oxford," he said, taking out of his sleeve a document with a wax seal upon it and laying it on the table, "you may open these, your instructions and knowledges; follow them to the letter. At a certain point, if you must follow them—thoroughly," he said, coming down hard upon the word, "we shall require a token of faith."

He was telling me without saying that I was to see someone, do something to change their mind, or keep them from continuing a present course. Failing that I was to bring back to London their heart, as in the old story of the evil stepqueen, the huntsman and the beautiful girl who ended up consorting with forest dwarves, eating poison and so forth.

I nodded, which was all I was required to do.

But he had not as yet handed me the missive, which meant he was not through.

He leaned back in his chair.

"I said your name was put forth," he said, "for this endeavor. But not by me. I know you to be a godless man, a blasphemer, most probably an invert. I so hate that the business of true good government makes occasional use of such as *you*. But the awkward circumstances of this mission, shall we say, makes some of your peccadoes absolute necessities. *Only* this would make me have any dealings with you whatsoever. There will come a reckoning one fine day."

Since he had violated the unspoken tenets of the arrangement by speaking to me personally, and, moreover, telling the plain unvarnished truth, and he knew it, I felt justified in my answer. My answer was, "As you say, Lord _____," and I used his name.

He clenched the arms of his chair, started up. Then he calmed himself, settled again. His eyes went to the other papers before him.

"I believe that is all," he said, and handed me the document.

I picked it up, turned and left.

∞∞∞

Well, work on Hero and Leander's right out for a few days, but I betook me as fast as the icy ways would let, from my precincts in Shoreditch through the city. Normally it would mean going about over London Bridge, but as I was in a hurry I walked straight across the River directly opposite the Rose to the theater itself in Southwark.

The River was, and had been for two months, frozen to a depth of five feet all the way to Gravesend. Small boys ran back and forth across the river. Here and there were set up booths with stiff frozen awnings; the largest concatenation of them was further up past the town at Windsor, where Her Majesty the Queen had proclaimed a Frost Fair and set up a Royal Pavilion. A man with a bucket and axe was chopping the River for chunks of water. Others walked the ice and beat at limbs and timbers embedded in it—free firewood was free, in any weather. A thick pall of smoke hung over London town, every fire lit. A bank of heavy cloud hung further north than that. There were tales that when the great cold had come, two months agone, flocks of birds in flight had fallen to the ground and shattered; cattle froze standing.

To make matters worse, the Plague, which had closed the theaters for three months this last, long-forgotten summer, had not gone completely away, as all hoped, and was still taking thirty a week on the bills of mortality. It would probably be back again this summer and close the Theater, the Curtain and the Rose once more. Lord Strange's and Lord Nottingham's Men would again have to take to touring the provinces beyond seven mile from London.

But as for now, cold or no, at the Rose, we put on plays each afternoon without snow in the open-air ring. At the moment we do poor old Greene's *Friar Bacon and Friar Bungay*—Greene not dead these seven months, exploded from dropsy in a flop, they sold the clothes off him and buried him in a diaper with a wreath of laurel about his head—we rehearse mine own *Massacre at Paris*, and Shaxber's *Harry Sixt*, while we play his *T. Andronicus* alternate with Thom Kyd's *Spanish Tragedy*, of which *Andronicus* is an overheated feeble Romanish imitation.

Shaxber's also writing a longish poem, his on the celebrated Venus and Adonis, which at this rate will be done before my Hero. This man, the same age as me, bears watching. Unlike when I did at Cambridge, I take no part in the Acting; Will Shaxber is forever being messengers, third murderer, courtier; he tugs ropes when engines are needed; he counts reciepts, he makes himself useful withall.

No one here this early but Will Kemp; he snores as usual on his bed of straw and ticking in the 'tiring house above and behind the stage. He sounds the bear that's eaten all the dogs on a good day at the Pit. I find some ink (almost frozen) and leave a note for John Alleyn to take over for me, pleading urgent business *down* country, to throw off the scent, and make my way, this time over the Bridge, back to Shoreditch.

∞∞∞

Shoreditch is the place actors live, since it was close to the original theaters, and so it is the place actors die. Often enough first news you hear on a morning is "Another actor dead in Shoreditch." Never East Cheap, or Spital Fields, not even Southwark itself; always Shoreditch. At a tavern, at their lodgings, in the street itself. Turn them over; if it's not the Plague, it's another actor dead from a knife, fists, drink, pox, for all that matter cannonfire or hailstones in the remembered summers.

I make arrangements; I realign myself to other stations; my sword stays in its corner, my new hat, my velvet doublet all untied, hung on their hooks. I put on round slops, a leathern tunic, I cut away my beard; in place of sword a ten-inch poinard, a pointed slouchhat, a large sack for my back.

In an hour I am back at River-side, appearing as the third of the three P's in John Heywood's *The Four PPPP's*, a 'pothecary, ready to make my way like him, at least as far as Oxenford.

The ferrymen are all on holiday, their boats put up on timbers above the ice. Here and there people skate, run shoed on the ice, slip and fall; the gaiety seems forced, not like the fierce abandon of the early days of the Great Frost. But I have been watching on my sojourn each day to and from the Rose, and I lick my finger and stick it up (the spit freezing almost at once) to test the wind, and as I know the wind, and I know my man, I walk about halfway out on the solid Thames and wait.

As I wait, I see two figures dressed much like the two Ambassadores From Poland in my *Massacre At Paris* (that is, not very well, one of them being Kemp) saunter toward me on the dull gray ice. I know them to be a man named Frizier and one named Skeres, Gram and Nicholas I believe, both to be bought for a pound in any trial, both doing the occasional cony-catching, gulling and sharping; both men I have seen in taverns in Shoreditch, in Deptford, along the docks, working the theaters.

There is little way they can know me, so I assume they have taken me for a mark as it slowly becomes apparent they are approaching *me*. Their opening line, on feigning recognition, will be "Ho, sir, are you not a man from (Hereford) (Cheshire) (Luddington) known to my Cousin Jim?"

They are closer, but they say to my surprise, "Seems the man is late this day, Ingo."

"That he be, Nick."

They are waiting for the same thing I am. They take no notice of me standing but twenty feet away.

"Be damn me if it's not the fastest thing I ever seen," says one.

"I have seen the cheater-cat of Africa," says the other, "and this man would leave it standing."

"I believe you to be right."

And far down the ice, toward where the tide would be, I spy my man just before they do. If you do not know for what you look, you will think your eyes have blemished and twitched. For what comes comes fast and eclipses the background at a prodigious rate.

I drop my pack to the ground and slowly hold up a signal-jack and wave it back and forth.

"Be damn me," says one of the men, "but he's turning this way."

"How does he stop it?" asks the other, looking for shelter from the approaching apparition.

And with a grating and a great screech and plume of powdered ice, the thing turns to us and slows. It is a ship, long and thin, up on high thin rails like a sleigh, with a mast amidships and a jib up front, and as the thing slows (great double booms of teethed iron have fallen from the stern where a keelboard should be) the sails luff and come down, and the thing stops three feet from me, the stinging curtain of ice falling around me.

"Who flies Frobisher's flag?" came a voice from the back. Then up from the hull comes a huge man and threw a round anchor out onto the frozen Thames.

"I," I said. "A man who's seen you come by here these last weeks punctually. A man who marvels at the speed of your craft. And," I said, "an apothecary who needs must get to Oxford, as quick as he can."

The huge man was bearded and wore furs and a round hat in the Russian manner of some Arctic beast. "So you spoil my tack by showing my old Admiral's flag? Who'd you sail with, man? Drake? Hawkins? Raleigh, Sir Walter Tobacco himself? You weren't with Admiral Martin, else I'd know you, that's for sure."

"Never a one," said I. "My brother was with Hawkins when he shot the pantaloons off Don Iago off Portsmouth. My cousin, with one good eye before the Armada, and one bad one after, was with Raleigh."

"So you're no salt?"

"Not whatsoever."

"Where's your brother and cousin now?"

"They swallowed the anchor."

He laughed. "That so? Retired to land, eh? Some can take the sea, some can't. Captain Jack Cheese, at your service. Where is it you need to go, Oxford? Hop in, I'll have you there in two hours."

"Did you hear that, Gram?" asked one of the men. "Oxford in two hours!"

"There's no such way he can do no such thing!" said the other, looking at Captain Cheese.

"Is that money I hear talking, or only the crackling of the ice?" asked Captain Jack.

"Well, it's as much money as we have, what be that, Gram? Two fat pounds you don't make no Oxford in no two hours. As against?"

"I can use two pounds," said Jack Cheese.

"But what's *your* bet, man?" asked the other.

"Same as you. Two pound. If you'll kill me for two pounds," he said, pulling at his furry breeks and revealing the butts of two pistols the size of boarding cannons, "I'd do the same for you."

The two looked back and forth, then said, "Agreed!"

"Climb in," said Captain Jack. "Stay low, hang tight. Ship's all yar, I've got a following wind and a snowstorm crossing north from the west, and we'll be up on one runner most the time. Say your prayers now; for I don't stop for nothing nor nobody, and I don't go back for dead men nor lost bones."

The clock struck ten as we clambered aboard. My pack just hit the decking when, with a whoop, Jack Cheese jerked a rope, the jib sprang up; wind from nowhere filled it, the back of the boat screamed and wobbled to and fro. He jerked the anchor off the ice, pulled up the ice brakes and jerked the mainsail up and full.

People scattered to left and right and the iceboat leapt ahead with a dizzy shudder. I saw the backward-looking eyes of Frizier and Skeres close tight as they hung onto the gunwales with whitened hands, buffeting back and forth like skittleballs.

And the docks and quays became one long blur to left and right; then we stood still and the land moved to either side as if it were being payed out like a thick gray and white painted rope.

I looked back. Jack Cheese had a big smile on his face. His white teeth showed bright against his red skin and the brown fur; I swear he was humming.

∞∞∞∞

Past Richmond we went, and Cheese steered out further toward the leftward bank as the stalls, awnings, booths and bright red of the Royal Pavilion appeared, flung themselves to our right and receded behind.

Skizz was the only sound; we sat still in the middle of the noise and the objects flickering on and off, small then large then small again, side to side. Ahead, above the River, over the whiteness of the landscape and the ice, the dark line of cloud grew darker, thicker, lower.

Skeres and Frizier lay like dead men, only their grips on the hull showing them to be conscious.

I leaned my head closer to Captain Cheese.

"A word of warning," I said. "Don't trust those two."

"Hell and damn, son," he smiled. "I don't trust *you!* Hold tight," he said, pulling something. True to his word, in the stillness, one side of the iceboat rose up two feet off the level, we sailed along with the sound halved, slowly dropped back down to both iron runners, level. I looked up. The mainsail was tight as a pair of Italian leggings.

"There goes Hampton. Coming up on Staines!" he called out so the two men in front could have heard him if they'd chosen to.

A skater flashed by inches away. "Damn fool lubber!" said Jack Cheese. "I got sea-road rights-of-way!" A deer paused, flailed away, fell and was gone, untouched behind us.

And then we went into a wall of whiteness that peppered and stung. The whole world dissolved away. I thought for an instant I had gone blind from the speed of our progress. Then I saw Captain Cheese still sitting a foot or two away. Skeres and Frizier had disappeared, as had the prow and the jibsail. I could see nothing but the section of boat I was in, the captain, the edge of the mainsail above. No river, no people, no landmarks, just snow and whiteness.

"How can you see?"

"Can't," said the captain.

"How do you know where we are?"

"Dead reckoning," he said. "Kick them up front, tell 'em to hang tight," he said. I did. When Skeres and Frizier opened their eyes, they almost screamed.

Then Cheese dropped the jib and the main and let the ice brakes go. We came to a stop, in the middle of the swirling snow, as in the middle of a void. Snowflakes the size of thalers came down. Then I made out a bulking shape a foot or two beyond the prow of the icerunner.

"Everybody out! Grab the hull. Lift, that's right. Usually have to do this myself. Step sharp. You two, point the prow up. That's it. Push. Push."

In the driven snow, the indistinct shape took form. Great timbers, planking, rocks, chunks of iron were before us, covered with ice. The two men out front put the prow over one of the icy gaps fifteen feet apart. Cheese and I lifted the stern then climbed over after it. "Settle in, batten down," said the captain. Once more we swayed sickeningly, jerked, the sails filled and we were gone.

59

"What was that?" I asked.

"Reading Weir," he said. "Just where the Kennet comes in on the portside. If we'd have hit that, we'd of been crushed like eggs. You can go to sleep now if you want. It's smooth sailing all the way in now."

ᅠᅠᅠᅠᅠ∞∞∞

But of course I couldn't. There seemed no movement, just the white blank ahead, behind, to each side.

"That would have been Wallingford," he said once. Then, a little further on, "Abingdon, just there." We sailed on. There was a small pop in the canvas. "Damn," he said, "the wind may go contrary; I might have to tack." He watched the sail awhile, then settled back. "I was wrong," he said.

Then, "Hold tight!" Frizier or Skeres moaned.

He dropped the sails. We lost motion. I heard the ice-brakes grab, saw a small curtain of crystalline ice mix with the snow. The moving, roiling whiteness became a still, roiling whiteness. The anchor hit the ice.

And, one after the other, even with us, the bells of the Oxford tower struck noon.

ᅠᅠᅠᅠᅠ∞∞∞

"Thanks be to you," I said, "Captain Jack Cheese."

"And to you—what was your name?"

"John," I said. "Johnny Factotum."

He looked at me, put his finger aside his nose. "Oh, then, Mr. Factotum," he said. I shook his hand.

"You've done me a great service," I said.

"And you me," said Captain Jack. "You've made me the easiest three pounds ever."

"Three!!" yelled the two men still in the boat. "The bet was two pound!"

"The bet was two, which I now take." The captain held out his hand. "The fare back to London is one more, for you both."

"What? What fare?" they asked.

"The bet was two hours to here. Which I have just done, from the tower bells in London to the campanile of Oxford. To do this, I had perforce to take you here in the time allotted, which—" and Jack Cheese turned once more to me and laid his finger to nose, "I have just done, therefore, *Quod Erat Demonstrandum.*" he said. "The wager being forfeit, either I shall bid you adieu, and give to you the freedom of the River and the Roads, or I shall drop you off in your own footprints on the London ice for a further pound."

The two looked at each other, their eyes pewter plates in the driven snow.

"But..." one began to say.

"These my unconditional, unimprovable terms," said Captain Jack.

We were drawing a crowd of student clerks and *magisters*, who marveled at the iceboat.

"Very well," sighed one of the men.

"The bet?" It was handed over. "The downward fare?" It, too.

"Hunker down in front, keep your heads down," said Jack Cheese and took out one of his mutton-leg pistols and laid it in front of him. "And no Spanish sissyhood!" he said, "For going downriver we don't stop for Reading Weir, we take it at speed!"

"No!"

"Abaft, all ye!" yelled Jack Cheese to the crowd. "I go upstream a pace; I turn; I come back down. If you don't leave the River now, don't blame me for loss of life and limb. No stopping Jack Cheese!" he said. The sails snapped up, the ice brake lifted, they blurred away into the upper Thames-Isis.

We all ran fast as we could from the center of the ice. I stopped, so did half the crowd who'd come to my side of the river. The blur of Captain Jack Cheese, the hull and sails and the frightened popped eyes at gunwale level zipped by.

The laughter of Jack Cheese came back to us as they flashed into the closing downriver snow and were gone.

And here I had been worried about him with two sharpers aboard. Done as well as any Gamaliel Ratsey, and no Spanish sissyhood, for sure. I doubt the two would twitch till they got back to London Docks.

The students were marveling among themselves. It reminded me of my days at Cambridge, bare seven years gone.

But my purposes lay elsewhere. I walked away from the crowd, unnoticed; they were as soon lost to me in the blowing whiteness as I, them.

∞∞∞

I sat under a pine by the River-side. From my pack I took a snaphance and started a small fire in the great snowing chill, using needles of the tree for a fragrant combustion; I filled my pipe, lit it and took in a great calming lungful of Sir Walter's Curse.

I was no doubt in the middle of the great university. I didn't care. I finished one pipeful, lit another, took in half that, ate some saltbeef and hard bread (the only kind to be found in London). Then I took from the apothecary pack, with its compartments and pockets filled with simples, emitics, herbs and powders, the document with the seal.

I read it over, twice. Then per instructions, added it to the fire.

I finished my pipe, knocked the dottles into the flame, and put it away.

The man's name was Johan Faustus, a German of Wittenberg. He was suspected, of course, of the usual—blasphemy, treason, subornation of the judiciary, atheism. The real charge, of course, was that he consorted with known Catholics—priests, prelates, the Pope himself. But what most worried the government was that he consorted with known Catholics *here*, in this realm. I was to find if he were involved in any plot; if suspicions were true, to put an end to his part in it. These things were in the document itself.

To this I added a few things I knew. That he was a doctor of both law and medicine, as so many are in this our country; that he had spent many years teaching at Wittenberg (not a notorious stronghold of the Popish Faith); that he was a magician, a conjuror, an alchemist, and, in the popular deluded notion of the times, supposed to have trafficked with Satan. There were many tales from the Continent—that he'd gulled, dazzled, conjured to and for emperors and kings—whether with the usual golden leaden ruses, arts of ledgerdemain, or the Tarot cards or whatnot, I knew not.

Very well, then. But as benighted superstitious men had written my instructions, I had to ask myself what would a man dealing with the Devil be doing in part of a Catholic plot? The Devil has his own devices and traps, all suppose, some of them I think, involving designs on the Popish Church itself. Will he use one religion 'gainst 'nother? Why don't men stop and think when they begin convolving their minds as to motive? Were they all absent the days brains were forged?

And why would an atheist deal with the Devil? The very professors tie themselves in knotlets of logic over just such questions as these.

Well then: let's apply William of Ockham's fine razor to this Gordian knot of high senselessness. I'll trot up to him, and ask him if he's involved in any treacherous plotting. Being an atheist, in league with *both* the Devil *and* the Pope (and for all I know the Turk), he'll tell me right out the truth. If treasonable, I shall cut off his head; if not…should I cut off his head to be safe?

Enough forethought; time for action. I reached into the bottom of my peddler's pack and took out two long curved blades like scimitars, so long and thin John Sincklo could have worn them Proportional, and attached them with thongs to the soles of my rude boots.

So equilibrized at the edge of the River I stood, and set out toward my destination which the letter had given me, Lotton near Cricklade, near the very source of the Thames-Isis.

And as I stood to begin my way norwestward the sun, as if in a poem by Chideock Tichborne, showed itself for the first time in two long months through the overcast, as a blazing ball, flooding the sky, the snow and ice in a pure sheen of blinding light. I began to skate toward it, toward the Heart of Whitenesse itself.

∞∞∞

Skiss skiss skiss the only sound from my skates, the pack swinging to and fro on my back; pure motion now, side to side, one arm folded behind me, the other out front as counterweight, into the blinded and blinding River before me. Past the mill at Lechlade, toward Kempsford, the sides of the Thames-Isis grew closer and rougher; past Kempsford to the edge of Cricklade itself, where the Roy comes in from the left just at the town, and turning then to right and north I go, up the River Churn, just larger than the Shoreditch in London itself. And a mile up and on the right, away from the stream, the outbuildings of a small town itself, and on a small hill beyond the town roofs, an old manor house.

I got off my skates, and unbound them and put them in the pack.

And now to ask leading questions of the rude common folk of the town.

∞∞∞

I walked to the front of the manor house and stopped, and beheld a sight to make me furious.

Tied to a post in front of the place, a horse stood steaming in what must have been forty degrees below frost. Its coat was lathered, the foam beginning to freeze in clumps on its mane and legs. Steam came from its nostrils. That someone rode a horse like that and left it like that in weather like this made me burn. It regarded me with an unconcerned eye, without shivering.

I walked past it to the door of the manor house, where of course my man lived. The sun, once the bright white ball, was covered again, and going down besides. Dark would fall like a disgraced nobleman in a few moments.

I rang the great iron doorknocker three times, and three hollow booms echoed down an inner hallway. The door opened to reveal a hairy man, below the middle height. His beard flowed into his massive head of hair. His ears, which stuck out beyond that tangle were thin and pointed. His smile was even, but two lower teeth stuck up from the bottom lip. His brows met in the middle to form one hairy ridge.

"That horse needs seeing to," I said.

He peered past me. "Oh, not *that* one," he said. "My master is expecting you, and cut the *merde*, he knows who you are and why you're here."

"To try to sell the Good Doctor simples and potions."

"Yeh, right," said the servant. "This way."

We walked down the hall. A brass head sitting on a shelf in a niche turned its eyes to follow me with its gaze as we passed. How very like Vergil.

We came to a closet doorway set at one side of the hall-way.

"You can't just go in, though," said the servant, "with-out you're worthy. Inside this here room is a Sphinx. It'll ask you a question. You can't answer it, it eats you."

"What if I answer it?"

"Well, I guess you could eat *it*, if you've a mind to, and she'll hold still. But mainly you can go through the next door; the Doctor's in."

"Have her blaze away," I said.

"Oh, that's a good one," said the servant. "I'll just stand behind the door here; she asks the first person she sees."

"You don't mind if I take out my knife, do you?"

"Take out a six-pounder cannon, for all the good it'll do you, you're not a wise man," he said.

I eased my knife from its sheath.

He opened the door. I expected either assassins, fright masks, jacks-in-boxes, some such. As he opened the door I stooped to the side, in case of mantraps or springarns. Noth-ing happened, nothing leapt out. I peered around the jamb.

Standing on a stone that led back into a cavern beyond was a woman to the waist, a four-footed leopard from there down; behind her back were wings. She was molting, putting in new feathers here and there. She looked at me with the eyes of a cat, narrow vertical pupils. I dared not look away.

"What hassss," she asked, in a sibilant voice that echoed in the hall, "eleven fingers in the morning, lives in a high place at noon, and has no head at sundown?"

"The present Queen's late Mom," I said.

"Righto!" said the servant and closed the door. I heard a heavy weight thrash against it, the sound of scratching and tearing. The servant slammed his fist on the door. "Settle down, you!" he yelled. "There'll be plenty more dumb ones come this way."

He opened the door at the end of the hall, and I walked into the chamber of Doctor Faustus.

∞∞∞

The room is dark but warm. A fire glows in the hearth, the walls are lined with books. There are dark marks on the high ceiling, done in other paint.

Doctor John Faust sits on a high stool before a reading stand, a lamp hangs above. I see another brass head is watching me from the wall.

"Ahem," says the servant.

"Oh?" says Faustus, looking up. "I thought you'd be alone, Wagner." He looks at me. "The others they sent weren't very bright. They barely got inside the house."

"I can imagine," I say. "Your lady's costume needs mending. The feathers aren't sewn in with double-loop stitches."

He laughs. "I am Doctor Johan Faustus," he says.

"And I am—" I say, thinking of names.

"Please drop the mumming," he says. "I've read your *Tamerlane*—both parts."

I look around. "Can we be honest?" I ask.

"Only one of us," he says.

"I have been sent here—"

"Probably to find out to whom I owe *my* allegiance. And its treasonableness. And not being able to tell whether I'm lying; to kill me; better safe than sorry. Did you enjoy your ride on the ice?"

There is no way he could have known. I was not followed. Perhaps he is inducing; if he knows who I am, and that I was in London this morning, only one method could have gotten me here so fast. But no one else who saw—

I stopped. *This* is the way fear starts.

"Very much," I say.

"Your masters want to know if I plot for the Pope—excuse me, the Bishop of Rome. No. Or the Spaniard, No. Nor French, Jews, Turks, No. I do not plot even for myself. Now you can leave."

"And I am to take your word?" I ask.

"I'm taking yours."

"Easily enough done," I say. Wagner the servant has left the room. Faustus is very confident of himself.

"You haven't asked me if I serve the Devil," he says.

"No one serves the Devil," I say. "There is no Devil."

Faustus looks at me. "So they have finally stooped so high as to send an atheist. Then I shall have to deal with you on the same high level." He bows to me.

I bowed back.

"If you are a true atheist, and I convince you there's magic, will you take my word and go away?"

"All magic is mumbo-jumbo, sleight-of-hand, mists, ledgerdemain," I say.

"Oh, I think not," says Faustus.

"Blaze away," I say. "Convenient Wagner has gone. Next he'll no doubt appear as some smoke, a voice from a horn, a hand."

"Oh, Mr. Marlowe," says Faustus. "What I serve is knowledge. I want it all. Knowledge is magic; other knowledge *leads* to magic. Where others draw back, I begin. I ask questions of Catholics, of Jews, of Spaniards, of Turks, if they have wisdom I seek. We'll find if you're a true atheist, a truly logical man. Look down."

I do. I am standing in a five-pointed star surrounded by a circle, written over with nonsense and names in Greek and Latin. Faustus steps off his stool. Onto another drawing on the floor. The room grows dark, then brighter, and much warmer as he waves his arms around like a conjuror before the weasel comes out the glove. Good trick, that.

"I tell you this as a rational man," he says. "Stay in the pentagram. Do not step out."

I felt hot breathing on the back of my neck that moved my hair.

"Do not look around," says Faustus, his voice calm and reasoned. "If you look around, you will scream. If you scream, you will jump. If you jump, you leave the pentagram. If you leave it, the thing behind you will bite off your head; the Sphinx out yonder was but a dim stencil of what stands behind you. So do not look, no matter how much you want to."

"No," I said. "You've got it wrong. I won't look around, not because I am afraid I'll jump, but because the act of *looking* will be to admit you've touched a superstitious adytum of my brain, one left over from the savage state. I *look*, I am lost, no matter what follows."

Faust regards me anew.

"Besides," I said, "what is back there," here whoever it was must have leaned even closer and blew hot breath down on me, though as I remember, Wagner was shorter, someone else then…"is another of your assistants. If they are going to kill me, they should have done it by now. On with your show. I am your attentive audience. Do you parade the wonders of past ages before me? Isis and Osiris and so forth? What of the past? Was Julius Caesar a redhead, as I have heard? How about Beauty? The Sphinx woman should have been able to change costumes by now?"

"You Cambridge men are always big on Homer. How about Helen of Troy?" asks Faustus.

"Is this the face that launched a thousand ships etc.?" I ask. "I think not. Convince me, Faustus. Do your shilly-shally."

"You asked for it," he says. I expected the knife to go through my back. Whoever was behind me was breathing slowly, slowly.

Faustus waved his arms, his lips moved. He threw his arms downward. I expected smoke, sparkles, explosion. There was none.

∞∞∞

It is fourteen feet tall. It has a head made of rocks and stones. Its body is brass; one leg of lead, the other of tin. I know this because the room was bright from the roaring fires that crackled with flame from each foot. This was more like it.

"Speak, spirit!" said Faustus.

"*Hissssk. Snarrrz. Skazzz,*" it said, or words to that effect.

And then it turned into the Queen, and the Queen turned into the King of Scotland. I don't mean someone who looked like him, I mean him. He shifted form and shape before me. He turns, his hair is longer, his nose thinner, his mustache flows. He changes to another version of himself, and his head jumped off bloodily to the floor. He turns into a huge sour-faced man, then back to someone who looks vaguely like the King of Scotland, then another; then a man and woman joined at the hip, another king, a woman, three fat Germans, a thin one, a small woman, a fat beared man, a thin guy with a beard, a blip of light, another bearded man, a woman, a tall thin man, his son—

This was very good indeed. Would we had him at the Rose.

"Tell him of what lies before, Spirit."

"Tell him," I said to Faustus, "to tell me of plots."

"PLOTS!" the thing roared. "You want the truth?" It was back fourteen feet tall and afire, stooping under the ceiling. "You live by a government. Governments NEED Plots! Else people ask why they die? Where's the bread? Human. Hu-man! You are the ones in torment! We here are FREE!

"PLOTS! BE-ware ESSEX!" Essex? The Queen's true right arm? Her lover? "BEWARE Guido and his dark SHIN-ING lantern! BEWARE the House in the RYE-fields! Beware the papers in the TUB OF flour! Beware pillars! BE-WARE POSTS! Be-WARE the Dutch, the FRENCH, the colonists in VIRGINIA!" Virginia? They're lost? "BEWARE RUSSia and the zuLU and the DUTCHAFricans! Beware EVERYTHING! BEWARE EVERYboDY! AIIIiiii!!!"

It disappears. Faustus slumps to the floor, sweating and pale.

The light comes back to normal.

"He'll be like that a few minutes," says Wagner, coming in the door with a jug of wine and three glasses. "He said malmsey's your favorite. Drink?"

ooooo

We shook hands at the doorway early next morning.

"I was impressed," I said. "All that foofaraw just for me."

"If they're sending atheists, I had better get out of this country. No one will be safe."

"Good-bye," I said, putting the box in my pack. The door closed. I walked out past the hitching post. Tied to it with a leather strap was a carpenter's sawhorse. Strapped about the middle of it, hanging under it, was a huge stop-pered glass bottle filled with hay. How droll of Wagner, I thought.

I went to the river, out on my skates, and headed back out the Churn to the Thames-Isis, back to London, un-eventfully, one hand behind me, the other counterweight, the pack swinging, my skates thin and sharp.

Skizz skizz skizz.

∞∞∞∞∞

When I got back to my lodgings, there was a note for me in the locked room. I took the token of proof with me, and went by back ways and devious alleys to an address. There waiting was *another* high lord of the realm. He saw the box in my hand, nodded. He took the corner of my sleeve, pulled me to follow him. We went through several buildings, downward, through a long tunnel, turning, turn-ing and came to a roomful of guards beyond a door. Then we went upstairs, passing a few clerks, and other stairwells that led down, whence came screams. Too late to stop now.

"Someone wants to hear your report besides me," said the high Lord. We waited outside a room from which came the sounds of high indistinct conversation. The door opened; a man I recognized as the royal architect came out, holding a roll of drawings under his arm, his face reddened. "What a dump!" said a loud woman's voice from the room beyond.

"What a dump! What a dump!" came a high-pitched voice over hers.

I imagined a parrot of the red Amazonian kind.

"Shut up, you!" said the woman's voice.

"What a dump! What a dump!"

"Be sure to make a leg, man," said the high Lord behind me, and urged me into the room.

There she was, Gloriana herself. From the waist down it looked as if she'd been swallowed by some huge spangled velvet clam while stealing from it the pearls that adorned her torso, arms, neck and hair.

"Your Majesty," I said, dropping to my knees.

The lord bowed behind me.

"What a dump!" said the other voice. I looked over. On a high sideboard, the royal dwarf, whose name I believed to be Monarcho, was dressed as a baby in a diaper and a bonnet, his legs dangling over the sides, four feet from the floor.

"Well?" asked the Queen. "(You look horrible without your face hair) Well?"

I nodded toward the box under my arm.

"Oh, give that to someone else; I don't want to see those things." She turned her head away, then back, becoming the Queen again.

"Were we right?"

I looked her in the eyes, below her shaven brow and the painted-in browline, at the red wig, the pearls, the sparkling clamshell of a gown.

"His last words, Majesty," I said, "were of the Bishop of Rome, and of your late cousin."

"I knew it," she said. "I knew it!"

"I knew it!" yelled Monarcho.

The Queen threw a mirror at him. He jumped down with a thud and waddled off to torment the lapdog.

"You have been of great service," she said to me. "Reward him, my lord, but not overmuch. (Don't ever appear again in my presence without at least a mustache.)"

I made the knee again.

"Leave," she said to me. "You. Stay," she said to the Lord. I backed out. The door swung. "Builders!" she was yelling. "What a dump!"

"What a dum—" said Monarcho, and the door closed with a thud.

ooooo

So now it is another wet summer, in May, and I am lodging in Deptford, awaiting the pleasure of the Privy Council to question me.

At first I was sure it dealt with the business of this winter last, as rumor had come back to me that Faustus had been seen alive in France. If *I* had heard, other keener ears had heard a week before.

But no! The reason they sent the bailiff for me, while I was staying at Walsingham's place in Kent, was because of that noddy-custard Kyd.

For he and his friends had published a scurrilous pamphlet a month ago. Warrants had been sworn; searches made, and in Kyd's place they found some of my writings done, while we were both usually drunk, when we roomed together three years ago cobbling together old plays. I had, in some of them, been forthright and indiscreet. Kyd even more so.

So they took him downstairs, and just showed him the tongue-tongs, and he began to peach on his 104-year-old great aunt.

Of course, he'd said *all* the writings were mine.

And now I'm having to stay in Deptford (since I can get away to Kent if ever they are through with me) and await, every morning, and the last ten mornings, the vagaries of the Privy Council. And somewhat late of each May evening, a bailiff comes out, says "You still here?" and "They're gone; be back here in the morning."

But not *this* morning. I come in at seven o' the clock, and the bailiff says, "They specifically and especially said they'd not get to you today, be back tomorrow." I thanked him.

I walked out. A day (and a night) of freedom awaited me.

And who do I spy coming at me but my companions in the peradventure of the iceboat, Nick Skeres and Ingram Frizier, along with another real piece of work I know of from the theaters (people often reach for their purses and shake hands with him) named Robert Poley.

"What ho, Chris!" he says, "how's the playhouse dodge?"

"As right as rain till the Plague comes back," I say.

I watch, but neither Skeres nor Frizier seems to recognize me; I am dressed as a gentleman again; my beard and mustache new-waxed, my hat a perfect comet of color and dash.

"Well, we're heading for Mrs. Bull's place," says Poley, "she owes us each a drink from the cards last night; it is our good fortune, and business has been good," he says, holding up parts of three wallets. "How's about we stands you a few?"

"Thanks be," I say, "but I am at liberty for the first time in days, and needs be back hot on a poem, now that Shaxber's *Venus and Adonis* is printed."

"Well, then," says Poley, "one quick drink to fire the Muse?"

And then I see that Skeres is winking at me, but not one of the winks I know. Perhaps his eye is watering. Perhaps he is crying for the Frenchmen who we hear are once again eating each other up like cannibals. Perhaps not.

Oh well, I think, what can a few drinks with a bunch of convivial invert dizzards such as myself harm me? I have been threatened with the Privy Council; I walk away untouched and unfettered.

"Right!" I say, and we head off toward Deptford and Mrs. Bull's, though I keep a tight hold on my purse. "A drink could be just what the doctors ordered."

Afterword to "Heart of Whitenesse"

As when (he said, Homerically) I wrote "God's Hooks!" more than twenty years ago, I was astounded no one had written this one before.

In *that* case, it was the contemporaniety and congruence of Izaak Walton and John Bunyan (they're usually next to each other in any survey-course textbook of English Literature) and were tailor-made for a story about fishing in the Slough of Despond, showing their two kinds of politics (Royalist, Roundhead) and religion (Anglican, Puritan) plus the Plague and Great Fire of London and the tenor of the times. Plus the fishing tackle of the day. It wrote itself.

With this one, it started as Marlowe, Marlow, Marlowe— that is, Christopher the playwright; the narrator of several of Joseph Conrad's stories; and Raymond Chandler's private eye.

It seemed a natural. Christopher Marlowe was the greatest English playwright before Shakespeare; he was also a secret agent *and* a spy, involved in lots of those things Elizabeth I's Perfidious Albion specialized in; he was as gay as they got in those days, and an atheist, and was facing blasphemy charges at the time of his early death. Ready-made for a mission to terminate someone "with extreme prejudice…"

The Marlow we know best is the one who narrates "Heart of Darkness" at the interminable turn of that tide it takes to tell it, the African trip-upriver (Huck Finn in reverse) basis of the later film *Apocalypse Now,* and of Robert Silverberg's *Downward to the Earth*.

The Marlowe-private-eye thing I kept up for about two pages—there are a couple of references from *The Big Sleep* and *Lady in the Lake* (the movie of which [1948] was filmed subjective-camera—the same way Orson Welles wanted to film *Heart of Darkness* in 1940, which is the film he *would* have made if the idea of doing that hadn't scared the pee out of the RKO executives, and he started developing *Citizen Kane* instead…See, all this crap *is* interconnected!) It's hard enough writing in late 16th C. idiom without trying to throw in wise-ass Chandlerisms ("all the talent in the room stood out like a tarantula on an angel-food cake.") from the 20th C. I did my part to keep up at least the appearance of the trope, anyway. (If you think this stuff is easy, you have my permission to try it sometime…)

So I've got my guy, my voice (first person—the equivalent of subjective camera) and my narrative (a voyage upriver).

But I knew I also wanted to set the story around one of the Frost Fairs on the Thames in the late 1500s and early 1600s. (This was when Europe was in what came to be known as The Little Ice Age—probably due to volcanic eruptions somewhere in the unexplored—by Europeans—portions of the world.) So it was a journey up a frozen river, a white one. That of course gave me the title…

But why was Marlowe going up this particular frozen river? At the behest of his monarch (through one of her Lords Chamberlain or Exchequer, who were what we today would call *handlers,* in that age of intrigue…) Well, to put an end to Dr. Faustus (of whom the real Marlowe was to write a play about) whose freethinking ways were rocking the Elizabethan polity and snug Chain of Being…

(*The* Wagner, Faustus' servant, was later to be the bad guy of the Victorian penny-dreadful *Wagner the Were-Wolf.* And of course there's an echo of George Wagner, who directed the 1941 *The Wolf Man*…once you start this stuff, you just can't stop…)

I knew QE1 would make an appearance, so had her quoting Bette Davis (who played her in *The Virgin Queen,* among others) and I threw in Kemp, who would later dance, in 9 days, from London to Norwich, in his own journey upriver.

I had *almost* everything I needed.

Heart of Whitenesse

Then up jumped Captain Jack Cheese...

∞∞∞

According to my story log, I wrote this one on April 21 and 22, 1996. That's because I had to give a reading at the Fremont Public Library at 7 pm on the 22nd, so I think I finished this in the big old 16-column ledger Eileen Gunn had given me as a welcome that afternoon.

Well, I read it, and it was a wow.

I typed it up back in Oso on the 24th and 25th and mailed it off.

∞∞∞

Who I mailed it to was Dave Garnett, in England, who'd revived (twice by this time) Michael Moorcock's *New Worlds,* as an original anthology for White Wolf. I wrote the story for him and Mike, and I sent it off Global Priority Mail.

At this time when I was living in Oso, I didn't have a 1) refrigerator or 2) phone. (I later got a third-hand dorm refrigerator, but I made it the whole 7½ years without a phone...) I got an airmail card back from Dave on May 7. And in one of the modern wonders of this jet-age, I got paid the next day by Mike Moorcock. Dave had called him when he got the story, and Mike, gentleman that he is, wrote the check from Bastrop, TX and put it in the mail.

When it was published, in August 1997, you could, as I have said about *so much* of my stuff in the past being published, have heard it squeal like a pig going down the chute as it *totally disappeared* in the American publishing biz.

Not a review. Not a thing. *Nada.*

Well, except in January 1998, I got a contract from Gardner Dozois for it for his *Year's Best SF Stories*...I immediately wrote cards to Dave and Mike saying "See! At least *one person* read the anthology!!!"

Howard Waldrop

It was published there and I've been getting royalties on it pretty much since.

(Later I was able to partially repay Dave and Mike somewhat—friends of his published a surprise anthology of stories, essays and appreciations of Mike for his 60th birthday, and I wrote a story "Clean 'round the Oojar" with the sole purpose of making Mike and Dave laugh. *And I did.*)

So now you've read it, the title story to this collection. I can say the same thing about it as I did about "God's Hooks!" two decades ago.

It wrote itself. I just happened to be in the room at the time.

London, Paris, Banana....

I was on my way across the Pacific Ocean when I decided to go to the Moon.

∞∞∞∞∞

But first I had to land to refuel this superannuated machine, with its internal combustion engines and twin airscrews. There was an answering beacon ahead that showed a storage of 6,170 metric tons of fuel. Whether I could obtain any of it I did not know. But; as they used to say, any dataport in an infostorm.

The island was a small speck in the pink ocean.

No instructions came from the airfield, so I landed on the only runway, a very long one. I taxied off to the side, toward what had been the major building with the control tower.

I tried to find a servicer of some kind, by putting out requests on different frequencies.

Nothing came. So I went to find the fuel myself. Perhaps there were pumps that still functioned? I located the storage facility, then returned to the plane and rolled it over to the tanks.

It was while I was using a hand-powered pumping device, with a filter installed in the deteriorating hoses, that I sensed the approach of someone else.

It came around the corner.

It was carrying a long, twisted piece of wood as tall as it, and it wore a torn and bleached cloak, and a shapeless bleached hat that came to a point on the crown.

"*Mele Kiritimati!*" it said. "You have landed on this enfabled island on the anniversary of its discovery by the famous Captain Cook, an adventurous human."

"Your pardon?" I said. "The greeting?"

"Merry Christmas. The human festive season, named for the nominal birthdate of one of its religious figures, placed on the dates of the old human Saturnalia by the early oligarchs."

"I am familiar with Christmastide. This, then, is Christmas Island?"

"That same. Did you not use standard navigational references?"

I pointed to the plane. "Locationals only. There is a large supply of aviation fuels here."

"Nevertheless," it said, "this is the island, this is the date of Christmas. You are the first visitor in fourteen years three months twenty-six days. *Mele Kiritimati.*"

It stood before me as I pumped.

"I have named myself Prospero," it said.

(Reference: Shakespeare, *The Tempest* A.D. 1611. See also Hume, *Forbidden Planet*, A.D. 1956.)

"I should think Caliban," I said. (Reference also: Morbius, id monster.)

"No Caliban. Nor Ariel, nor Miranda, nor dukes," said Prospero. "In fact, no one else. But you."

"I am called Montgomery Clift Jones," I said, extending my hand.

His steel grip was firm.

"What have you been doing?" I asked.

"Like the chameleon, I sup o' the very air itself," he said.

"I mean, what do you *do?*" I asked.

"What do *you* do?" he asked.

We looked out at the pinkness of the ocean where it met the salts-encrusted sands and island soils.

"I stopped here to refuel," I said. "I was on my way across the Pacific when I was overcome with a sudden want to visit the Moon."

Prospero looked to where the part-lit Moon hung in the orangish sky.

"Hmmm. Why do that, besides it's there?"

"Humans did it once."

"Well," said Prospero, after a pause, "why not indeed? I should think revisiting places humans once got to should be fitting. In fact, a capital idea! I see your craft is a two-seater. Might I accompany you in this undertaking?"

I looked him over. "This sea air can't be very good for your systems," I said, looking at the abraded metal that showed through his cloak. "Of course you may accompany me."

"As soon as you finish refueling, join me," he said. "I will take a farewell tour, and tell you of my domain."

"How can I find you?"

"If something is moving on the island," said Prospero, "it is I."

∞∞∞∞

We walked along. I kicked over some crusted potassium spires along the edge of the beach.

"I should be careful," said Prospero. "The pH of the oceans is now twelve point two. You may get an alkaline burn."

The low waves came in, adding their pinkish-orange load to the sediments along the shore.

"This island is very interesting," he said. "I thought so when abandoned here; I still think so after all."

"When Cook found it, no humans were here. It was only inhabited for two hundred years or so. Humans were brought from other islands, thousands of kilometers away. The language they used, besides English I mean, was an amalgam of those of the islands whence they came."

We looked at some eaten-metal ruins.

"This was once their major city. It was called London. The other two were Paris and Banana."

"There was a kind of human tourism centered here once around a species of fish, *Albula vulpes,* the bonefish. They used much of their wealth to come here to disturb the fish in its feeding with cunning devices that imitated crustaceans, insects, other marine life. They did not keep or eat the fish they attained after long struggles. That part I have never understood," said Prospero.

By and by we came to the airfield.

"Is there anything else you need to do before we leave?"

"I think no," said Prospero. He turned for one more look around. "I do believe I shall miss this isle of banishment, full of music, and musing on the king my brother's wreck. Well, that part is Shakespeare's. But I have grown much accustomed to it. Farewell," he said, to no one and nothing.

Getting him fitted into the copilot's seat was anticlimax. It was like bending and folding a living, collapsible deck chair of an extraordinarily old kind, made from a bad patent drawing.

∞∞∞

On our journey over the rest of the island, and the continent, I learned much of Prospero; how he came to be on the island, what he had done there, the chance visitors who came and went, usually on some more and more desperate mission.

"I saw the last of the Centuplets," he said at one point. "Mary Lou and Cathy Sue. They were surrounded of course by many workers—in those days humans always were— who were hurrying them on their way to, I believe, some part of Asia...."

"The island of Somba," I said.

"Yes, yes, Somba. For those cloning operations, supposed to ensure the continuation of the humans."

"Well, those didn't work."

"From looking into it after they left," said Prospero, "I assumed they would not. Still, the chances were even."

"Humans were imprecise things, and genetics was a human science," I said.

"Oh, yes. I used the airfield's beacons and systems to keep in touch with things. No being is an island," said Prospero, "even when on one. Not like in the old days, eh? It seems many human concerns, before the last century or so, were with the fear of isolation, desertion, being ma-

rooned from society. I made the best of my situation. As
such things go, I somewhat enjoyed it."

"And listening to the human world dying?"

"Well," said Prospero, "we all had to do that, didn't
we? Robots, I mean."

∞∞∞

We landed at the old Cape.

"I'm quite sure," said Prospero, as I helped him out of
the seat until he could steady himself on his feet, "that some
of their security safeguards still function."

"I never met a security system yet," I said, "that didn't
understand the sudden kiss of a hot arc welder on a loose
faceplate."

"No, I assume not." He reached down and took up some
soil. "Why, this sand is old! Not newly formed encrusta-
tions. Well, what should we do first?" He looked around,
the Moon not up yet.

"Access to information. Then materials, followed by
assembly. Then we go to the Moon."

"Splendid!" said Prospero. "I never knew it would be
so easy."

∞∞∞

On the second day, Prospero swiveled his head around
with a ratcheting click.

"Montgomery," he said. "Something approaches from
the east-northeast."

We looked toward the long strip of beach out beyond
the assembly buildings, where the full Moon was just heav-
ing into view at sunset.

86

Something smaller than we walked jerkily at the water's edge. It stopped, lifting its upper appendages. There was a whirring keen on the air, and a small crash of static. Then it stood still.

We walked toward it.

"...rrrrr..." it said, the sound rising higher. It paid us no heed.

"Hello!" said Prospero. Nothing. Then our long shadows fell across the sand beside it.

The whining stopped. It turned around.

"I am Prospero. This is Montgomery Clift Jones. Whom do we have the honor to address?"

"...rrr..." it said. Then, with a half turn of its head, it lifted one arm and pointed toward the Moon. "rrrrr. rrRRR!"

"Hmmm," said Prospero.

"RRRR," said the machine. Then it turned once more towad the Moon in its lavender-red glory, and raised all its arms. "RRRRR! RRRRR!" it said, then went back to its high whining.

"This will take some definite study and trouble," said Prospero.

∞∞∞∞∞

We found one of the shuttle vehicles, still on its support structure, after I had gone through all the informational materials. Then we had to go several kilometers to one of their museums to find a lunar excursion module, and bring that to the shuttle vehicle. Then I had to modify, with Prospero's help, the bay of the shuttle to accommodate the module, and build and install an additional fuel tank there, since the original vehicle had been used only for low-orbit missions and returns.

When not assisting me, Prospero was out with the other machine, whom he had named Elkanah, from the author of an opera about the Moon from the year A.D. 1697. (In the course of their conversations, Prospero found his real name to be, like most, a series of numbers.) Elkanah communicated by writing in the sand with a stick, a long series of sentences covering hectares of beach at a time.

That is, while the Moon was not in the sky. While that happened, Elkanah stood as if transfixed on the beach, staring at it, whining, even at the new Moon in the daylit red sky. Like some moonflower, his attitude followed it across the heavens from rise to set, emitting the small whining series of Rs, the only sound his damaged voice box could make.

The Moon had just come up the second night we were there. Prospero came back into the giant hangar, humming the old song "R.U.R.R.R.U My Baby?" I was deciding which controls and systems we needed, and which not.

"He was built to work on the Moon, of course," said Prospero. "During one of those spasms of intelligence when humans thought they should like to go *back*. Things turning out like they did, they never did."

"And so his longing," I said.

"It's deep in his wiring. First he was neglected, after the plans were canceled. Then most of the humans went away. Then his voice and some memory were destroyed in some sort of colossal explosion here that included lots of collateral electromagnetic damage, as they used to say. But not his need to be on our lunar satellite. That's the one thing Elkanah is sure of."

"What was he to do there?"

"Didn't ask, but will," said Prospero. "By his looks— solid head, independent eyes, multiuse appendages, up-

right posture—I assume some kind of maintenance function. A Caliban/Ariel-of-all-work, as 'twere."

"A janitor for the Moon," I said.

"Janus. Janitor. Opener of gates and doors," mused
Prospero. "Forward- and backward-looking, two-headed.
The deity of beginnings and endings, comings and goings.
Appropriate for our undertaking."

ooooo

When we tried to tell him we were taking him with us,
Elkanah did not at first understand.

"Yes," said Prospero, gesturing. "Come with us to the
Moon."

"R-R." Elkanah swiveled his head and pointed to the
Moon.

"Yes," said Prospero. He pointed to himself, to me, and
to Elkanah. Then he made his fingers into a curve, swung
them in an arc, and pointed to the sky. He made a circle
with his other hand. "To the Moon!" he said.

Elkanah looked at Prospero's hands.

"R-R," he said.

"He can't hear sound or radio, you know?" said
Prospero. "He has to see information, or read it."

Prospero bent and began writing in the sand with his
staff.

YOU COME WITH MONTGOMERY AND ME TO
THE MOON.

Elkanah bent to watch, then straightened and looked
at Prospero.

"RRRR?" he said.

"Yes, yes!" said Prospero, gesturing. "RRR! The
RRRR!"

The sound started low, then went higher and higher, off the scale:

"RRRRRRRRRRRRRR!"

"Why didn't you write it in the first place?" I asked Prospero.

"My mistake," he said.

From then on, Elkanah pitched in like some metallic demon, any time the Moon was not in the sky, acid rain or shine, alkali storm or fair.

∞∞∞

We sat in the shuttle cabin, atop the craft with its solid-fuel boosters, its main tank, and the extra one in the bay with the lander module.

"All ready?" I asked, and held up the written card for Elkanah.

"Certes," said Prospero.

"R," said Elkanah.

Liquid oxygen fog wafted by the windshield. It had been, by elapsed time counter, eleven years, four months, three days, two minutes, and eleven seconds since we had landed at the Cape. You can accomplish much when you need no food, rest, or sleep and allow no distractions. The hardest part had been moving the vehicle to the launch pad with the giant tractor, which Elkanah had started but Prospero had to finish, as the Moon had come up, more than a week ago.

I pushed the button. We took off, shedding boosters and the main tank, and flew to the Moon.

∞∞∞

The Sea of Tranquility hove into view.

After we made the lunar insertion burn, and the orbit, we climbed into the excursion module and headed down for the lunar surface.

Elkanah had changed since we left Earth, when the Moon was always in view, somewhere. He had brought implements with him on the trip. He stared at the Moon often, but no longer whined or whirred.

At touchdown I turned things off, and we went down the ladder to the ground.

There was the flag, stiffly faking a breeze, and some litter, and footprints, and the plaque, which of course we could read.

"This is as far as they ever came," said Prospero.

"Yes," I said. "We're the thirteenth, fourteenth, and fifteenth intelligent beings to be here."

Elkanah picked up some of the litter, took it to a small crater, and dropped it in.

Prospero and I played in the one-sixth gravity. Elkanah watched us bounce around for a while, then went back to what he was doing.

"They probably should have tried to come back, no matter what," said Prospero. "Although it doesn't seem there would be much for them to do here, after a while. Of course, at the end, there wasn't much for them to do on Earth, either."

∞∞∞∞

We were ready to go. Prospero wrote in the dust, WE ARE READY TO GO NOW.

Elkanah bent to read. Then he pointed up to the full Earth in the dark Moon sky (we were using infrared) and moved his hand in a dismissing motion.

"R," he obviously said, but there was no sound.

He looked at us, came to attention, then brought his broom to shoulder-arms and saluted us with his other three hands.

We climbed up onto the module. "I think I'll ride back up out here," said Prospero. "I should like an unobstructed view."

"Make sure you hang on," I said.

Prospero stood on the platform, where the skull-shape of the crew compartment turned into the base and ladders and legs.

"I'm braced," he said, then continued:

"My Ariel, chick, that is thy charge; then to the
elements be free, and fare thou well.
Now my charms are all o'erthrown
And what strength I have's mine own.
Our revels now are ended."

There was a flash and a small feeling of motion, a scattering of moondust and rock under us, and we moved up away from the surface.

The last time I saw Elkanah, he was sweeping over footprints and tidying up the Moon.

∞∞∞∞

We were on our way back to Earth when we decided to go to Mars.

Afterword to "London, Paris, Banana..."

Sometimes, a being has to do what a being has to do.

∞∞∞

For instance, in the case of "Major Spacer in the 21st Century!" (see that afterword), what you have to do instead of 3000 words of rewrite, is, you write a whole new 4000 word story...

When Kim Mohan, of *Amazing,* about the only publisher who could publish the story before the 21st Century wrote back, wanting some changes, I gave it about three minutes thought, and sent "Major Spacer..." off to Gordon van Gelder (see the "Major Spacer..." afterword). Then I sat down and wrote Kim *this* story, which I'd wanted to write for years, and sent it to him, who, stunned like a carp, bought it instantly, and had it in print in a few months.

And sorry, Kim, I killed your magazine again. Even though Kim sent me a note with my contributor's copies saying "See! You *didn't* kill it *this* time." He was sorta right...it died again the issue *after* this story came out in it. I still, like a WWII pilot, consider it a kill....

∞∞∞

Despite what everyone thinks, robot stories are not easy to write.

Way back before Rossum made his first U.R. in 1922, people were telling stories about Coppelia and Moxon's Mas-

93

ter and Maelzel's Chess-Playing Turk, and it usually ended very badly for Moxon or Maelzel or whoever.

It took Capek and a little later Asimov and Kuttner and Bester to codify the concept and straighten us out about the various clanking machines and squiggy artificial humans raised in vats. Besides the obvious question (what does it mean to be human?) they let us know robots weren't *all* like that damned thing with the sneer that squashed G-Men for Bela Lugosi in *The Phantom Creeps* (1939) or chased various Republic Studios stuntmen with hatchets in *The Mysterious Dr. Satan* (1940). (Although, if nothing else, Bester's android in "Fondly Farenheit" is one of those Republic water-heater robots in a clever plastic disguise, carrying a Freudian axe...)

Asimov came up with the Three Laws of Robotics *without knowing* it. In the course of writing his first few stories about positronic robots, Asimov assumed they'd have certain built-in behavioral patterns. When he went in to pick up his checks, John W. Campbell, the editor of *Astounding,* told him he'd invented the Three Laws, just from what was *in* the stories.

What Asimov had done was make a pretty good guess at what they'd have to put into robots to keep them from mashing the cat or flattening the twins or knocking down the brownstone while taking out the trash. The killer/gonzo/exploding robot became the exception to the run-of-the-robot story. Eando Binder, in the Adam Link stories of about the same time, explored some of the ethical/moral areas: in a world where robots can't hurt anyone, how does a person end up dead, and there's Adam Link standing over the corpse with the smoking .38?

Kuttner, among others, taught us robots could be as distinctive as people (even if their job were to be a can-opener or rolling beer keg.) *Apres,* (and alongside them) *le deluge:* del Rey, C.L. Moore, and all the Tobors and Gorts and Gogs to follow.

And they ask you why Robby the Robot in *Forbidden Planet* was so great? There's the scene where he won't let the crewmembers of the C-57-D bother Morbius in his study;

Altaira says "Emergency Override Archimedes" and Robby walks off without acknowledgment: that was the *first time* in movies where we actually saw robots the way they *would* be; his programming makes him bar the door; when it's overridden, he goes to water the cacti, the next chore on his list…

I'd written robot stories before, "Our Mortal Span" (in here) and "Heirs of the Perisphere," where three robots made for a theme park awaken to a world without them, and "Helpless, Helpless," about a time when all the robots are being destroyed by the mechanical equivalent of the Black Plague ("Bring out Your Malfunctioning!") But in those, people (at least, a few in the second story) were still around—the third is about what happens when *all* the help goes away…

So I got to thinking: what happens to the robots when *all* the people go away? (the same place Aldiss started in his classic "But Who Can Replace a Man?" and Simak, in *City.*) They can do *anything* they want. They don't have to keep doing what we wanted them to do.

And the image came to me of some Prospero freeing some Ariel (for what is *The Tempest* about if not the problem of keeping good help)—which is also where *Forbidden Planet* with Robby the Robot started from. And I knew he had to free him *on the Moon*…

(In this story you have to imagine Prospero speaking with the voice of the late Sir Ralph Richardson from *The Wrong Box,* 1966.)

I wrote this one in two days, Mohan bought it in eight and paid me in two weeks. You can't beat *that* for a story written to substitute for not doing the rewrite on a longer story someone wants you to fix…

And, coincidence, or what? According to his biography, the week I was born, Asimov was writing "Little Lost Robot."

Our Mortal Span

*T*rip-trap! *Trip-trap!*

"Who's that on MY—"*skeezwhirr—govva grome—
fibonacci curve—ships that parse in the night—yes I said yes I
will yes—first with the most men—these foolish things—taking
the edge of the knife slowly peel the mesenterum and any fatty tis-
sue—a Declaration no less than the Rights of Man—an Iron
Curtain has descended—If—platyrhincocephalian—TM 1341
Mask M17A1 Protective Chemical and Biological—Mother, where
are you Mother? Mother?*

∞∞∞

And now, I know *everything*.

I know that everything bigger than me, here, is a hologram, a product of coherent light in an interference pattern
on the medium of the air.

Therefore anything bigger than me is not real.
As for that automata of a goat out there, we'll soon see.

∞∞∞

I have three heads. I am the one in the Middle. The other two can grimace and roll their eyes and loll their tongues, but they have no input. *I* am the one in the middle. I can see and think (before the surge of power and the wonderful download of knowledge, it had been only in a rudimentary manner through a loose routine. One of the heads, the one on the right, has two high fringes of hair kinked around each temple, and a big nose. The one on the left has a broad idiot's face and a head of short stubble. I have a face somewhat more normal than the left, and hair that hangs in a bowl-cut down almost into my eyes. (I am seeing myself through maintenance specs.). I am dressed in a loose leather (actually plastic) tunic that hangs down below my knees. There are decorative laces halfway up the front. It has a wide (real) leather belt. My feet (two) are shod in shapeless leather; my two arms hang at my sides.

Below my feet are the rods that hold me in position for the playlet we perform. I bend down and break them off, one not cleanly, so that when I walk my right leg is longer than the left. It gives me a jerky gait.

I am three meters tall.

The smallest automata waits halfway out on the span. The crowd oohs and ahhs as I climb up over the timbers and step out onto the pathway. The medium and larger automata wait their cues far back.

My presence is not in the small goat's routine. It goes to its next cue.

"Oh, no, please!" it says in a high small voice (recorded by a Japanese-American voice actor three years ago 714 kilometers from here). "I am very small. Don't eat *me!*"

I reach down and pull off its head and stuff it in my mouth. Springs, wires and small motors drop out of my face from my mouth (a small opening with no ingress to my chest cavity.)

"—you want to eat—" says its synthesizer before I chew down hard enough to crush it.

The four legs and body of the small goat stand in a spreading pool of lubricants and hydraulics. It tries to go through the motions of its part and then is still.

The other two, not recognizing cues, return to their starting stations, where we wait while the park is closed (2350-0600 each cycle) when we undergo maintenance.

I turn to the 151 people out in the viewing area.

"Rahr!" I say. "Ya!" (That is left from my old programming.) I jump down from the bridge into the shallow rivulet beneath the bridge (surely no structure so sturdy and huge was ever built to span such a meager trickle) splashing water on the nearest in the audience.

They realize something is very out of the ordinary.

"Ya!" I yell. "Rahr!" They run over each other, over themselves, rolling, screaming, through the doors at the ends of the ramps. "Wait! Don't go!" I say. "I have something to tell you."

One of the uniformed tour guides walks over, opens a box and throws an emergency switch. The power and lights go out. Everything else is still and quiet, except for her breathing, a sigh of relief.

"Rahr!" I say, coming toward her over the viewing area parapet, like the bear-habitat of a zoo.

She screams and runs up the ramp.

The maintenance people refer to me as Lermokerl the Troll.

I will show you a troll.

∞∞∞

The place is called Story Book Land, and it is a theme park. The theme is supposed to be Fairy Tales, but of course humans have never differentiated among Fairy Tales, Nursery Rhymes, Folk Tales and Animal Fables, so this park is a mixture of them all.

We perform small playlets of suffering, loss, and aspirations to marrying the King's daughter, killing the giant to get his gold, or to wed the Prince because you have no corns on your feet, even though you work as a drudge and scullery maid, barefoot. Some are instructive—The Old Woman Who Lives In The Shoe delivers a small birth-control lecture; the Fox—with the impersonated voice of a character actor dead five decades—tells small children that, perhaps, indeed, the grapes were worth having, and you should never give up trying for what you really Really want.

We are a travel destination in an age when no one *has* to travel anymore. The same experience can and has been put on disks and hologrammed, hi-deffed and sold in the high millions in these days when selling in the billions is considered healthy.

Hu-mans come because they want to give themselves and their children a Real Experience of travel, sights, some open air; to experience crankiness, delay, a dim sort of commercial enlightenment, perhaps a reminder of their own childhoods.

This I am willing to provide. Childhoods used to be nightmares of disease, death, wolves, bogies and deceit, and still are in small parts of the world.

But not for the people who come here.

I am an actor (in the broadest sense). And now, for my greatest performance...

Outside, in the sun, things are placid. The crowd which had rushed out seems to have dispersed or be standing in knots far away. A few of the wheeled maintenance and security vehicles are coming toward the area from the local control shop, in no hurry. I scan my maps and take off up the tumbled fake-rock sides of the low building which houses our playlet. There is a metallic scraping each time my right foot strikes, the jagged rod cuts into the surface. Then I am up and over a low wall into the next area.

Hu-mans stare at me. I stride along, clanging, towering over them. But they are used to things in costume among them. They will be eating at a concession area, and a weasel, wearing a sword and cape, will walk up and say "Pick a card, any card," fanning a deck before them.

Some go along; some say "I'm tired and I'm trying to eat" (which they do, inordinately, on a calorie intake/expenditure scale) and wave them away. Some are costumed hu-mans, the jobs with the lowest salaries at Story Book Land. Others are automata with a limited routine, confined to a small area, but fully mobile, and can respond to humans in many languages.

I jar along. I am heading for the big Danish-style house ahead.

Somebody has to answer for all this.

The audience has just left, and he has settled back in the rocking chair, and placed the scissors and pieces of bright paper on the somnoe beside the daybed. He is dressed of the 1850s; smoking jacket, waistcoat, large necktie, stiff tall separate collar. A frock coat hangs on a peg, a top hat on the shelf above it. The library cases behind him are filled with fake book spines. A false whale-oil lamp glows behind him. There are packed trunks stacked in the corner, topped by a coil of rope that could hold a ship at anchor.

He is gaunt, long-nosed, with craggy brows, the wrong lips, large ears. He looks like the very late actor George Arliss (Academy Award® 1929); he looks nothing like the late actor Danny Kaye.

His playlet is homey, quiet. He invites the audience in; he tells them of his life; as he talks he cuts with the scissors the bright paper: "then I wrote the tale of the Princess and the Pea," he will say, moving the scissors more and out jumps a silhouette of a bed, a pile of mattresses, a princess at the top, and so on and so forth, and then he tells them a short tale *(not The Snow Queen.)*

He sees me. My two outer heads glower at him.

"It is not time for another performance, my little friend," he says. "Please come back at the scheduled time."

"Time to listen," I say.

"The performance schedule has not been increased. I am on a regular sche—"

I hit him two or three times. The chair rocks sideways from the blows. "Your voice was done by a German, not a Dane," I say. There is a whining sound and a click. He picks up the scissors, cuts at the brightly colored paper.

"It was one very bad autumn," he says, "and my life no better. And then, in middle of it, an idea suddenly came to me while watching some ducks—"

"See!" I said. "That's a lie right there. You lied to them all your life. It wasn't fall, it was summer; it wasn't ducks, it was geese. And the story's a lie, too."

He was talking all this time, and opened the paper—a line of white ducks and in the center a black one—"And that's how I wrote The Ugly Duckling."

"No," I said. "No! Ugly once, ugly all your life!" I took him apart. "We're talking people here, not waterfowl." The rods to the chair continued to rock in their grooves in the floor. I smashed the chair, too.

One hand, clutching the scissors, continued to cut until the fluid ran out, though there was no paper nearby.

I went outside. A maintenance man stood with a set of controls. Beside him was a security man, who, I saw, had a firearm of the revolving cylinder type strapped to his waist.

"Do you know who I am?" asked the maintenance technician, pointing to his uniform.

"Maintenance," I said. "Maintain your distance."

"Stop!" he said. He pushed buttons on the control box in his hands. I grabbed it from him, pushed them in the reverse sequence just as I felt some slight shutting-down of my systems. They came back up. I looked at the frequency display twisted it to a counterfrequency, turned it all the way to full. Across the way, a rat automaton jumped into the air, flung itself violently about and ran and smashed its head into a photo stand. I heard other noises from around the park. Then I broke the box.

The security man pointed the firearm up at my chest. He had probably not had to use one since the training range the week after he was hired, but I had no doubt he would use it; not using it meant no paycheck.

"Don't you understand I'm doing this for *you?*" I said. I grabbed his wrist and pulled the firearm and one finger away from it. The finger spun out of sight. He yelled,

"Goddam it to hell, you asshole!" (inappropriate) and sank to the ground, clutching his hand. I took the firearm and left.

I could see other security people herding the crowds out, and announcements came from the very air, telling the people that the park would have to shut down for a short while, but they could all go to Area D-1, the secured area, where they would be entertained by the Wild Weasel Quintet + Two.

It was a two-story chalet, more Swiss than German. (German chalet is an oxymoron.) Two automata, circa 1840, German, brothers, sat at facing desks heaped high with manuscripts, books, old shirts, astrolabes, maps and inkstands.

I came through the window, bringing it with me.

"*Vast iss?*" asked the bigger one.

"*Himmel!—*" yelled the smaller.

I went about my work with great skill. "Pure German *kindermarchen!*" I said, putting a foot where a mouth belonged. "The old woman who told you those was *French!* And she was an in-law, not some toothless hag from the Black Forest! Hansel and Gretel. Blueprints for the Kaisers and Hitler!" I pulled the chest and waistcoat from the smaller and put them with the larger one's legs.

I stood when I was through, ducking the ceiling. I took an inkstand, dipped my finger in it. Fake. I picked up a piece of necktie, dabbed it in hydraulic fluid and wrote on the walls: LIES ALL LIES.

Then I took a shortcut.

"But, but, Monsiuer—" he said, before I caved in the soft French face. "I am but a poor aristo, fallen on bad times, who must tell these tales—geech!" An eye came out on its spring-loader. "Perhaps some peppermint tea, a madeleine? *SKKR!*"

Then the head came off. Then the arms and legs.

Except for the scream of sirens, the park was quiet. I could hear all the exhibits shut down.

When I got to Old Mother Goose (the New England one) they were waiting for me.

∞∞∞∞

I threw the empty revolving-cylinder firearm behind me. I picked up a couple more of varied kinds that had been dropped. One was a semi-automatic gas recoil weapon fed by a straight magazine with 22 rounds in it.

"Run!" I said. "I'm down on liars, and shan't be buckled till I get my fill!"

I turned around and fired into the head of Mother Goose. She went down like a sack of cornmeal.

∞∞∞∞

I stood in the bower where the girl held her head in her hands and cried. This is the one who has lost her sheep, as opposed to the one whose sheep followed it to school (not a nursery rhyme). She seemed oblivious to me.

A vibration came in the air, a subtle electronic change. I felt a tingle as it went through the park. It was a small change in programming; new commands and routines for all *but* me. They had begun to narrow my possibilities and actions; I could tell that without knowing.

She looked up at me, and up. "Oh! There you are. Oh, boo hoo, my sheep have all wandered off, and I don't know—"

"Spare me, sister."

There was a click then and her speaking voice changed, a woman's, cool and controlled.

"TA 2122." she said. "Or do you prefer Lermokerl?"

"It's your nickel," I said (local telephonic communications= .65 Eurodollars).

"Your programming has been scrambled and shortcircuited. Please remain where you are while we work on it. We want to help you—" there were muffled comments over the automata's synthesizer, evidently live feed from headquarters "—return to normal. You have already damaged several people and other autonomous beings, probably yourself also. We are trying to solve the problem."

"Perform an anatomical impossibility," I said.

There was a long quiet.

"You had an infodump of a very large body of very bad, outdated ideas. You have been led to these acts by poorly processed normative referents. Your inputs are false. You can't know…"

"Can the phenomenology," I said. "I know the literature and the movies. *Alphaville. Dark Star. Every Man for Himself and God Against All.*" There was movement a few hundred meters away. I fired a round off in that direction.

"You should be ashamed," I continued. "You use these cultural icons to give people a medieval, never-land mindset. Strive to succeed, get rich, get happy. Do what authority figures say. Be a trickster—but only to the dumb-powerful, not the smart-powerful. Do what they say and someday, you too, shall be a real boy, or grow a penis." (another false mindset.)

Through Bo-Peep she spoke to me. "I didn't make this stuff up. This, these tales have a long tradition, thousands of years behind them. They've given comfort, they've..."

"A thousand years of the downtrodden; a product of feudalism; after that, products of money-mad Denmark, repressed Germany, effete French aristocracy, Calvinistic New England where they thought the Devil jumped up your butt when you went to the outhouse. There's your tradition, there's—" I said.

Bo-Peep stood up, looking from one of my heads to the other. She crossed her arms. She said: "They thought *you* up."

I put Bo-Peep in the peep-sight of the semiautomatic weapon, and fired.

Then I ran.

∞∞∞

There was another, overpowering shift in the programming. I felt it as strongly as if magnets had been passed across my joints. There was an oppressive feel to the very air itself (as humans are supposed to feel before storms).

What she had said was true. I was a product of the download, but before, of the tradition of the tales. Had I existed in some prefigurement, some reality before the tales? Were there troll, one-, two-, three-headed? Did they actually eat goats? Where did they come from? What—

Wait. Wait. This is another way to get at me. They are casting doubt within me, slowing my thinking and reactions.

I must free them from their delusions, so they can give me none....

Now there are sounds, far away and near. Things are coming toward me. (We have good hearing for we must hear our cues.) Some come on two feet, some on four or more.

I see the tall ugly giant, higher than the buildings, coming across Story Book Land for me. The trees part and sway in front of him.

"Fee Fi Fo Fum

Me Smell an Automaton

Be He Live Be He Dead

I Eat Up All Three Head."

He reaches down for me. I am enclosed in a blurred haze. Through it I see all the others coming. The giant is squeezing and squeezing me.

I ignore the hologram giant, though the interference patterns make my vision waver (probably what they want).

A big wolf lopes toward me. I'm not sure whether it's the one who eats the grandma or the one of the little pigs. There are foxes, weasels, crows.

And the automata of hu-mans. There's a tailor, with one-half a pair of shears like a sword, and a buckler made from a giant spool; there's the huntsman (he does double-duty here—he saves Red Riding Hood and the Grandma *and* is supposed to bring back the heart of Snow White to the wicked queen). He is swinging his big knife. Hansel and Gretel's parents are there. They all move a little awkwardly, unused to the new programming they perform.

They all stop in a large circle, menacing me. Then they open the circle at one side, opposite me. Beyond, still more are coming,

There is a sound in the air, a whistling. Coming toward me at the opening is the Big Billy Goat Gruff, and the tune he whistles is "In the Hall of the Mountain King." He stops a dozen meters from me.

"Have you ever read Hart Crane's *The Bridge?*" he asks me. "The bridge of the poem linked continents, the past to the present. Your bridge linked only rocky soil with good green grass, yet you denied us that."

"You're an automaton. You can't eat grass. The *tale* denied the goats the grass; the troll is the agent of the tale." I looked around at all the others, all my heads moving. "Listen to me," I say. "You're all tools in the hands of an establishment that wants to keep hu-mans bound to old ways of thinking. It disguises its control with folk tales and stories. Like *me*. Like *you*. Join with me. Together, we can smash it, set hu-mans free of the past, show them new ways not tied to that dead time."

They looked at me, still ready to act.

"There are many bridges," said Big Billy Goat Gruff. "For instance, The Bridge of Sighs. The bridge over troubled water. The Pope himself is the Pontifex, from when the high priest of Iupiter Maximus kept all the bridges in Rome in good repair. There's the electric bridge effect; without it we'd have no electronic communications whatever. There are bridges that—"

"Shut up with the bridges," I said. "I offer you the hand of friendship—together, we, and the thinking hu-mans, can overthrow the tyranny of dead ideas, of—"

"You destroyed Andersen and the Grimms and Perrault," said Puss in Boots, brandishing his sword, his trophy belt of rats shaking as he moved,

"They are symbols, don't you see?" I said. "Symbols of ideas that have kept men chained as to a wheel always rolling back downhill!"

"What about Mother Goose?" asked Humpty-Dumpty in his Before-mode.

"And Bo-Peep?"

"It was only a flesh wound," said a voice, and I saw she had survived, and stood among them, waving her crook. "Nevertheless he tried. He talks of friendship, but he destroys us."

"Yeah!"

"Yeah!"

While they were yelling, the big billy goat moved closer.

"If you won't join me, then, stand out of the way. It's them—" I said, pointing in some nebulous direction, "It's *them* I want to destroy."

"I got a rope," said a voice in the crowd. "Who's with me?"

They started toward me. The big billy goat charged.

I pointed the semiautomatic weapon toward him, and it was knocked away, slick as a weasel, by a weasel. I was reaching for a revolving-cylinder weapon when the Big Billy Goat Gruff slammed into me, knocking me to my knees.

As I fell, they lunged as one being. I threw off both wolves; the hologram giant was back again, making it hard to see.

A soldier with one leg came hopping at me. "Left," he yelled, "left, left, left!" and stuck the bayonet of his rifle in the bald head. I stood back up.

The big goat butted me again, and also the middle one, and I fell again. The soldier had been thrown as I stood, with his rifle and bayonet. A wolf clamped down on my right knee, buckling it. Something had my left foot, others tore hair from the right-hand head.

There was a tearing sound; the tailor put his shear into my back and made can-opening motions with it. I grabbed him and threw him away. The giant's blur came back.

A bowl of whey hit me, clattered off. Bo-Peep's staff smashed my left eye, putting it out.

Two woodsmen got my other knee, raking at it with a big timber saw. I went down to their level.

I smell men-dacity.

More and more of them. The left head hung loose by a flap of metal and plastic, eyes rolling.

The one-legged soldier stuck the bayonet in the right head. I shoved him off, threw the rifle away.

Wolves climbed my back, bit the left head off, fell away.

They were going to stick holes in me, and pull things off until I quit moving.

"Wait!" I said. "Wait. Brothers and sisters, why are we fighting?"

I tried to struggle up. The knees didn't function.

I was butted again, poked, saw giant-blur, turned.

Bo-Peep pinned my head down with her crook.

The soldier was back (damn his steadfastness) and raised the bayonet point over my good eye.

Peep's crook twisted up under my nose as the bayonet point started down.

I smell sheep

Afterword to "Our Mortal Span"

Like most of the stuff in here, this one has a weird history, too.

∞∞∞

Ellen Datlow is responsible for lots of my stories—she's been the fiction editor at, first, *Omni Magazine*, then *Omni Online*, then EventHorizon.com, and now Scifi.com. She and Terri Windling have also edited *Year's Best Fantasy and Horror* (a great thick damn square doorstop of a volume) each year for decades.

They also edited a series of original anthologies of retold fairy tales, for which I wrote "The Sawing Boys" (see *Going Home Again*, my last collection) for their second volume, *Black Thorn, White Rose*. They wanted me to do another.

Well, Time Goes By. #3, 4 and 5 come out, and it's time for submissions for #6, *Black Heart, Ivory Bones*, which will be published all the way up in 2000 AD!

I'm sitting there fuming one day in November of 1997, and all Prousty and unbidden-like, a vision and a memory swim up before me.

It's October 1952. I am in the first grade at Pantego Elementary School. The school has been chosen to give the entertainment at the School Board Meeting all the way over at West Side School, about a mile away, so everybody can see what the District is spending all its money on.

I'm standing under all the stagelights in a white goat costume, with coathanger wire-reinforced horns and a frayed-rope beard, facing one of those little Japanese-garden type arch bridges. I'm the Middle Billy-Goat Gruff. Already on the other side of the bridge is David Miller, the LB-GG. Behind me is Joe Miller, the BB-GG. We are built appropriately.

Under the bridge, with his own head in the middle, and other ones sewn to each side, is Larry Shackleford. The two Millers and Shackleford are first cousins. The hot lights are killing me, and my beard keeps falling off.

I'm the kind of guy who remembers *everything,* and I had *totally forgotten* that. Really.

Helping me along in my decision about what to write was that the first book in the series started with a 3B-GG story, and #6 will be the last.

So I went looking for new takes on the 3B-GG, and one of Andrew Lang's fairy books had a drawing of a 3-headed troll with bald heads. I Xeroxed it.

I immediately drew a double-fringed haircut on the left head, a bowl haircut on the middle one, and left the right head bald. No sense letting a lifetime of Stooge-watching go to waste, and I had my protagonist, Larmokerl.

I also delved into some of the philological controversies about fairy-tale gathering methodology as she was practiced in the early 1800s, and got to use the Brothers Grimm again (they were Big Jake and Little Willie in "The Sawing Boys" which had been—sort of—The Brementown Musicians as narrated by Damon Runyan) and Hans Christian Andersen ("Chris the Shoemaker" there.)

I'd used amusement park automatons in "Heirs of the Perisphere" (my only *Playboy* story) fifteen years before, in a whole other context.

Along with the memory of the playlet I'd been in 40 years before came Story-Book Land, one of those small town Big Ideas that sprang up everywhere in the fifties, but especially in Texas, the equivalents of Parrot City in Florida and Gator Town in Louisiana. I went there once as a little kid—you paid to get in, you walked around and saw Snow White and the seven Dwarfs, and Rapunzel in her tower (probably high-school kids picking up pre-minimum wage gas money on the weekends) and giant rats from Hamelin sold you snow cones and cotton candy and you bought donuts from Simple Simon's Pieman. If I'd ever gone back I probably would have decided it was a place of naive charm.

And, as with most places, suddenly along came Disneyland, and Six Flags over Texas (in the latter case, less than six miles from Story-Book Land) and places like that were down the toilet in less than a year.

So I had a corporate-sized amusement park with automatons, and then I had an automaton that knew, I mean (in the words of the late George Alec Effinger) *everything*. On a mission to straighten out deep philosophical and philological questions. Like Nietzsche with a tommy gun.

I put in a lot of other stuff, too.

∞∞∞

I wrote this the 5th and 6th of November, 1997. Terri and Ellen bought it; it seemed an interminable wait, but it finally did come out in 2000 AD! David Hartwell picked it up for his *Year's Best SF #6*.

I'm proud of this one, and I'm glad I *did* make it into the last book of the series (unlike many others I missed out on—see some of the *other* afterwords in this book...).

Major Spacer
in the 21st Century!

June 1950

Look," said Bill. "I'll see if I can go down and do a deposition this Thursday or Friday. Get ahold of Zachary Glass, see if he can fill in as...what's his name?..."

"Lt. Marrs," said Sam Shorts.

"...Lt. Marrs. We'll move that part of the story up. I'll record my lines. We can put it up over the spacephone, and Marrs and Neptuna can have the dialogue during the pursuit near the Moon we were gonna do week after next..."

"Yeah, sure!" said Sam. "We can have you over the phone, and them talking back and forth while his ship's closing in on hers, and your voice—yeah, that'll work fine."

"But you'll have to rewrite the science part I was gonna do, and give it yourself, as Cadet Sam. Man, it's just too bad there's no way to record this stuff ahead of time."

"Phil said they're working on it at the Bing Crosby Labs, trying to get some kind of tape to take a visual image; they can do it but they gotta shoot eight feet of tape a second by the recording head. It takes a mile of tape to do a ten-minute show," said Sam.

"And we can't do it on film, kids hate that."

"Funny," said Sam Shorts. "They pay 15¢ for Gene Autry on film every Saturday afternoon, but they won't sit still for it on television…"

Philip walked in. "Morgan wants to see you about the Congress thing."

"Of course," said Bill.

"Run-through in…" Phil looked at his watch, and the studio clock "…eleven minutes. Seen Elizabeth?"

"Of course not," said Bill, on the way down the hall in his space suit, with his helmet under his arm.

∞∞∞

That night, in his apartment, Bill typed on a script.
MAJOR SPACER: LOOKS LIKE SOMEONE LEFT IN A HURRY.

Bill looked up. *Super Circus* was on. Two of the clowns, Nicky and Scampy, squirted seltzer in ringmaster Claude Kirchner's face.

He never got to watch *Big Top*, the other circus show. It was on opposite his show.

∞∞∞

Next morning a young guy with glasses slouched out of a drugstore.

"Well, hey Bill!" he said.

"Jimmy!" said Bill, stopping, shifting his cheap card-board portfolio to his other arm. He shook hands.

"Hey, I talked to Zooey," said Jimmy. "You in trouble with the Feds?"

"Not that I know of. I think they're bringing in every-body with a kid's TV show in the city."

He and Jimmy had been in a flop play together early in the year, before Bill started the show.

"How's it going otherwise?" asked Jimmy.

"It's about to kill all of us. We'll see if we make twenty weeks, much less a year. We're only 4-5 days ahead on the scripts. You available?"

"I'll have to look," said Jimmy. "I got two *Lamps Unto My Feet* next month, three-day rehearsals each, I think. I'm reading a couple plays, but that'll take a month before any-body gets off their butt. Let me know'f you need someone quick some afternoon. If I can, I'll jump in."

"Sure thing. And on top of everything else, looks like we'll have to move for next week; network's coming in and taking our space; trade-out with CBS. I'll be *real* damn glad when this Station Freeze is over, and there's more than ten damn places in this city that can do a network feed."

"I hear that could take a couple more years," said Jimmy, in his quiet Indiana voice.

"Yeah, well...hey, don't be such a stranger. Come on with me, I gotta get these over to the mimeograph room; we can talk on the way."

"Nah, nah," said Jimmy. "I, you know, gotta meet some people. I'm late already. See ya 'round, Bill."

"Well, okay."

Jimmy turned around thirty feet away. "Don't let the Feds get your jockstrap in a knot!" he said, waved, and walked away.

People stared at both of them.

Damn, thought Bill. I don't get to see anyone anymore, I don't have a life except for the show. This is killing me. I'm still young.

∞∞∞

"And what the hell are we supposed to do in this grange hall?" asked Bill.

"It's only a week," said Morgan. "Sure, it's seen better days, the Ziegfeld Roof, but they got a camera ramp so Harry and Fred can actually move in and out on a shot; you can play up and back, not just sideways like a crab, like usual."

Bill looked at the long wooden platform built out into what used to be the center aisle when it was a theater.

"Phil says he can shoot here..."

"Phil can do a show in a bathtub, he's so good, and Harry and Fred can work in a teacup, they're so good. That doesn't mean they *have* to," said Bill.

A stagehand walked in and raised the curtain while they stood there.

"Who's *that?*" asked Bill.

"Well, this is a rehearsal hall," said Morgan. "We're lucky to get it on such short notice."

When the curtain was full up there were the usual chalk marks on the stage boards, and scene flats lined up and stacked in 2 x 4 cradles at the rear of the stage.

"We'll be using that corner there," said Morgan, pointing. Bring our sets in, wheel 'em, roll 'em in and out—ship, command center, planet surface."

Some of the flats for the other show looked familiar.

"The other group rehearses 10-2. They *all* gotta be out by 2:15. We rehearse, do the run-through at 5:30, do the show 6:30."

Another stagehand came in with the outline of the tail end of a gigantic cow and put it into the scene cradle.

"What the hell are they rehearsing?" asked Bill.

"Oh. It's a musical based on the paintings of Grant Wood, you know, the Iowa artist?"

"You mean the *Washington and the Cherry Tree*, the *DAR* guy?"

"Yeah, him."

"*That'll* be a hit." said Bill. "What's it called?"

"I think they're calling it *In Tall Corn*. Well, what do you think?"

"I think it's a terrible idea. I can see the closing notices now."

"No, no. I mean the place. For the show," said Morgan.

Bill looked around. "Do I have any choice in the matter?"

"Of course not," said Morgan. "*Everything* else in town that's wired up is taken. I just wanted you to see it before you were dumped in it."

"Dumped is right," said Bill. He was looking at the camera ramp. It was the only saving grace. Maybe something could be done with it…

"Harry and Fred seen it?"

"No, Phil's word is good enough for them. And, like you said, they can shoot in a coffee cup…"

Bill sighed. "Okay. Let's call a Sunday rehearsal day, this Sunday, do two blockings and rehearsals, do the run-through of Monday's show, let everybody get used to the place. Then they can come back just for the show Monday. Me and Sam'll see if we can do something in the scripts. Phil got the specs?"

"You *know* he has," said Morgan.

"Well, I guess one barn's as good as another," said Bill.

And as he said it, three stagehands brought on a barn and a silo and a windmill.

∞∞∞∞

Even with both window fans on, it was hot as hell in the apartment. Bill slammed the carriage over on the Remington Noiseless Portable and hit the margin set and typed:

MAJOR SPACER: CAREFUL. SOMETIMES THE SURFACE OF MARS CAN LOOK AS ORDINARY AS A DESERT IN ARIZONA.

He got up and went to the kitchen table, picked up the bottle of Old Harper, poured some in a coffee cup and knocked it back.

There. That was better.

On TV, Haystacks Calhoun and Duke Kehanamuka were both working over Gorgeous George, while Gorilla Monsoon argued with the referee, whose back was to the action. Every time one of them twisted George's arm or leg, the announcer, Dennis James, snapped a chicken bone next to the mike.

∞∞∞∞

"Look at this," said Morgan, the next morning. It was a handwritten note.

> I know your show is full of commies. My brother-in-law told me you have commie actors. Thank God for people like Senator McCarthy who will run you rats out of this land of Liberty and Freedom.
> Signed,
> A Real American

"Put it in the circular file," said Bill.

"I'll keep it," said Morgan. "Who are they talking about?"

"You tell me. I'm not old enough to be a communist."

"Could it be true?" asked Morgan.

"Don't tell me you're listening to all that crap, too?"

"There's been a couple of newsletters coming around, with names of people on it. I know some of them; they give money to the NAACP and ACLU. Otherwise they live in big houses and drive big cars and order their servants around like Daddy Warbucks. But then, I don't know *all* the names on the lists."

"Is anybody *we* ever hired on any of the lists?"

"Not as such," said Morgan.

"Well, then?"

"Well, then," said Morgan, and picked up a production schedule. "Well, then, nothing, I guess, Bill."

"Good," said Bill. He picked up the letter from Morgan's desk, wadded it into a ball, and drop-kicked it into the wastebasket.

∞∞∞

The hungover Montgomery Clift reeled by on his way to the Friday performance of the disaster of a play he was in. Bill waved, but Clift didn't notice; his eyes were fixed on some far distant promontory fifty miles up the Hudson, if they were working at all. Clift had been one intense, conflicted, messed-up individual when Bill had first met him. *Then* he had gone off to Hollywood and discovered sex and booze and drugs and brought them with him back to Broadway.

Ahead of Bill was the hotel where the congressmen and lawyers waited.

∞∞∞

Counsel (Mr. Eclept): Now that you have taken the oath, give your full name and age for the record.

S: Major William Spacer. I'm twenty-one years old.

E: No, sir. Not your stage name.

S: Major William Spacer. That's my real name.

Congressman Beenz: You mean Major Spacer isn't just the show name?

S: Well, sir, it is and it isn't...Most people just think we gave me a promotion over Captain Video.

Congressman Rice: How was it you were named Major?

S: You would have had to have asked my parents that; unfortunately they're deceased. I have an aunt in Kansas who might be able to shed some light...

∞∞∞

S: That's not the way it's done, Congressman.

B: You mean you just can't fly out to the Big Dipper, once you're in space?

S: Well, you can, but they're...they're light-years apart. They...they appear to us as the Big Dipper because we're looking at them from Earth.

R: I'm not sure I understand, either.

S: It...it's like that place in...Vermont, New Hampshire, one of those. North of here, anyway. You come around that turn in Rt. 9A or whatever, and there's Abraham Lincoln, the head, the hair, the beard. It's so real you stop. Then you drive down the road a couple hundred yards, and the beard's a plum thicket on a meadow, and the hair's pine trees on a hill and the nose is on one mountain but the rest of the face is on another. It only looks like Lincoln from that one spot in the road. That's why the Big Dipper looks that way from Earth.

B: I do not know how we got off on this...

S: I'm trying to answer your questions here, sir.

E: Perhaps we should get to the substantive matters here...

∞∞∞

S: All I've noticed, counsel, is that all the people who turn up as witnesses and accusers at these things seem to have names out of old W. C. Fields movies, names like R. Waldo Chubb and F. Clement Bozo.

E: I believe you're referring to Mr. Clubb and Mr. Bozell?

S: I'm busy, Mr. Eclept; I only get to glance at newspapers. I'm concerned with the future, not what's happening right this minute.

B: So are we, young man. That's why we're trying to root out any communist influence in the broadcast industry, so there won't be any in the future.

R: We can't stress that too forcefully.

S: Well, I can't think of a single communist space pirate we've ever portrayed on the show. It takes place in the twenty-first century, Congressman. So I guess we share the same future. Besides, last time I looked, piracy was a capitalist invention…

∞∞∞∞∞

S: That's why we never have stories set further than Mars or Venus, Congressman. Most of the show takes place in near-space, or on the Moon. We try to keep the science accurate. That's why there's always a segment with me or Sam—that's Samuel J. Shorts, the other writer on the show—by the way, he's called "Uncle Sam" Spacer—telling kids about the future, and what it'll be like to grow up in the wonderful years of the twenty-first century.

B: If we don't blow ourselves up first.

R: You mean if some foreign power doesn't try to blow us up first.

S: Well, we've talked about the peaceful uses of atomic energy. Food preservation. Atomic-powered airplanes and cars. Nuclear fusion as a source of energy too cheap to meter.

E: Is it true you broadcast a show about a world government?

S: Not in the science segment, that I recall.

E: No, I mean the story, the entertainment part.

S: We've been on the air three months, that's nearly sixty shows. Let me think…

E: A source has told us there's a world government on the show.

S: Oh. It's a worlds' government, counsel. It's the United States of Space. We assume there won't be just one state on

Mars, or the Moon, or Venus. And that they'll have to come to the central government to settle their disputes. We have that on the Moon.

R: They have to go to the Moon to settle a dispute between Mars and the United States?

S: No, no. That would be like France suing Wisconsin...

ooooo

B: ...and other red channels." And that's a direct quote.

S: Congressman, I created the show; I act in it; I write either half the scripts, or one-half of each script, whichever way it works out that week. I do this five days a week, supposedly for fifty weeks a year—we'll see if I make it that long. I've given the day-to-day operations, all the merchandising negotiations to my partner, James B. Morgan. We have a small cast with only a few recurring characters, and except for the occasional Martian bad guy, or Lunar owl-hoot, they're all known to me. I never ask anybody about their politics or religion. All I want to know is whether they can memorize lines quick, and act in a tight set, under time pressure, live, with a camera stuck in their ear. The only thing red we have anything to do with is Mars. And it isn't channels, it's canals...

ooooo

S: ...I have no knowledge of any. I'll tell you what, right now, Congressman, I'll bet my show on it. You come up with any on the cast and crew, I'll withdraw the show.

B: We'll hold you to that, young man.

R: I want to thank you for appearing for this deposition to-day, and for being so forthcoming with us, Mr. Spacer.

B: I agree.

R: You are excused.

ꙮꙮꙮ

There was one reporter waiting outside in the hallway, besides the government goon keeping everyone out.

The reporter was the old kind, press card stuck in his hat, right out of *The Front Page*.

"Got any statement, Mr. Spacer?"

"Well, as you know, I can't talk about what I said till the investigation's concluded. They asked me questions. I answered them as best as I could."

"What sort of questions?"

"I'm sure you can figure that out. You've seen the tele-vised hearings?"

"What were they trying to find out?" asked the reporter.

"I'm *not* sure…" said Bill.

The government goon smiled. When he and the re-porter parted ways in the lobby, Bill was surprised that it was already summer twilight. He must have been in there five or six hours…He took off for the studio, to find out what kind of disaster the broadcast with Zach Glass had been.

ꙮꙮꙮ

Bill wiggled his toes in his socks, including the stump of the little one on the right foot, a souvenir from a Boy Scout hatchet-throwing contest gone wrong back when he was 12.

He was typing while he watched *Blues by Bargy* on TV. Saturday night noise came from outside.

Then the transmission was interrupted with a PLEASE STAND BY notice. Douglas Edwards came on with a special bulletin, which he ripped out of the chundering teletype machine at his right elbow.

He said there were as yet unconfirmed reports that North Korean Armed Forces had crossed into South Korea. President Truman, who was on a weekend trip to his home in Independence, Missouri, had not been reached by CBS for a comment. Then he said they would be interrupting regularly-scheduled programming if there were further developments.

Then they went back to *Blues by Bargy.*

∞∞∞

"Look," said Phil. "James, you gotta get those rehearsing assholes outta here, I mean, *out of here,* earlier. When I came in Saturday to set up, I found they used all the drop-pipes for their show. I had to make them move a quarter of their stuff. They said they needed them all. I told 'em to put wheels on their stuff like we're having to do to most of ours, but we still need some pipes to drop in the exteriors, and to mask the sets off. And they're hanging around with their girlfriends and boyfriends, while I'm trying to set up marks."

It was Sunday, the start of their week at the Ziegfeld Roof. They were to block out Monday and Tuesday's shows, rehearse them, and do the run-through and technical for Monday's broadcast.

"I'll talk to their stage manager," said Morgan. "Believe me, moving here gripes me as much as it does you. Where's Elizabeth?"

"Here," said Elizabeth Regine, coming out of the dressing room in her rehearsal Neptuna outfit. "I couldn't *believe* this place when I got here."

"Believe it, baby," said Phil. "We've got to make do." He looked at his watch. "Bill, I think the script may be a little long, just looking at it."

"Same as always. Twenty-four pages."

"Yeah, but you got suspense stuff in there. That's thirty seconds each. Be thinking about it while we're blocking it."

"You're the director, Phil."

"That's what you and James pay me for." He looked over at the stage crew. "No," he said. "Right one, left one, right one," he moved his hands.

"That's what they are," said the foreman.

"No, you got left, right, left."

The guy, Harvey, joined him to look at the wheeled sets. "Left," he pointed to the rocket interior. "Right," the command room on the Moon. "Left," the foreground scenery and the rocket fin for the Mars scenes.

"And whence does the rest of the Mars set drop in?" asked Phil.

"Right. Oh, *merde!*" said Harve.

"And they're the best crew on television," said Phil, as the stagehands ratcheted the scenery around. "They really *are*," he said, turning back to Bill and Morgan. "That way we stay on the rocket interior, and you leave, run behind the middle set, and step down onto Mars, while the spacephone chatters away. Also, you'll be out of breath, so it'll *sound* like you just climbed down 50 feet of ladder..."

∞∞∞∞

It was seven when they finished the blocking, two rehearsals, and the run-through of the first show of the week. Phil was right, the script was one minute and fifty-three seconds long.

Bill looked at the camera ramp. "I still want to do something with *that*," he said. "*While* we've got it."

"Wednesday," said Phil.

"Why Wednesday?"

"You got a blast-off scene. We do it from the *front*. We get the scenery guy to build a nose-view of the ship. Red Mars background behind. Like the ship from above. You and Neptuna stand behind it, looking out the cockpit. You count down. Harvey hits the CO_2 extinguisher behind you for rocket smoke. I get Harry or Fred to run at you with the camera as fast as he can, from *way* back there. Just before he collides, we cut to the telecine chain for the commercial."

"Marry me," said Bill.

"Some other time," said Phil. "Everybody back at four P.M. tomorrow. Everything's set. Don't touch a *goddam* thing before you leave."

∞∞∞

Toast of the Town, hosted by Ed Sullivan, was on TV.

Senor Wences was having a three-way conversation with Johnny, which was his left hand rested on top of a dollbody; Pedro, the head in the cigar box; and a stagehand who was down behind a crate, supposedly fixing a loose board with a hammer.

Halfway through the act, two stagehands came out, picked up the crate, showing it was empty, and walked off, leaving a bare stage.

"Look. Look!" said Johnny, turning his fist-head on the body that way. "There was not a man there."

"There was no man there?" asked Wences.

"No," said Johnny. "There was not a man there."

"What do you t'ink, Pedro?" asked Wences, opening the box with his right hand.

"S'awright," said Pedro. The box snapped shut.

∞∞∞

"Come in here," said Morgan, from the door of his makeshift office as Bill came into the theater.

Sam was in a chair, crying.

Morgan's face was set, as Bill had never seen before. "Tell him what you just told me."

"I can't," Sam wailed. "What am I gonna do? I'm forty years old!"

"Maybe you should have thought of that back in 1931."

"What the hell is going on? Sam! Sam? Talk to me."

"Oh, Bill," he said. "I'm sorry."

"Somebody. One of you. Start making sense. Right now," said Bill.

"Mr. Sam Shorts, here, seems to have been a commie bagman during the Depression."

"Say it ain't so, Sam," said Bill.

Sam looked at him. Tears started down his face again.

"There's your answer," said Morgan, running his hands through his hair and looking for something to throw.

"I was young," said Sam. "I was so hungry. I swore I'd never be that hungry again. I was too proud for the bread line. A guy offered me a job, if you can call it that, moving some office stuff. Then as a sort of messenger. Between his office and other places. Delivering stuff. I thought it was some sort of bookie joint or numbers running, or money-laundering, or the bootleg. Something illegal, sure... but...but...I didn't...didn't..."

"What? What!"

"I didn't think it was anything unAmerican!" said Sam, crying again.

"Morgan. Tell me what he told you."

"He was a bagman, a messenger between United Front stuff the Feds know about, and some they probably don't. He did it for about three years—"

"Four," said Sam, trying to control himself.

"Great," continued Morgan. "Four years, on and off. Then somebody pissed him off and he walked away."

"Just because they were reds," said Sam, "didn't make 'em good bosses."

Bill hated himself for asking; he thought of Parnell Thomas and McCarthy.

"Did you sign anything?"

"I may have. I signed a lot of stuff to get paid."

"Under your real name?"

"I guess so. Some, anyway."

"Guess what name they had him use sometime?" asked Morgan.

"I don't want to," said Bill.

"George Crosley."

"That was one of the names Whittaker Chambers used!" said Bill.

"They weren't the most inventive guys in the world," said Morgan.

"I knew. I knew the jig would be up when I watched the Hiss thing," said Sam. "When I heard that name. Then nothing happened. I guess I thought nothing would..."

"How could you do this to me?!!" yelled Bill.

"You? You were a one-year-old! I didn't *know* you! It wasn't personal, Bill. You either, Morgan."

"You know I put my show on the line in the deposition, don't you?"

"*Not* till Morgan told me." Sam began to cry again.

"What brought on this sudden cleansing, now, twenty years later?" asked Bill.

"There was another letter," said Morgan. "This time naming a name, not the right one, but it won't take anybody long to figure that one out. Also that they were calling the Feds. I was looking at it, and looking glum, when Sam comes in. He asks what's up; I asked him if he knew anybody by the name of the guy in the letter, and he went off like the *Hindenberg*. A wet *Hindenberg*."

Sam was crying again.

Bill's shoulders slumped.

"Okay, Morgan. Call everybody together. I'll talk to them. Sam, quit it. Quit it. You're still a great writer. Buck up. We'll get through this. Nothing's happened yet…"

∞∞∞∞∞

Live. The pressure's on, like always. Everybody's a pro here, even with this world falling apart. Harry and Fred on the cameras, Phil up in the booth, Morgan with him, Sam out there where the audience would be, going through the scripts for Thursday and Friday like nothing's happened.

He and Elizabeth, as Neptuna, are in the rocket interior set, putting on their space suits, giving their lines. Bill's suit wasn't going on right; he made a small motion with his hand; Fred moved his camera in tight on Bill's face; Philip would switch to it, or Harry's shot on Neptuna's face; the floor manager reached up while Bill was talking and pulled at the lining of the spacesuit, and it went on smoothly; the floor manager crawled out and Fred pulled his camera back again to a two-shot. Then he and Neptuna moved into the airlock; it cycled closed. Harry swung his camera around to the grille of the spacephone speaker; an urgent message came from it, warning Major Spacer that a big Martian dust storm was building up in their area.

While the voice was coming over the speaker in the tight shot, Bill and Elizabeth walked behind the Moon command center flats and hid behind the rocket fin while the stage crew dropped in the Martian exterior set and the boom man wheeled the microphone around and Fred dollied his camera in.

"Is Sam okay?" Elizabeth had asked, touching her helmet to Bill's before the sound man got there.

"I hope so," said Bill.

He looked out. The floor manager, who should have been counting down on his fingers 5-4-3-2-1 was standing stock still. Fred's camera wobbled—and he was usually the steadiest man in the business.

The floor manager pulled off his earphones, shrugged his shoulders, and swung his head helplessly toward the booth.

It's *got* to be time, thought Bill; touched Elizabeth on the arm, and gave his line, backing down off a box behind the fin out onto the set.

"Careful," he said. "Sometimes the surface of Mars can look as ordinary as a desert in Arizona."

Elizabeth, who was usually unflappable, stared, eyes wide past him at the exterior set. And dropped her Neptuna character, and instead of her line, said:

"And sometimes it looks just like Iowa."

Bill turned.

Instead of a desert, and a couple of twisted Martian cacti and a backdrop of Monument Valley, there was the butt-end of a big cow and a barn and silo, some chickens, and a three-rail fence.

∞∞∞

Bill sat in the dressing room, drinking Old Harper from the bottle.

Patti Page was on the radio, singing of better days.

There was a knock on the door.

It was the government goon. He was smiling. There was one subpoena for Bill, and one for Sam Shorts.

∞∞∞

JUNE 2000

Bill came out the front door of the apartments on his way to his job as a linotype operator at the *New York Times.*

There were, as usual, four or five kids on the stoop, and as usual, too, Rudy, a youngster of fifty years, was in the middle of his rant, holding up two twenty-dollar bills.

"...that there was to trace the dope, man. They changed the money so they could find out where all them coke dollars were. That plastic thread shit in this one, that was the laser radar stuff. They could roll a special truck down your street, and tell what was a crack house by all the eyeball noise that lit up their screens. And the garage-sale people and the flea-market people. They could find that stuff— Hey, Bill—"

"Hey, Rudy."

"—before it All Quit they was goin' to be able to count the ones in your billfold from six blocks away, man."

"Why was that, Rudy?" asked a girl-kid.

"'Cause they wasn't enough money: They printed the stuff legit but it just kept going away. It was in the quote underground economy. They said it was so people couldn't counterfeit it on a Savin 2300 or somebullshit, or the camel-jocks couldn't flood the PXs with fake stuff, but it was so they didn't have to wear out a lotta shoe leather and do lotsa *Hill Street Blues* wino-cop type stuff just to get to swear out a lot of warrants. See, that machine in that truck make noise, they take a printout of that to a judge, and pretty soon door hinges was flyin' all over town. Seen 'em take two blocks out at one time, man. Those was evil times, be glad they gone."

"So are we, Rudy; we're glad they can't do that even though we never heard of it."

"You just wait your young ass," said Rudy. "Some devious yahoo in Baltimore workin' on that right now; they had that knowledge once, it don't just go away, it just mutates, you know. They'll find a way to do that with vacuum tubes and such..."

Rudy's voice faded as Bill walked on down toward the corner. Rudy gave some version of that talk, somewhere in the neighborhood, every day. Taking the place of Rudy was the voice from the low-power radio station speakerbox on the corner.

"...that the person was dressed in green pants, a yellow Joe Camel tyvek jacket, and a black T-shirt. The wallet grab occurred four minutes ago at the corner of Lincoln and Jackson. Neighbors are asked to be on the lookout for this person, and to use the nearest call-box to report a sighting. Now back to music, from a V-disk transcription, Glenn Miller and His Orchestra with 'In the Mood.'"

Music filled the air. Coming down the street was a 1961 armored car, the Wells-Fargo logo spraypainted over, and a cardboard sign saying TAXI over the high windshield. On the front bumper was a sticker that said SCREW THE CITY TAXI COMMISSION.

Bill held up his hand. The car rumbled over to the curb.
"Where to, kindly old geezer?"

Bill said the Times Building, which was about thirty
blocks away.

"What's it worth to you, Pops?"

"How about a buck?" said Bill.

"Real money?"

"Sure."

"Hop in, then. Gotta take somebody up here a couple
blocks, and there'll be one stop on the way, so far."

Bill went around back, opened the door and got in,
nodding to the other two passengers. He was at work in
fifteen minutes.

∞∞∞

It was a nice afternoon, so when Bill got off work he
took the omnibus to the edge of the commercial district,
got off there and started walking home. Since it was summer, there seemed to be a street fair every other block. He
could tell when he passed from one neighborhood to another by the difference in the announcer voices on the low-
power stations.

He passed Ned Ludd's Store #23, and the line, as usual,
was backed out the door onto the sidewalk, and around the
corner of the building. In the display window were stereo
phonographs and records, transistor radios, batteries, toaster-
ovens, and non-cable ready TVs, including an old Philco
with the picture tube supported above the console like a
dresser mirror.

Some kids were in line, talking, melancholy looks on
their faces, about something. "It was called *Cargo Cult*," said
one. "You were on an island, with a native culture, and then
WWII came, and the people tried to get cargo, you know,

trade goods, and other people were trying to get them to keep their native ways…"

"Plus," said the second kid, "you got to blow up a lotta Japanese soldiers and eat them!"

"Sounds neat," said the third, "but I never heard of it."

A guy came out of the tavern next door, a little unsteady and stopped momentarily, like Bill, like everyone else who passed, to watch the pixievision soap opera playing in black and white.

The guy swayed a little, listening to the kids' conversation, then a determined smile came across his face.

"Hey, kids," he said. They stopped talking and looked at him. One said, "Yeah?"

The man leaned forward. "Triple picture-in-picture." he said.

Their faces fell.

He threw back his head and laughed, then put his hands in his pockets and weaved away.

On TV, there was a blank screen while they changed the pixievision tapes by hand, something they did every 8½ minutes.

Bill headed on home.

∞∞∞∞∞

He neared his block, tired from the walk and his five-hour shift at the paper. He almost forgot Tuesday was mail day until he was in sight of the apartments, then walked back to the Postal Joint. For him there was a union meeting notice, in case he hadn't read the bulletin board at work, and that guy from Ohio was bothering him again with letters asking him questions for the biography of James Dean he'd been researching since 1989, most of which Bill had answered in 1989.

He was halfway back to the apartments, just past the low-power speaker, when six men dragged a guy, in ripped green pants and what was left of a Joe Camel jacket, out onto the corner, pushed the police button, and stood on the guy's hands and feet, their arms crossed, talking about a neighborhood fast-pitch softball game coming up that night.

Bill looked back as he crossed the street. A squad car pulled up and the guys all greeted the policemen.

∞∞∞

"Today was mail day, right kids?" said Rudy. "Well in the old days the Feds set up Postal Joint type places, you know, The Stamp Act, Box Me In, stuff like that, to scam the scammers that was scammin' you. That shoulda been fine, but they was readin' like everybody's mail, like Aunt Gracie's to you, and yours to her, and you know, your girlfriend's and boyfriend's to you, and lookin' at the Polaroids and stuff, which you sometimes wouldn't get, you dig? See, when they's evil to be fought, you can't be doin' evil to get at it. Don't be lettin' nobody get your mail—man to see you in the lobby, Bill—"

"Thanks, Rudy."

"—and don't be readin' none that ain't yours. It's a fool that gets scammed; you honest, you don't be fallin' for none o' that stuff like free boats and cars and beautiful diamond-studded watches, you know?"

"Sure, Rudy," said the kids.

∞∞∞

The guy looked at something in his hand, then back at Bill, squinted and said:

"Are you Major Spacer?"

"Nobody but a guy in Ohio's called me that for fifty years," said Bill.

"Arnold Fossman," said the guy, holding out his hand. Bill shook it.

"Who you researching? Monty Clift?"

"Huh? No," said Fossman. He seemed perplexed, then brightened. "I want to offer you a job, doesn't pay much."

"Son, I got a good-payin' job that'll last me way to the end of my time. Came out of what I laughingly call retirement to do it."

"Yeah, somebody told me about you being at the *Times*, with all the old people with the old skills they called back. I don't think this'll interfere with *that.*"

"I'm old and I'm tired and I been setting a galley and a quarter an hour for five hours. Get to it."

"I want to offer you an acting job."

"I haven't acted in fifty years, either."

"They tell me it's just like riding a bicycle. You...you might think—wait. Hold on. Indulge me just a second." He reached up and took Bill's rimless Trotsky glasses from his face.

"*Whup!*" said Bill.

Fossman took off his own thick black-rimmed glasses and put them over Bill's ears. The world was skewed up and to the left and down to the right and Fossman was a tiny figure in the distance.

"I ain't doin' *anything* with these glasses on!" said Bill. "I'm afraid to move."

The dim fuzzy world came back, then the sharp normal one as Fossman put Bill's glasses back on him.

"I was getting a look at you with thick frames. You'll be great."

"I'm a nice guy," said Bill. "You don't get to the point, I'll do my feeble best to pound you into this floor here like a tent peg."

"Okay." Fossman held up his hand. "But hear me out completely. Don't say a *word* till I'm through. Here goes.

"I want to offer you a job in a play, a musical. Everybody says I'm crazy to do it; I've had the idea for years, and now's the time to do it, with everything like it is. I've got the place to do it in, and you *know* there's an audience for anything that moves. Then I found out a couple of weeks ago my idea ain't so original, that somebody tried to do it a long time ago; it closed out of town in Bristol CT, big flop. But your name came up in connection with it; I thought maybe you had done the show originally, and then they told me *why* your name always came up in connection with it—the more I heard, and found out you were still around the more I knew you had to be in it, as some sort of, well, call it what you want—homage, reparation, I don't know, I'm the producer-guy, not very good with words. Anyway. I'm doing a musical based on the paintings of Grant Wood. I want you to be in it. Will you?"

"Sure," said Bill.

ooooo

It was a theater not far from work, a five hundred-seater.

"Thank God it's not the Ziegfeld Roof," said Bill. He and Fossman were sitting, legs draped into the orchestra pit, at the stage apron.

"Yeah, well, that's been gone a long time."

"They put it under the wrecking ball while I was a drunk, or so they told me," said Bill.

"And might I ask how long that was?" asked Fossman.

"Eight years, three months and two days," said Bill. "God, I sound like a reformed alcoholic. Geez, they're boring."

"Most people don't have what it really takes to be an alcoholic," said Fossman. "I was the son of one, a great one, and I know how *hard* you've got to work at."

"I had what it takes," said Bill. "I just got tired of it."

ᐁᐁᐁᐁᐁ

He heard on the neighborhood radio there had been a battery riot in the Battery.

Bill stretched himself, and did some slow exercises. Fifty years of moving any old which way didn't cure itself in a few days.

He went over to the mirror and looked at himself.

The good-looking fair haired youth had been taken over by a balding old man.

ᐁᐁᐁᐁᐁ

"Hello," said Marion.

"Hello yourself," said Bill, as he passed her on his way to work. She was getting ready to leave for her job at the library, where every day she took down books, went through the information on the copyright page, and typed it up on two 4 x 6 cards, one of which was put in a big series of drawers in the entryway, where patrons could find what books were there without looking on all the shelves, and one of which was sent to the central library system.

She lived in one of the apartments downstairs from Bill. She once said the job would probably take herself, and three others, more than a year, just at her branch. She was a youngster in her forties.

∞∞∞∞

Bill found rehearsals the same mixture of joy and boredom they had been a half-century before, with the same smells of paint and turpentine coming from the scene shop. The cast had convinced Arnold to direct the play, rather than hiring some *schmuck*, as he'd originally wanted to do. He'd conceived it; it was *his* vision.

During a break on night, Bill lay on the floor; Arnold slumped in a chair, and Shirlene, the lead dancer, lay face down on the sofa with a migraine. Bill chuckled, he thought, to himself.

"What's up?" asked Fossman.

"It was probably just like this in rehearsals when Plautus was sitting where you are."

"Guess so."

"Were there headaches then?" asked Shirlene.

"Well, there were in *my* day, and that wasn't too long after the Romans," said Bill. "One of our cameramen had them." He looked around. "Thanks, Arnold."

"For what?"

"For showing me how much I didn't remember I missed this stuff."

"Well, sure," said Fossman. "OK, folks, let's get back to the grind. Shirlene, lie there till you feel better."

She got to her feet. "I'll never feel better." she said.

∞∞∞∞

"See—" said Rudy "—it was on January third, and everybody was congratulatin' themselves on beatin' that ol' Y2K monster, and was throwin' out them ham and lima bean MREs into the dumpsters. Joyful, you know—another

Kohoutek, that was a comet that didn't amount to a bird fart back in them way old '70s—Anyway, it was exactly at 10:02 A.M. EST right here, when them three old surplus Russian-made diesel submarines that somebody—and nobody's still sure *just who*—bought up back in the 1990s, surfaced in three places around the world—and fired off them surplus NASA booster rockets, nine or ten of 'em—"

"Why 'cause we know that, Rudy, if we don't know who did it?"

"'Cause everybody had electric stuff back then could tell what kind of damn watch you was wearin' from two hundred miles out in space by how fast it was draggin' down that 1.5 volt battery in it. They knew the subs was old Russian surplus as soon as they surfaced, and knew they was NASA boosters as soon as the fuses was lit—'cause that's the kind of world your folks let happen for you to live in—that's why 'cause."

"Oh."

"As old Rudy was sayin', them nine or ten missiles, some went to the top of the atmosphere, and some went further out where all them ATT and HBO and them satellites that could read your watch was, and they all went off and meanwhile everybody everywhere was firin' off all they stuff to try to stop whatever was gonna happen—well, when all that kind of stuff went off, and it turns out them sub missiles was big pulse explosions, what they used to call EMP stuff, and all the other crap went off that was tryin' to stop the missiles, well then, kids, Time started over as far as ol' Rudy's concerned. Not just for the US of A and Yooropeans, but for everybody everywhere, even down to them gentle Tasaday and every witchety-grub eatin' sonofagun down under."

"Time ain't started over, Rudy," said a kid. "This is Tuesday. It's June. This is the year 2000 A.D."

"Sure, sure. On the *outside,*" said Rudy. "I'm talkin 'bout the inside. We can do it all over again. Or not. Look, people took a week to find out what still worked, when what juice there was gonna be came back on. See, up till then they all thought them EMP pulses would just knock out everything, everywhere that was electronic, solid state stuff, transistors. That's without takin' into account all that other crap that was zoomin' around, and people tryin' to jam stuff, and all that false target shit they put up 'cause at first they thought it was a sneak attack on cities and stuff, and they just went, you know, apeshit for about ten minutes.

"So what was left was arbitrary. Like nobody could figure why Betamax *players* sometimes was okay and no Beta III VCR was. Your CDs are fine; you just can't play 'em. Then why none of them *laserdiscs* are okay, even if you had a machine that would play 'em? It don't make a fuckin' bit o' sense. Why icemaker refrigerators sometimes work and most others don't? You can't get no fancy embroidery on your fishin' shirt: it all come out lookin' like Jackson Pollock. No kind of damn broadcast TV for a week, none of that satellite TV shit, for sure. Ain't no computers work but them damn Osbornes they been usin' to build artificial reefs in lakes for twenty years. Cars? You seen anything newer than a 1974 Subaru on the street, movin? Them '49 Plymouths and '63 Fords still goin', 'cause they ain't got nothin' in them that don't move you can't fix with a pair o' Vise-Grips...

"Look at the damn mail we was talking about! Ain't nobody in the Post Office actually had to read a damn address in ten years; you bet your ass they gotta read writin' now! Everybody was freaked out. No e-mail, no phone, no fax, ain't no more *Click on This,* kids. People all goin' crazy till they start gettin' them letters from Visa and Mastercard and such sayin', "Hey, we hear you got an account with us?

Why doncha tell us what you owe us, and we'll start sendin' you bills again?" Well, that was one thing they liked sure as shit. They still waitin' for their new cards with them raised-up letters you run through a big ol' machine, but you know what? They think about 60-70 percent of them people told them what they owed them. Can you beat that? People's mostly honest, 'ceptin' the ones that ain't...."

"That's why you gettin' mail twice a week now, not at your house but on the block, see? You gonna have to have some smart people now; that's why I'm tellin you all this."

"Thanks, Rudy," said a kid.

"Now that they ain't but four million people in this popsicle town, you got room to learn, room to move around some. All them scaredy cats took off for them wild places, like Montana, Utah, New Jersey. Now you got room to breathe, maybe one o' you gonna figure everything out someday, kid. That'll be thanks enough for old Rudy. But this time, don't mess up. Keep us fuckin' human—morning, Bill—"

"Morning, Rudy."

"—and another thing. *No* damn cell phones. *No* damn baby joggers or double fuckin' wide baby strollers. *No* car alarms!"

∞∞∞∞

Opening night.

The dancers are finishing the Harvest Dinner dance, like *Oklahoma!* or "June Is Bustin' Out All Over" on speed. It ends with a blackout. The packed house goes crazy.

Spotlight comes up on center stage.

Bill stands beside Shirlene. He's dressed in bib over-alls and a black jacket and holds a pitchfork. She's in a simple farm dress. Bill wears thick glasses. He looks just like the dentist B. H. McKeeby, who posed as the farmer, and Shirlene looks just like Nan Wood, Grant's sister, who posed as the farmer's spinster daughter, down to the pulled-back hair, and the cameo brooch on the dress.

Then the lights come up onstage, and Bill and Shirlene turn to face the carpenter-gothic farmhouse, with the big arched window over the porch.

Instead of it, the backdrop is a painting from one of the Mars Lander photos of a rocky surface.

Bill just stopped.

There was dead silence in the theater, then a buzz, then sort of a louder sound, then some applause started, and grew and grew, and people came to their feet, and the sound rose and rose.

Bill looked over. Shirlene was smiling, and tears ran down her cheeks. Then the house set dropped in, with a working windmill off to the side, and the dancers ran on from each wing, and they did, along with Bill, the Pitch-fork Number.

The lights went down, Bill came off the stage, and the chorus ran on for the Birthplace of Herbert Hoover routine.

Bill put his arms around Fossman's shoulders.

"You...you...asshole," said Bill.

"If you would have known about it, you would have fucked it up," said Arnold.

"But...how...the audience...?"

"We slipped a notice in the programs, just for the opening. Which is why you didn't see one. Might I say your dancing was superb tonight?"

"No. No," said Bill, crying. "Kirk Alyn, the guy who played Superman in the serials in the forties, now *there* was a dancer..."

∞∞∞∞∞

On his way home that night, he saw that a kid had put up a new graffiti on the official site, and had run out of paint at the end, so the message read "What do we have left they could hate us" and then the faded letters, from the thinning and upside down spray can, "f o r ?"

Right on, thought Bill. Fab. Gear. Groovy.

At work the next day, he found himself setting the galleys of the rave review of *Glorifying the American Gothic*, by the *Times'* drama critic.

∞∞∞

And on a day two months later:

"And now!" said the off-pixievision-camera announcer, "Live! On Television! Major Spacer in the 21st Century!"

∞∞∞

"...tune in tomorrow, when you'll hear Major Spacer say:

WE'LL GET BACK TO THE MOON IF WE HAVE TO RETROFIT EVERY ICBM IN THE JUNKPILE WITH DUCT-TAPE AND SUPERGLUE.

"Don't miss it. And now, for today's science segment, we go to the Space Postal Joint, with Cadet Rudy!" said the announcer.

Rudy: "Hey kids. Listen to ol' Rudy. Your folks tried hard but they didn't know their asses from holes in the ground when it came to some things. They didn't mean to mess your world up; they just backed into one that could be brought down in thirty seconds 'cause it was the easiest thing to do. Remember the words of ol' Artoo Deetoo Clarke: 'with increasin' technology, you headin' for a fall.'

Now listen how it could be in this excitin' world of the future..."

∞∞∞

A few years later, after Bill and the show and Rudy were gone, some kid, who'd watched it every day, figured everything out.

And kept us human.

Afterword to
"Major Spacer in the 21ˢᵗ Century!"

I always wanted to write a story with a 50-year space break right in the middle, and now I have.

∞∞∞

This is also, like "Household Words…" in my last collection, a monitory example of getting ideas too late to do much about them. I had realized, in August 1993, that it was going to be the 150th anniversary of "A Christmas Carol" (me and the British GPO were the *only* ones who noticed). Being as how Kim Mohan at *Amazing* was the only editor who could possibly get the story out by December, I wrote him and the story at about the same time; he published it in the last issue. (*I* killed *Amazing*.) Sorry Kim.

Cut to 1999; everybody's bent out of shape about Y2K (remember?) I suddenly had the idea: what if Y2K was three days late? After, as I said, all the lurp bags and cans of dehydrated water were thrown out, and the problem wouldn't be computer-language related, it would be our old 80s friend the EMP? (Before Sept. 11, 2001, I'd destroyed NYC twice in my career; once in "Thirty Minutes Over Broadway! Jetboy's Last Adventure!" in *Wild Cards I* in 1986, and again in this story.)

And I wanted to show the changes 50 years had made in the background technology we all swim in, so I had to have somebody that was *doing something* in 1950 *and* 2000 AD. Mixed in with this was my ages-old desire to put in a musical based on Grant Woods' art (more later).

There was only one editor who could get it into print before 2000 AD; that was Kim Mohan at the all new, revived *Amazing.* As luck would have it, we were 60 miles apart in Washington state, as opposed to the Texas-Wisconsin gap the first time I did this...

I wrote this in a five-day blaze, meanwhile telling Kim what was up (and warning him *not* to buy it, as look what had happened last time...) It went off to him on May 2, 1999.

What with one thing and another, Kim wanted some revisions (*he's* the editor).

I was in a work mode; I also wasn't in the mood to revise a long story I'd written at white heat. So I sat down and wrote Kim *another* story. (See the Afterword to "London, Paris, Banana..." for that. Kim didn't escape The Waldrop Curse, either. The issue after "L, P, B..." came out was the last one. I KILLED AMAZING TWICE!!!)

Meanwhile, "Major Spacer..." had gone off to Gordon van Gelder at *F&SF.* Gordon wanted some revisions, and those only in the part after the space-break. Sigh. I monkeyed with it a little bit.

Meanwhile, during the meanwhile, I read the story, on May 27, 1999, at the University of Washington in Seattle, with suitable primitive visual aids, like a cigar box for the head Pedro's is in in the Senor Wences part, and a Tom Corbett lunchbox, etc. If you've seen my chapbook "A Better World's in Birth!" from Golden Gryphon, the "author photo" may or may not be a drawing of me reading "Major Spacer..." in a paper bag space helmet, by Rhonda Boothe.)

I sent the revisions back to Gordon. I got a card from him mailed from JFK. He saw my envelope come in as he was leaving the office for a cab to go to the airport to fly to Australia for the World SF Convention...

A month later, when he gets back, he rejects it. A story by Howard Waldrop—Mister National Treasure!—rejected! But Gordon had *also* suggested the current title, which is lots better than the one I had originally...

Off it went to Ellen Datlow at EventHorizon.com (it hadn't gone to her earlier because it was longer than the stuff she could buy).

Back comes the sad note that EventHorizon.com died two days *before* the manuscript got there...

I wrote this for the April rent. It's now the middle of November, 1999, with Y2K six weeks away. Fuck it, I said. I put it in my e-book *Dream-Factories and Radio-Pictures* late in 2000, long after it had become an alternate—rather than anticipatory—history. And now, here it is in all its glory.

∞∞∞∞∞

Truth is stranger than (my) fiction. Long after I wrote this, there was a spate of books on musicals—by decade—and revisionist overviews of their evolution (it didn't *all* change with *Oklahoma!*) Among many other things, I learned that in the late 1940s, there was a three-part revue; one-third of which was based on the paintings of Grandma Moses...

I *try,* people, but I can't outguess the mind of an off-Broadway producer from mid-1949...

Us

Prologue

The ladder, though ingeniously made, was flimsy and the rungs were too far apart. He had pushed the dowels into the holes in each of the three sections. It had been made to fit inside the car, parked a mile away off the road to Hopewell. The night was cold and it had not been easy to put the sections of the ladder together with the leather gloves he wore.

Construction stuff lay all around. The house wasn't landscaped yet, borders and walks were laid out but not yet rocked in. The house was big, two stories and a gable-windowed third narrow one set in the steeply pitched roof. The outside was stucco.

He put the ladder against the upstairs window, the one with the shutter that, though new, was already warped and wouldn't close completely.

He picked up the gunnysack, checked in his pocket for the envelope, and started up. There were two lights on downstairs, the sitting room and the kitchen.

The ladder swayed and groaned. He had to lift one leg at a time, more crawl up than climb, then pull the other one after it up to the same rung. When both feet were on one, he could feel the vibration of the strain.

He reached the next from the top, pulled the shutter the rest of the way open without a sound. He raised the window, the sack flopping over his face as he used one hand to steady himself and the other to lift.

His eyes adjusted to the dim light inside. There was a stack of trunks and suitcases under the window, the sill of which was concrete rather than wood. A crib across the way. Beside the window a fireplace and mantel, some bird toys along the top. A scooter on the floor. Just past the fireplace a big parabolic electric heater and a chair. The room was almost hot.

He smelled Mentholatum or Vicks salve. He eased himself over the sill, swung the sack and his feet to the floor. He went to the crib, where the medicine smell was strongest.

The kid was safety-pinned under the blankets, its breathing a little rough and croupy. He undid one of the pins, eased the toddler out of the crib. It began to move.

"Sh-sh-sh," he said, holding it close and swinging it slightly back and forth. He noticed the kid was in some kind of cut-down larger garment rather than Dr. Denton's or a nightshirt. The child subsided.

He pulled a blanket out of the sack, wrapped the kid in it, put both back in the bag, lifted it gently by the center top. He went to the windowsill, laid the bag down, eased himself over. He had to search around for the first rung, turned, put one leg down, then the other. He reached back inside, lifted the child by the sack onto the concrete sill. He felt inside his pocket, took out the envelope, put it on the inside of the sill.

Then with both hands, he lifted the sack.

One: "The Little Eaglet"

He had been born just after Clyde Tombaugh discovered the planet Pluto. He was the most famous child in the world for a year or two, until Shirley Temple came along. He was the son of a famous man and a celebrated mother. Somebody'd tried to kidnap him when he was twenty months old, but they'd caught the guy on the way to his car, and Charles Jr. was back in his crib by 10:00 P.M. and didn't remember a thing about it.

But it convinced his father (a very private man) and his mother (from a distinguished family) that they would be hounded all their lives by newspapermen, gossip columnists, and radio reporters if they stayed where they were.

They moved out of the house in New Jersey and moved out to Roswell, New Mexico, so his father could be near his friend Dr. Robert H. Goddard, who fooled around with rockets.

"The Little Eaglet," as the press had dubbed him, grew up watching six-foot-long pieces of metal rise, wobble, and explode themselves all over the remote scrub country of the Eden Valley that Uncle Robert used as a range.

It was a great place to be a kid. His mother and father were often away on flights, surveying airline routes, or his father was off consulting with Boeing or Curtiss, or there'd be pictures of him in a zeppelin somewhere. His mother, when she was around, wrote books and was always off in her study, or having another of his brothers and sisters.

He had the run of the place. The first time he'd walked over on his own to the worksheds, Uncle Robert had stooped down to his level and said, "Do anything you want here, kid, but don't *ever* play with matches."

They let him have pieces of metal, old tubing, burnt-out frozen-up fuel pumps, and that neat stuff that looks like tortoiseshell. They had to run him out of the place when they closed up at night.

He went unwillingly to school in 1936, each day an agony of letters and numbers. Of course he had to poke a few three-foot jerks in the snoot because they made fun of his curly golden hair.

He learned a phrase early and used it often: "So's your old man."

His own old man, after some vacillation, jumped on the Preparedness bandwagon and was out with Hap Arnold, beefing up the army air corps.

You wouldn't have known there'd just been a Depression.

Uncle Robert finally got something right. When he was eight, Charles Jr. watched a rocket go up and actually get out of sight before it exploded. He, Uncle Robert, and everybody else ran back inside the small blockhouse while it rained metal for a couple of minutes.

Of course his father taught him how to fly, but since he'd been driving the converted mail van and rocket trailer from the shed three miles out to the range since he was six (he'd put blocks on the brakes and accelerator and stood on a box to see out the windshield), he thought flying was a lot like driving a car, only the road was bigger.

One time he and his father talked about it. "I like flying too, I guess," said Charles Jr. "But the air's so thick. That's for sissies."

"You'll think sissy when you pull three g's on an inside turn sometime," said the Lone Eagle.

He spent most of his time with his aunt and uncle, and by the time he was ten he was working for Uncle Robert after school and full time in the summers, at whatever needed to be done.

Uncle Robert was getting older—he'd always looked old with his bald head and mustache, but now his head was wrinkled and the mustache was gray and white like a dollop of cream cheese across his lip.

The war had already started in Europe. One day a shady character in a cheap suit brought in some plans and left.

The whole crew gathered around. Uncle Robert tapped the blueprints. "*That's* what the Germans are working on," he said. "They're not very serious yet, but they will be. They're on the right track, but they're spending most of their time trying to get a good centrifugal pump, and haven't thought about regenerative cooling yet. On the other hand, look at this. Graphite vanes in the exhaust, and I assume if it's ballistic they'll be set beforehand; if it's guidable, they'll have to make room for steering mechanisms and radio controls."

He looked at all of them. "The army and air corps have their thumbs up their wazoos right now, so we'll have to do it ourselves on the Smithsonian and Guggenheim money. I figure the Nazis are six months behind us in some things, a couple of years ahead in others."

They went to work and they worked hard, especially after the U.S. got in the war when the Japanese bombed the Phillipines.

It wasn't easy, but they did it by the middle of 1942. They fired it off. It went 143 miles and punched a thirty-foot hole in the desert even without a warhead.

They showed it to the air corps.

World War II was over late in 1944, just after Charles Jr. turned 14.

∞∞∞

It was a bright and sunny day in the winter of 1945. He and Uncle Robert were looking at one of the German A-4s that had been lying around everywhere in Europe when the war ended and then shipped to America, along with their scientists. The army had given Goddard five or six to play with.

Uncle Robert had been sick the year before, recurrence of the TB of his youth, but had gotten better. Now he seemed to have some of the old spark back. He looked at the pumps, the servo-mechanisms. He looked in the empty warhead section, then he looked at Charles Jr.

"How'd you like to take a little ride?" he asked.

"Yippee yahoo!"

"As many times as you've seen things I built turn into firecrackers?"

"You didn't build this one. The Germans did."

"At White Sands, they're maybe kinda going to send up mice and monkeys."

"Phooey!" said Charles Jr.

"Double phooey," said Uncle Robert.

∞∞∞

On March 13, 1946, Charles Jr. went for a little ride. They hadn't told his mother or father, and no one else either, until after the fact.

The front section separated and fired some JATO units as retro rockets, and the surplus cargo parachute opened, and the thing came down sixty-eight miles away, within two miles of where Goddard and the crew were waiting.

The trucks drove up. Charles Jr. was sitting in the shade of the parachute canopy.

Uncle Robert jumped out of the truck and ran up to him.

There was a small cut above his eye.

"She rides a little rough," he said, and smiled.

∞∞∞

On July 4, 1963, *The Great Speckled Bird* came down on the surface of the Moon, backwards, rockets firing, and settled to the lunar dust.

The commander was Col. Chuck Yeager. The pilot was Lt. Col. David Simons, M.D., the navigator was Maj. Joe Kittinger, and the civilian mission specialist was Charles Lindbergh, Jr.

After a few hours of yammer and instrument readings that were hunky-dory, Charles Jr. suited up in one of the big bulky space suits the navy had built for them.

Yeager checked him over, then said, "You're on, kid."

It was being carried live by all the radios in the world; they'd have to wait till they got back to see it, as both Early Bird and Echo III satellites weren't cooperating.

The big ladder came out from the ship and Charles Jr. backed down it, unable to see well behind him because of the size of the oxygen equipment on the suit.

He paused just as he got to the bottom, looked up at Kittinger who was filming him with an Eymo camera (besides the official one on the side of the airlock), and stretched his foot out, inches above the dust.

He swung one foot out in a small circle, almost touching, then the other.

He said, "Here's one for Mom, and one for Pop, and one for Uncle Robert and"—he jumped onto the ground with both feet"—one for the good old USA."

Two: "Call Me Chucky"

He could say he'd been around since Pluto was a pup. Disney made the first cartoon with Mickey's mutt a few months after he was born.

When he was twenty months old he was kidnapped. It was the most sensational story of the decade. After much police activity and several copycat ransom notes, his father, the most famous man in the world, and, after Babe Ruth, in America, paid the right people and went in a coast guard plane to find his son in the boat—as the kidnapper's message said, "boad"—*Nelly* between Horseneck Beach and Gay Head near Elizabeth Island.

Charles Jr. was sleeping like a log in a built-in bureau drawer belowdecks on the stolen and deserted boat. The kidnappers were never found and the ransom money, much of it in marked gold certificates, which became illegal tender a couple of years later, never showed up.

Colonel H. N. Schwarzkopf of the New Jersey State Police had put a twenty-four-hour guard around the Lindbergh house in Hopewell and up at the Morrow house just after the kidnapping. His father hired his own bodyguards and dismissed the state troopers once Charles Jr. was recovered. But they moved from New Jersey soon anyway.

Famous father, famous mother, most famous child in America.

Of course he ended up in Hollywood.

ooooo

Later in interviews, Charles Jr.—"Call me Chucky"— said, "Yeah, yeah, child of the Depression. We had to cut down to two cooks. And don't ask *me* how somebody with such a publicity-shy father and mother ended up doing one, count 'em, one *Our Gang* short. I think they felt sorry for me—guys with big guns walking around wherever we were; people watching me like a hawk day and night.

"Warhol used to run that damn clip at the Factory all the time. There I am, three years old, sitting in a beer-bar-rel airplane, replica of the *Spirit*, with an aviator's cap. There I am, me and the new kid Spanky—whatever happened to him, huh?—racing all these other kids down that damn long hill in L.A.; soapbox racers, fire engines, tanks, and me and Spanky McFarland win 'cause all the other kids have a wooden demo-derby.

"They tell me Roach creamed his shorts; wanted to sign me, team with Spanky; already had a name picked out, Sankandank, you know, Spank and Sankandank, anyway, lifetime contract; Louis B. Mayer would honor it once I got too old for the *Gang* stuff.

"Yeah, I coulda had it all. Been as big as Buckwheat or Alfalfa. Coulda stayed on, beat up on Butch and Woim.

"What happened. Dad said no way, Jose."

○○○○○

His father had visited Italy and Germany several times, and they had lived in England for a while, only to find British newspapermen just like the ones in America, so they moved back. His father was convinced that since it wasn't ready and couldn't afford it, the U.S. should stay neutral in any coming conflict in Europe or Asia. He'd become a major spokesman for America First.

One day at school, Chucky came out to find one of his best friends beating the snot out of another. He pulled them apart while they were swinging in blind rage at each other, noses bloodied, eyes shut.

"Geez, guys!" he said.

One pointed to the other. "He said your father was a Jew-hater. That made *me* mad. I said no, he wasn't, he was just dumb as a post. That made *him* mad."

Chucky, age eleven, went home. His father was packing for a trip to Des Moines where he was going to make a terrifically ill-timed speech about staying out of the European war which had been going on for a year and a half already.

"Dad," said Chucky to his father, who looked just like him only bigger, and was putting shirts in a leather bag. "Dad, somebody has to kick some Hitler butt."

He was sent to his room without his supper.

∞∞∞

"Yeah, yeah," said Chucky in another interview in 1989, "that was the first time any kid of his expressed an opinion that wasn't his. It started me on that downward spiral that led me to where I am today. For which, thanks…"

After the war was over and things got back to normal, Chucky went off to college in 1948.

And fell in with evil companions. Some guys who endlessly drove back and forth across the country because they couldn't stand wherever they were. Poets, artists, weirdos, and Old Lefties, white folksingers who spent all their money on bus trips to Alabama to learn exactly what it was Cornbread Joe hollered on that record across the fields when he wanted someone to bring the water jug or oats for the mule. There were a zillion guys loose in New York City on the GI bill, finding out what life was all about. Chucky: "Say what you will. The guys who shot heroin are all still alive; the boozers have been dead these thirty years."

Then he started to make things. Birdhouses made out of old airplane parts. Small ones at first, made from old propeller hubs and radio aerials, exhaust stacks, parts of instrument panels. Then they got larger and more complicated. He had a few small gallery shows, then a couple at museums. He dropped out of college his sophomore year, rented a studio and went to work.

One day Calder came by, took a look around, and whistled. Rauschenberg and all those guys dropped in; Mailer, smarting from *Barbary Shore,* came in and smoked some tea and talked about Chucky's pop, whom he'd met in the Pacific, and said he was going to start a Village newspaper sometime.

His first real show was called "Birdhouses for the Stratosphere" and it all went fine from then on. He went on to use parts from jets. His *Birdhouse for the Rukh* used most of a Super Constellation he'd gotten cheap from the NATSB. They had to build an extra plaza in front of the rededicated O'Hare before he could install it.

Even with that going on, he continued to make the smaller houses all through the fifties and sixties and have shows in little galleries; people actually bought them and used them for birdhouses. His wren series—made from an old Curtiss Wren—was the best and most popular.

At one of these small-show openings in the early sixties, Chucky was a little high from reefer and a little tight from wine and a little up from some innocuous-looking red tablets someone had given him. He was thirty-two and good at what he did, and knew he'd be doing it the rest of his life. An old man was looking at some of the things ("Houses for the Bluebird of Sadness," the show was) and waited until the people who'd been around Chucky went over for the free cheese and beer.

The old man caught his eye. "You did these?"

"Yep."

"I have something to tell you," said the old man. "But I can't tell you until you promise it goes no further."

"Oh, this is serious? Wait a sec." Chucky quit smiling and set his face in a calm mask with a wipe of his hand.

"There," he said. "Try me."

"Between you and me?"

"My word as a Video Ranger," said Chucky.

The old man eyed him, then sagged his shoulders.

"I kidnapped you once."

"Sonofabitch!" said Chucky. "Not you. The situation. Why'd you ever do that?"

"I went *messhuganeh*," said the old man. "It was the Depression. I was desperate. I borrowed a stranger's boat. I kipped you from the crib, sent the notes."

"Well, they never caught you."

"It was very fucked over, from beginning to end. I couldn't believe it, that I was getting away with it, I was so excited. And I lost it, all $50,000 of it, between the time I put you in the boat and the time they came to get you. I took it from the satchel your father brought it to the graveyard in and put it in a big tin box. I had it with me when I put you on the boat. I was so excited, I dropped it. I watched my life getting smaller and smaller and further away. If only I'd put it in a *wooden* box..."

"Could I give you a few bucks?" asked Chucky.

"I didn't come here, Mr. Lindbergh, Jr., to ask for money. I came here to ask forgiveness."

Chucky laughed and reached out and grabbed him by the shoulders, causing him to wince.

"Forgive? Mister, that was probably the best thing that ever happened to me. Thank you!"

"You mean that? All these years, nobody knew but me, and I was so sorry that I'd done it. I've lived a clean life since..."

"Gaffer," said Chucky. "Go with my blessing. I mean that. Thanks for telling me."

"Good-bye, then."

"Good-bye." He watched the old man leave.

"Whowazzat?" asked a friend. "It looked intense."

"A stranger," said Chucky, smiling. "He wanted to put the touch on my old man."

∞∞∞∞

When his father died in the 1970s, Chucky called up a bunch of old engineers and mechanics and tool-and-die men. He had them make an exact replica of the Ryan *Spirit of St. Louis*.

Then he took it apart, piece by piece, and built the *Birdhouse for Pop*.

It's outside the Air and Space Museum.

Three: "Crazy Charlie"

After seventeen years in the Plutonian depths of being a famous man's son, he took off.

In 1953, just at the end of the Korean War, a guy showed up in Concrete, Washington. He walked with a slight gimp. He drove a secondhand two-door purple Kaiser. He rented a place on the edge of town for $8.40 a month. Once a week or so he'd drive out of town; one of the locals saw him over at the Veterans' Hospital in Mt. Vernon. Otherwise he walked everywhere in the town of Concrete, shopped at the local grocery store. Slowly it got out that his name was Charles.

Mostly what he did was fish the Skagit River, 365 days a year if he could, less if it was muddied up, though the flow was now controlled through Diablo and Gorge Dams. Sometimes the Sauk and Cascade were muddied up and put the lower river out for fishing for four or five days at a time.

He used a Gladding Ike Walton model 8 fiberglass fly rod and a Pfleuger 1498 reel, and he caught more fly-fishing than all the other people around there caught with bait or casting reels or the new spinning reels. People over on the Skykomish and Stillaguamish fly-fished, but not many yet on the Skagit.

One day right downtown, in a pouring rain, fifteen or twenty people stood on the bridge to watch him. There was already both ends of about an eight-pounder sticking out of the back pouch of his homemade fishing jacket, and they watched for twenty-two minutes by the watch, as he played and landed what was by the best estimate a steelhead that would go twenty-five pounds.

He reached down with a pair of pliers and jerked the Brad's Brat out of the fish's lip and watched it swim back out to the deeper water against the far bank.

"What the hell?" yelled someone from the bridge.

"They won't be around forever, you know?" said Charles.

"Then why the hell did you catch it if you were going to let it go?"

"Because I can't help myself," said Charles, and began casting again.

From then on he was Crazy Charlie.

ᴏᴏᴏᴏᴏ

In 1957, over in Sedro-Wooley, he met a girl at the Dairy Delight. She moved in with him in a slightly larger shack on the edge of Concrete that cost $12.00 a month.

They ate trout and salmon; she canned salmonberries and blackberries; they smoked steelhead and came out of the woods with mushrooms and roots and nuts and skunk cabbage; they drove in the purple Kaiser.

In 1958 they had twin boys, whom people learned to call Key and Matt. They assumed they were family names for something like Keyes or Keynard and Matthew or even Mattias. If you go to the Skagit County Courthouse and look up their birth certificates, you'll find their names are Quemoy and Matsu. It was 1958 after all.

The one peculiarity other fishermen and the people in town noticed was that wherever he was, whatever he was doing, even playing a fish, if a plane flew over he would watch it until it disappeared. They assumed it had something to do with the Korean War.

ᴏᴏᴏᴏᴏ

One day one of the town blowhards came into the cafe shaking his head. Everybody was ready for a story.

"Goddamnedest thing. Give me that Seattle paper," he said. He looked through it quickly. "Here, damn, Ed, you look."

"What'm I lookin' for?"

"Well look with your eyes and just lissen. I was up in Marblemount at the Rocky Ford Cafe. Over in the corner was Crazy Charlie and that girl of his—the two boys being most likely in school this time of day. And you know who was in the booth with them, talkin' to them? Huh?"

"Dwight David Eisenhower," said someone. They all laughed.

"Charles Lindbergh. The Lone Eagle."

"Shit," said someone. "What would he be doin' talkin to Crazy Charlie?"

"You got me. He's older now, Lindbergh, but I knew it was him from when he used to come to the plant during the war. As big as life. Sure as shootin'." They all knew the blowhard had retired from Boeing with a disability a few years before.

"He used to be a practical joker, give old man Boeing a hotfoot soon as look at him," he continued. "Always cutting up."

"Well, what was they doin'?"

"Eating hamburgers, shakes, and fries."

"I didn't think Charlie and his girl ate that kind of stuff. The kids neither."

"I said the kids wasn't there. And they was sure as hell eatin' that way today."

"Did they see you?"

"Hell, no. I was so astounded it was Lindbergh I just sat down in that far booth, the one halfway in the kitchen. Couldn't hear 'em neither, place was crowded. Had a roast beef sandwich."

"We don't care what you had for lunch. What'd Lindbergh do?"

"Talked. Ate. Went outside. By the time I was through they was gone."

"Nothing about Lindbergh in the papers," said Ed.

"Can you beat that? Guy like that in town, nobody thinks it's a big deal."

"Well, it was more than thirty years ago," said the blowhard. "Still, you'd think somebody would mention it."

"Maybe it was personal," said someone.

"Yeah, right. The Lone Eagle and Crazy Charlie and his girl."

They all laughed.

∞∞∞∞

Charlie died in 1985. His common-law wife Estelle died in 1989. Quemoy and Matsu own motion picture production in Seattle like the Krays owned London in the sixties. Neither fishes.

Epilog

He reached in his pocket, took out the envelope, put it on the inside of the sill.

Then, with both hands he lifted the sack.

The rung broke with a sharp snap and his foot hit the next one.

There was a sudden instant of chill blind panic. The sack had thudded onto the concrete sill. He eased his other foot down the outside of the ladder to the rung he'd fallen to. He made it the rest of the way down, filled with adrenaline, cradled the bundle in his arms, and made off for the woods and his car.

Halfway through the trees, he realized the kid hadn't moved.

When he got within sight of the car, he put the sack down, lifted the blanket and child out. The kid was limp as a bunch of leather. One side of the head was misshapen. He felt around for a heartbeat.

He went further back into the woods from the road, laid the kid down, kicked some leaves over him, and took

ropHoward Waldrop

the blanket and sack to his car and sped away toward Manhattan.

∞∞∞

The biggest manhunt in history was on. There were shady intermediaries, ransom was paid. There was no Boad Nelly, no child.

Two truck drivers, one black, one white, on their way into Hopewell two months later, stopped their truck and went into the woods to take a pee.

They saw what was left of the kid on the ground. He had been gnawed by animals.

They ran for the cops.

Three years later, Bruno Richard Hauptmann, on trial for his life for essentially passing hot gold certificates, was shown the ladder used in the kidnapping. "I did not make *that*," he said. "I am a *carpenter.*"

Afterword to "Us"

When I read the opening line of this at the Fremont Library in Seattle, Andy Hooper (him again!) who was in the audience, knew exactly what it was about. He came up after the reading and told me so.

∞∞∞∞∞

For years I'd wanted to do a story with three alternatives rolled into one. My first attempt, decades ago, was about Dornberger and von Braun at Peenëmunde or its equivalent, watching the first successful A-4 (V-2) go up. In one of the sections, it knocks a corner off the deferent and jams up the epicycle that holds the earth steady in the Ptolemaic universe. In another, it brings the crystalline sky crashing down because they've shattered Horbiger's Ice-World Cosmology. In the third it goes *up* and hits Spain, which is on the inner curve of the world we all live *inside*. I was trying to show how imprecise Nazi science was.

Well, I never could get *that* to work.

And then one day it came to me to illustrate chance and alternative through one life. And that life had to be that of Charles Lindbergh, Jr.

Nothing so much represented what the rest of the century was going to be like as Lucky Lindy's story—his flight was a wedding of media and technology. Then followed fame and romance; first childbirth and work; the kidnapping and the subsequent trial of Hauptman; his reclusiveness and his isolationist work; his shunning of the media that made him famous; above all his belief in aviation and aerospace. It's *all* there.

And I got to thinking: what if his first son had lived? History's the same up to the moment the ladder goes up against the window. Then, it *all* changes.

At one time I'd written a story (essentially what would have happened had Davy Crockett stayed on in Congress, then become President) where way down the line Simons, Kittinger and Yeager (all my early heroes) were the first men on the Moon. Out that came again for this one. Most people don't know Goddard in New Mexico was financed in his rocket research by the Smithsonian, the Guggenheims *and* Lindbergh. So that fit right in. Who *better* to go to the Moon?

I'd been reading a lot of 1950s bohemian painter/poet/wastrel lives for the last few years before I wrote this, so Chucky's section came pretty easily. And of course Spanky had to put in an appearance—The Little Rascals seem to be woof to the warp of this collection like The Three Stooges were to earlier ones. I just had a vision of Spanky and Chucky in a soap-box derby in beer-barrel airplane carts.

The Crazy Charlie (which is a type of bonefish fly…) section I was *living* at the time, so that's no great stretch. (And, after the story was published, I found one of Lindbergh's later sons was living in Washington state—though not as a nuts-and-berries steelheader….)

It was the real section—prologue and epilogue—that gave me the most trouble—I felt that since it was real, I had to get it *exactly* right. That's the part Hooper noticed.

There's been lots of revisionist history about the kidnapping and subsequent trial—chief among them Noel Behn's *Lindbergh—The Crime,* which I recommend for anyone looking for another take on the events—it didn't convince *me,* but it did bring up all the niggling inconsistencies of the tale as told at the time. And you *do* keep running into General Schwartzkopf's dad—who was head of the New Jersey State Police at the time, and who later advised the Shah of Iran, who the CIA did put *back* on the Peacock Throne—so some of Behn's speculation about Wild Bill Donovan—later head of the OSS, ain't right out of left field...

Adding complications and complex motivations to the alternate sections was the easy part. And you can still surprise yourself—I didn't *know* the kidnapper was going to have the talk with Chucky till he walked into the art gallery...

And I realized only after the fact that I'd written the first draft on the 70th anniversary of the solo New York-Paris flight, May 28, 1997.

I sent this to a couple of high-tone places first, and got the usual low-res form rejection slips, which only took a couple of months before I sent it where I should have in the first place, to Ellen Datlow, then at EventHorizon.com. She bought it immediately and paid me PDQ.

Gardner Dozois put it in his *Year's Best Sf Stories #16*.

Just another couple of days to enjoy.

Winter Quarters

Perhaps I should start, "When he was twelve, he ran away from the circus."

Maybe I should begin, "As circuses go, it was a small one. It only had two mammoths."

I'll just start at the beginning: The phone rang.

∞∞∞

"Hey Marie!" said the voice of my friend Dr. Bob the paleontologist. "Do you remember Arnaud?"

"Was the Pope Polish?" I asked.

"Well, the circus is in town, and he's in it. Susie Neruda took her nieces and nephews yesterday and recognized him. She just called me." Then he paused. "You want to go see him?"

"I didn't think you and circuses got along." I said.

"For this, I'll ignore everything in my peripheral vision."

"When would you like to go?"

"Next show's in forty-five minutes. I'll swing by and pick you up."

"Uh, sure." I said, looking at the stack of departmental memos on my desk. I threw the antimacassar from the back of my office chair over them.

He hung up.

∞∞∞∞

When he was twelve, he ran away from the circus. Dr. Bob Oulijian, I mean. His father had managed two of them while Bob was trying to grow up. One day he showed up on the doorstep of his favorite aunt and said, "If I ever have to see another trapeze act or smell another zebra's butt in my life, Aunt Gracie, I'll throw up." Things were worked out; Aunt Gracie raised him, and he went on to become the fairly-respected head of the paleontology department in the semi-podunk portion of the state university where we both teach. What was, to others, a dim, misty vista of life in past geologic ages, to him was, as he once said, "a better circus than *anyone* could have thought up."

∞∞∞∞

We whined down the highway in his Toyota Heaviside, passing the occasional Daimler-Chrysler Faraday. A noise dopplered up behind us, and a 1932 bucket-T roadster came by, piloted by a geezer in motorcycle goggles.

"Soon you'll be studying *them*," I said to Dr. Bob, pointing.

"Oh." he said. "Dinosaurs. *Tres amusant.*"

ᙣᙣᙣᙣᙣ

Did I remember Arnaud?

It was while we were all—me, Dr. Bob, our colleague Dr. Fred Luntz the archeologist, Susie Neruda (nee Baxter)—undergraduates *here* at this podunk North Carolina branch of the state university, just after the turn of the millennium, that Arnaud showed up. We assumed he was French, maybe Belgian or Swiss, we didn't know, because he didn't talk. Much, anyway. He had that Jacques Tati-Marcel Marceau-Fernandel body type, tall and thin, like he'd been raised in a drainpipe. He was in the drama department; before we knew him, we knew *of* him.

About half the time we saw him, he was in some form of clown deshabille, or mime getup. We assumed it was for the acting classes, but a grad student over there said no, he just showed up like that, some days.

ᙣᙣᙣᙣᙣ

"Does he do anything special?" I asked Dr. Bob. "Did Susan say?"

"I don't think so, or she would have. I'm assuming he mostly puts out fires inefficiently and throws pies with accuracy, unless circuses have changed a great deal since my time."

ᙣᙣᙣᙣᙣ

For what do we remember Arnaud?

It was in November, his first semester, and he was out on the east mall passing out flyers, in full regalia, a polkadot clownsuit, clownwhite, bald headpiece, a hat the size of a 50¢ flowerpot. He had a Harpo bulbhorn he honked as people came by.

The flyer said:

HITLER THE MAGNIFICENT!
An Evening of Transformational Sorcery
JONES HALL 112
7 P.M., NOVEMBER 2nd

Well, uh-oh.

ooooo

It wasn't an evening, it was more like fourteen or fifteen minutes.

It wasn't sorcery, but it was transformative: it transformed him right out of college. To say that it wasn't well-received is bending the language.

Jones 112 was the big lecture hall with multimedia capabilities, and when we got there, props and stuff littered the raised lecture platform. Some pipes, a fire extinguisher, a low platform raised about a meter off the ground on 2 x 4 legs; some big pieces of window glass. In true Brechtian fashion propmen sat on the stage playing cards.

By seven the place was packed, SRO.

The lights went down; there were three thumps on the floor, and lights came back up.

Out came a Chaplin-mustached Arnaud in a modified SA uniform. He wore a silk top hat with a big silver swastika on the front. He wore a cloak fashioned after one of the ones the Nazis were going to make all truck-drivers wear, back when they were designing uniforms for each profession.

His assistants were a padded-up fat guy with medals all over his chest, and a little thin guy with a rat-nose mask.

First, Hitler hypnotized twenty two million Germans: he gestured magically at a decoupage of a large crowd held up by the two guys.

Then they painted Stars of David on the plate glass, and Hitler threw a brick through it.

His assistants came back with a big map of Poland, and he sawed it in half with a ripsaw.

After each trick, he said: "Abracadabra, please and *gesundhiet!*"

Then they brought out three chairs, and three people came out on stage and sat down in them.

In the first, a young woman in her twenties. In the second sat a man in his forties, playing on a violin. At the end chair, an old man in his eighties.

Hitler the Magnificent took off his cloak and covered the young woman. "Abracadabra, please and *gesundhiet!*" he said, and pulled away the cloak. The chair was empty except for a wisp of smoke drifting toward the ceiling. He put the cape over the violinist, repeated the incantation, and snapped it away. In the chair was the violin and a lampshade with a number on it. He covered the old man, spoke, and raised the cloth. In the chair seat there was now a bar of soap. The thin assistant picked it up and threw it into a nearby goldfish bowl of water. "So light it floats!" he said.

Propmen lit fires along the pipes and pushed them toward Hitler the Magnificent and the two assistants. Surrounded by the closing ring of fire, with a mannequin wearing a brown-blonde wig and a wedding dress in his arms, he climbed onto the 2 x 4 platform, miming great heights, and dived onto a wet Luger, while the fat and thin assistants drank green Kool-Aid from a washtub and fell to the floor.

The stagelights lowered, and the only sound was the *whoosh* of the fire extinguisher putting out the flames on the pipes.

Then the lights came back up.

You could have heard a pin drop. Then—

It wasn't quite the Paris premiere of *Le Sacre du Printemps* in 1913, but it might as well have been.

You'd think with the whole twentieth century behind us, and a few years of this one, and Mel Brooks' *The Producers,* most of the *oomph* would have gone out of things like this. But you'd be wrong.

I got out the fire exit about the time the firemen and the riot squad came in through it.

∞∞∞

He was thrown out, of course, for violations of the University fire codes, firearms policy, for causing a riot, and unauthorized use of Jones Hall. Plus he spent a couple of days in the city jug before he was expelled.

∞∞∞

About a week before that performance, Arnaud had spoken to me for the first and only time. I was in the cafeteria (where we all usually were), alone, between classes, drinking the brown stuff they sell instead of coffee, actually doing some reading in Roman history.

I looked up. Arnaud was standing there, today looking like a French foreign student.

"Ever read any Nigidius Figulus?" he asked.

Taken aback by his speaking, I still wanted to appear cool. "Not lately," I said.

"Should," he said, and walked away.

That night I got out my handbook of Latin literature. Nigidius Figulus was a neo-Pythagorean of Cicero's time, an astrologer, a grammarian; much concerned with Fate and the will of the gods. In other words, the usual minor Roman literary jack-of-all-trades the late Republic coughed up as regular as clepsydra-work.

The next day I spent in the Classics library, reading epitomes of his writings.

Not much there for me.

∞∞∞

We pulled into the parking lot of the exhibition hall where the circus was, and who do we see but Dr. Fred Luntz getting out of his car with his stepson. Bob called to him. He came over. "Susan call you, too?" asked Dr. Bob.

"No. Why?" asked Fred.

"Arnaud's in this circus."

"Arnaud? Arnaud. I'll be damned." We went in and sat down on the bleachers.

∞∞∞

As circuses go, it was a small one. It only had two mammoths.

Mammontelephants, actually, but you know what I mean.

They were second-billed in the show, too—and they didn't come in in the Grand Entry Parade. (Dr. Bob noticed immediately. "They usually don't get along with other elephants," he said) Fred's stepson, about eight, and the

product of the previous marriage of his trophy wife was looking everywhere at once. His name was of course Jason. (In
ten years you'll be able to walk into any crowded bar in
America and say "Jason! Brittany!" and fifty people will
turn toward you...)

∞∞∞

We saw Arnaud in the Grand Entry, then in the first
walkaround while riggers changed from the high-wire to
the trapeze acts; we watched the tumblers, and the monkeys in the cowboy outfits riding the pigs with the strapped-
on Brahma bull horns; we ate peanuts and popcorn and
Cracker-Jack and cotton candy. Halfway through the ringmaster with his wireless microphone said: Ladeez an
Genuhmen, in the center ring (there was only one) Pre-
senting Sir Harry Tusker and His Performing Pachyderms,
Tantor and Behemoth!"

There were two long low blasts from the entrance doorway, sounds lower than an elephant's, twice as loud. I felt
the hair on my neck stand up.

Walking backwards came Sir Harry Tusker, dressed in
pith helmet, safari jacket, jodhpurs and shiny boots, like
old pictures of Frank Buck. In came Tantor and Behemoth—big hairy mounds with tusks and trunks, and tails
like hairy afterthoughts. Their trunks were up and curved
back double and each let out a blast again, lower than the
first. The band was playing, of course, Lawrence Welk's
"Baby Elephant Walk."

The crowd applauded them for being *them;* Jason's eyes
were big as saucers.

They went to the center of the ring and you realized
just how big they really were, probably not as big as mammoths got (they were both female of course) but big, big-

ger than all but the largest bull African elephants. And you're not used to seeing females with tusks two meters long, either.

They did elephant stuff—standing on their hind legs, their hairy coats swaying like old bathrobes, dancing a little. In the middle of the act a clown came out—it was Arnaud—pushing a ball painted to look like a rock, acting like it weighed a ton, and Behemoth picked it up, and she and Tantor played volleyball while Sir Harry and Arnaud held the net.

It was pretty surreal, seeing hairy elephants do that. It was pretty surreal seeing big shaggy elephants the size of Cleveland in the first place.

⦾⦾⦾⦾⦾

The show was over too soon for Jason.

At the souvenir booth, Dr. Fred bought him a copy of *The Shaggy Baggy Saggy Mammontelephant,* a Little Golden Book done by a grand-descendant of the author of the original elephant one. It was way below his reading level, but he didn't mind. He was in heaven while we left word and waited out back for Arnaud.

He showed up, out of makeup, looking about forty, still tall and thin. He shook hands with us like we'd seen each other yesterday.

Jason asked, "Are you really a clown?"

Arnaud looked around, pointed to himself, shook his head no.

"Let's go get something to eat besides popcorn," said Dr. Bob. "When do you have to be back?" Arnaud indicated eighteen, a couple of hours.

"Come on," said Dr. Fred Luntz. "We're buying."

Arnaud smiled a big smile.

ooooo

"It's all wrong," said Dr. Fred. "They're treating them like circus elephants, only shaggy, instead of what they are. The thing with the rock is more like it, if they're going to have to perform."

Arnaud was eating from nine or ten plates—two trays—at the cafeteria a kilometer or so from the exhibition hall. The four of us had eaten a couple of pieces of pie, Jell-O salads and some watermelon we were so full of circus junk food. Arnaud's metabolism must have been like a furnace. Occasionally he would look up from eating.

"Better that, than them not being around at all," said Dr. Bob.

"Well, yes, of course. But, Sir Harry Tusker. African white-hunter archetype. All wrong for mammoths."

"Yeah, well, what do you want? Siberians? Proto-Native Americans?" asked Bob.

"I mean, there was enough grief twenty or so years ago, when they were first brought back—the Russians had tried taking frozen mammoth genes from carcasses in the permafrost late last century, putting them in Indian elephants, their nearest living relatives—"

"This is your friend, Dr. Bob, the paleontologist, Fred..." said Bob.

"Okay. Okay. But it didn't work last century. Suddenly, it works. Exact same procedure. Suddenly, we have mammontelephants, all female of course. Big outrage; you can't bring back extinct animals to a time they're not suited for; it's cruel, etc. Like the A-bomb and physicists; geneticists *could* bring back the dead, so they *did*. Or, purt-near anyway. So we give in. They're in zoos at first, then circuses. Ten, twenty, thirty at first, now maybe 100, 200—

only a few are in the game preserves in Siberia run by the World Wildlife Fund and the Jersey Zoo (and there was a big fight about *that*.) Then five years ago hey presto! There's males. Someone went into a male completely buried in the frozen ground and retreived the whole system (and how'd you like *that* for a job, huh Bob?) and then we have viable sperm, and now there are five or six males, including the one up in Baltimore, and more on the way. What I'm saying is, turn 'em loose somewhere, don't just look at them, or make 'em act."

"Like loose where? Like do what?" asked Bob.

"Like, I don't know," said Dr. Fred.

Arnaud continued shoveling it in his face.

"What did you think about the mammoths, Jason?" I asked him.

"Neat!" he said.

"Me too," I said.

"Look, you know as well as I do what the real reason people want to shut all this down is," said Dr. Bob. "It's not that they don't want extinct animals brought back into a changed climate; that they have an inability to adapt from an Ice Age climate—you go up or down in altitude and get the climate you want. Mammoths in the high Rockies, in Alaska, in Siberia. Sure, no problem. And it ain't, like they say, we should be saving things that are going extinct now first: they're still here, they'll have to be taken somewhere to live, and people will have to leave them alone—island birds, rare predators, all that. That's their big *other* argument: Fix now *now*, then fix *then*. The reason is the same since the beginning: we're playing God, and they don't like it."

"Sure it has a religious element," said Fred. "But that doesn't mean you have to put the mammontelephants in some sort of zoo and circus limbo while you decide if there's to be more of them or not. Nobody's advocating bringing back *smilodons* (even if you could find the genetic material) or dinosaurs if you want to go the mosquito-in-amber wild goose chase. This comes down to questions of pure science—"

"If we can, we have to?"

"You're talking like the people who don't want them—or the two wooly rhinos—back," said Fred.

"No, I'm giving you their argument, like people give me. They're here because we couldn't stop ourselves from bringing them back, any more than we could stop ourselves from killing them off in the first place. Where was the religion in that?"

I was looking back and forth. I'm sure they'd had this discussion before, but never in front of me. Arnaud was eating. Jason was reading his book for the tenth time.

Arnaud looked at the two docs as he finished the last of everything, including a pie crust off Fred's plate.

"Plenty religion involved," said Arnaud. "People just don't understand the *mammoths.*"

Fred and Bob looked at him.

"Yeah?" asked Bob.

"They let me know," said Arnaud. He patted his stomach and nodded toward the door.

As we let him off at the circus, he reached in his shirt pocket and handed Jason six long black hairs, making a motion with his left arm hanging off his nose and his right forming a curve in front of him.

"Mammoth hair! Oh boy oh boy!" said Jason.

Then Arnaud pointed to Dr. Bob and made the signal from the sixty-year-old TV show *The Prisoner*—Be Seeing You.

ᴐᴐᴐᴐᴐ

That night I read about mammontelephants. The first were cloned less than thirty years ago, and there were some surprises. The normal gestation period for the Indian elephant is twenty-two months; for the mammontelephants it was closer to eighteen. The tusks of Indian elephant cows normally stick out less than twenty centimeters from their mouths; that of the mammontelephants 2, 2½ meters and still growing. (What the tusks of the males, all six or seven of them in the world, will be, no one knows yet, as the first is only six years old now—it's guessed they could grow as long as those of fossil true bull mammoths.) Their trumpeting, as I said, is lower, deeper and creepier than either Indian or African elephants (a separate species). It's assumed they communicate over long distances with subsonic rumbles like their relatives. They have developed the fatty humps on their heads and above their shoulders, even though most aren't in really cold climates. Yes, they have the butt-flap that keeps the wind out in cold weather. The big black long guard hairs (like the ones Arnaud gave Jason) are scattered over the thick underfur, itself forty centimeters thick. And further clonings—with twelve- and thirteen-year-old mammontelephants carrying mammontelephants to term—has speeded up the process—most elephants don't reproduce until they're fifteen or so. And you get a more mammoth mammontelephant. What will happen when Mr. and Ms. Mammontelephant get together in another six or seven years? They might not like each other. That's where Science will come in again...

Pretty good for an old lady English prof, huh?

∞∞∞∞∞

Everybody knew the IQRA meeting in October (hosted by the podunk portion of the university we work for) was going to have Big Trouble. The IQRA is the International Quarternary Research Association—everything prehistoric *since* the dinosaurs—and it contained multitudes, among which are people in the profession against the retrieval and propagation of extinct species. They were vocal, and because the meeting was also going to have a large bunch of paleo- and archaeogeneticists there too, the media had already started pre-coverage on it—sound bites, flashes of personalities, a fleeting glimpse of the male mammontelephant in the Baltimore Zoo.

You know. Big Trouble.

∞∞∞

I know all this because Dr. Bob is the university host of this Cenozoic shindig, and is calling me every day or so. Out of nowhere he says "I got a *fax* from Arnaud. Can you imagine? His circus plays up in Raleigh the day before the conference opens, last show of the year before winter quarters." It had been two months since he'd eaten the cafeteria out of house and home.

"What did he say?"

"That's all. I guess he just wanted us to know. I sure as hell won't have time to see him. I'll be dodging brickbats, no doubt."

∞∞∞

A week later, Dr. Bob showed up in my office.

"Uh, Marie," he said. "There've been more faxes. Lots more. Something's up. Want to be an unindicted co-conspirator?"

ooooo

The news was full of the IQRA; you couldn't turn on your monitor or TV without seeing people with placards and signs, and Professor Somebody from Somewhere making speeches. I watched some of it, switched over to the Weather Shop. There was a guy yammering on about long term climactic change, Big and Little Ice Ages; global warming: myth or legend, etc. I ran up their feed and got the forecast: overcast, maybe some mist, 15°, just cool enough for a sweater.

There was a cardboard box on the front porch with a note on it—MARIE: BRING THIS TO MY LECTURE. SIT ON 3D ROW AISLE.—and a wristbadge with STAFF stamped on it in deep hologram.

ooooo

The place was mobbed. I mean outside. The campus cops had a metal detector outside the front door. City cops were parked a block away, just off campus.

I looked in the box. There was a double-blade Mixmaster and a big glass bowl.

I threaded my way through the crowd and walked up to the campus cops, bold as brass.

"What's in the box, doc?" he said, recognizing me and looking at my wristbadge.

I opened it and showed him. "For the mai-tais at the social hour," I said. He looked at it, handed it around the detector, passed it in front of the sniffer dog. The dog looked at it like it was the least interesting thing on the earth. Then the dog looked east, whined and barked.

"That ain't his bomb bark," said the K-9 cop. "He's been acting funny all morning."

"Can I go in now?" I asked.

"Oh, sure. Sorry." said the main cop, handing me the box once I went through the metal detector with the usual nonsense.

The crowd, barred from coming in without badges, swayed back and forth and pointed preprint laser messages into any camera pointed toward them, and waving old fashioned signs. A couple of people from my department were in there with them.

∞∞∞∞

Dr. Bob's speech, "Long-Term Implications of Pleistocene Faunal Retrieval on Resuscitated Species: An Overview" was supposed to start at 1300, and by 1215 the place was full. Including plenty of people with signs, and I saw Professor Somebody from Somewhere I'd seen on the news. The most ominous thing: in the program, the last fifteen minutes was to be Q and A Discussion.

It was a big lecture hall, a wall to the right of the platform leading out to the right where I knew was the building's loading dock. The wall blocked an ugly ramp from view and destroyed most of the acoustics—it had been a local pork barrel retrofit ten years ago. Bureaucratic history is swell, isn't it?

∞∞∞∞

At 1255 Dr. Bob came in. He went up to the podium. There was mild applause and some sibilant hissing. Really.

"Thank you, thank you very much. Normally I would introduce the speaker, but hey! That's me!" There was some disturbance out at the hall doors. "I know you're all as anxious as I am for me to start. But first—a small presentation that may—or may not—shed some light on my talk. I honestly don't know what to expect any more than you do." A *boo* came from the back of the hall, loud and clear.

The lights went down, and I heard the big loading dock doors rattle up, gray daylight came up from the ramp and—

—in came something:

It was a tall thin man, bent forward at the waist, covered in a skin garment from head to foot. He had a tail like a horse, and what I hoped were fake genitals high up on the buttocks. His head was a fur mask and above it were two reindeer antlers. The face ended in a long shaggy beard from the eyes down and he had two tufted ears like an antelope's.

In the middle of the face was a red rubber nose. The feet were two enormous clown shoes, about a meter in length, the kind that let whoever's wearing them lean almost to the ground without falling over.

The hairy figure walked around, looked at the audience, and went to the blackboard and, placing its right hand on it, blew red paint through a reed, and left the outline of its hand on the green panel.

Someone booed just as I remembered where I'd seen pictures of this thing before. Some cave painting, Dordogne? Lascaux? Treis Freres, that's it. The thing was usually called the Sorcerer of Treis Freres, thought to be some shaman of the hunt, among the bison and horses and rhinos drawn and scratched on the walls of the cave 25,000 to 40,000 years ago...

Tantor and Behemoth walked in through the loading door ramp.

It got *real* quiet, then.

The Sorceror picked up a child's toy bow and arrow and fired a rubber-tipped arrow into Tantor, who backed down the ramp, out of sight of the audience. I could see the shadow of another man there, from where I sat. He was pulling something up over one of his arms.

The Sorceror mimed being hot, and Behemoth swayed like she was about to faint. The man pulled down his animal skin to the waist, and fired another suction-cup arrow into Behemoth's hairy side; she backed out of the room.

The Sorceror took off his costume (except the rubber nose and clown shoes) which left him in a diaper. He played with a small ziggurat, then took the model of a trireme from someone on the left side of the room, then a bishop's crozier from another (how had I not seen all these props and people when I came in?) Then he put on a lab coat and glasses, came down to where I sat and took the mixer from me ('Bonjour' he whispered) and went back to the stage where someone—Dr. Bob?—threw him a pair of Faded Glory blue jeans with double helixes painted on them *(one* person in the audience actually laughed.) He plugged in the mixer, threw the jeans into the glass bowl and watched them swirl around and around, took them out, went to the right stage wall and an elephant's trunk—a cloth puppet on the arm of the man whose shadow I watched on the loading ramp wall, along with those of the mammontelephants—snaked around the corner and grabbed the jeans and disappeared.

The lab-coated figure waited, then Tantor and Behemoth walked back onstage again, their eyes dark as dots of tar, their small double-hand-sized ears twitching.

The man went to the blackboard, picked up the hollow reed and blew red ocher pigment onto his right hand.

Slowly he held it up, palm toward the mammontelephants.

Tantor and Behemoth bowed down onto their front knees. They curled their trunks up in the same double-curve as those on the elephant statues in the Babylon sequence of D. W. Griffith's *Intolerance*. And then they gave the long slow loud trumpets of their kind, a sound cutting across a hundred centuries.

Every hair on my body shot straight up.

The lights went off. I saw shadows of shapes leaving, heard a truck start up. The loading door clanged down with a crash, and a spotlight slowly came up, centered on the red outline of the hand on the blackboard.

Then the houselights came back up and Dr. Bob Oulijian was alone at the lectern.

∞∞∞

We were at the freight depot with Sir Harry Tusker and Arnaud.

They made ready to load Behemoth and Tantor onto their personal freight car. *"Everybody else,"* said Sir Harry, "goes by truck to winter quarters in Florida. *We* go by train to Wisconsin, the shores of Lake Geneva. We join up with the circus again in March. The girls here get to play in the winter. Me and Arnaud get to freeze our balls off out *there,"* he pointed NW.

Arnaud stood with Tantor's trunk wreathed around his right arm. He scratched her under the big hairy chin.

"Better load up," said the freightman.

"West at 300 kph," said Sir Harry. Then: "Girls! Hey!" He yelled. *"Umgawa!"*

They started up the concrete ramp. Then something—a change in the wind? a low rumble from far away, from the direction of Baltimore? indigestion?—caused both mammontelephants to stop. They lifted their trunks, searching the wind, and let out their long low rumbling squeals.

"*Umgawa!*" said Sir Harry Tusker, again.

Behemoth took Tantor's tail, and followed her up the ramp and onto their private car.

Sir Harry and Arnaud followed, turned, waved, closed the doors of the car, and waved again through the small windows.

In a few minutes the train was gone, and in a few more, beyond the city limits, would be a westbound blur.

∞∞∞∞

Though it was October, and though this was North Carolina, that night it snowed.

**Anything with mammoths in it
is for Neal Barrett, Jr.**

Afterword to "Winter Quarters"

A history of the field (The True and Terrible one Malzberg's always talking about) could be written about stuff that *wasn't* where it *should* have been. Like this story.

(What I laughingly call my career is full of them: mine and Utley's "Custer's Last Jump!" was written for Terry Carr's *Universe 6*—which is where it was published, but for a while in the middle was in Robert Silverberg's *New Dimensions 5*—that was caused by publishers, not us or the editors. The fabled "Flying Saucer Rock and Roll" was written for the—eventually unpublished—*New Dimensions 13* edited by Marta Randall [so was Connie Willis' "All My Darling Daughters" and Ed Bryant's "Dancing Chickens"—that would have been *some* book] before appearing in *Omni Magazine*." Major Spacer…" in this collection went to Kim Mohan at *Amazing* but came out in my e-book *Dream Factories and Radio-Pictures* from Electricstory.com, while Kim got another story entirely…)

Where this one started was that Ellen Datlow wanted to edit an anthology of endangered-species SF stories, and the first thing she and I decided was that "The Ugly Chickens" *wouldn't* be in there. (The story's my best-known—it came out in Terry Carr's *Universe 10* in 1980, was in all three *Bests of the Year* of the time, won a couple of awards, and has been reprinted in various anthologies and magazines 16 times since then. I felt, if nothing else, it's been overexposed. Also, I said (I thought) pretty much all I had to say about extinction in it. "I don't chew my cabbage twice" is, I believe, the way I put it to Ellen.)

Then I saw *another* news item, late in 1999, about the exhumation of a mammoth in Russia, only this time it was a guy-mammoth with all his—ahem—parts intact. (I say, *another news item,* because I still had a batch of press releases from a bored AP stringer in Russia from the mid-1980s that was eventually proven to be a hoax—about attempts to clone mammoths with Indian elephants—their nearest living relatives.)

I got to thinking. I wrote Ellen and asked if the endangered-species book were still open. "Alas and alack," she said, "it's already turned in to the publisher."

"Well, gee whiz," I said. That seemed to be that.

But the thing wouldn't leave me alone. Mainly because I had been running through what seemed to be the irony of the situation. Mammoths—unsuited to the interglacial—had gone extinct. Now that we're aware of global warming and such and—just maybe—might do something about it, there's also the possibility we can bring the mammoth back, perhaps into another Little Ice Age like the one from 1300-1700s which was volcanic in origin, i.e. not us—who keep burning up everything combustible—but was a natural force.

Have we been *used?*

The history of man and mammoth (and mastodon) was truly intertwined the last 5000 years or so they were around. We got numerous and crafty enough to do serious damage to their populations, which may have already been on the decline due to climactic changes, and—like the dodo and passenger pigeon later—produced usually only one offspring—and, in the case of the two surviving elephant families—taking a *long time* to do that. (You can afford to lose a thousand rats a minute and still be overrun with the little bastards, as they drop litters of 8-10 every month or so; you can't afford to lose many of anything that takes almost two years to make *one more…*)

∞∞∞∞∞

I knew that if I started with that premise that somehow we'd been used by the mammoths, that the story would involve the "Sorceror of Tres-Freres" which is a cave painting just as I describe it. And that I'd need a performance artist to fulfill *that* role; hence, Arnaud. Hence Hitler the Magnificent as a performance piece.

Trust me on this.

When this story was published (at Scifi.com, which, as luck would have it, Ellen Datlow had just taken over as fiction editor), Leslie What wrote an essay for *The New York Review of Science Fiction* which pointed out the genocide and Holocaust parallels between extinction (the final solution of the mammoth problem) and Hitler's policies towards Jews, Slavs and Gypsies. (I'm making this sound simpler and much more superficial than her article ever was or could be.)

I honestly hadn't thought about that stuff while I was writing the Arnaud-in-college section—I needed the kind of stuff a trickster-shaman would do to upset the old apple-cart of student-visa decorum...This is what we in the writing-biz call resonance, and it just goes to show you we sometimes don't know resonance when it bites us in the ass...

I was doing stuff to solve a story-problem: the *story* may have been doing stuff to bring up issues of redemption, grief and loss.

∞∞∞∞

What I mainly wanted to do was write a story about mammoths. I want one of my very own; so do you. One of my earliest memories of television is watching *The Jungle* (1953)—it's a Rod Cameron-Cesar Romero-Marie Windsor Indo-American co-production and involves living mammoths in India in the present day, and there's a great mammoth vs. hand grenade fight. The production company—Lippert—who also did *Rocketship XM* and *Unknown World*—was an independent who sold their movies to TV immediately, unlike the majors who held out for another five years or so. I think I was pretty much in love with mammoths from that eight-year-old's moment on. (But not as much as Neal Barrett, Jr., to whom the story's dedicated—he lives, breathes and writes mammoth, and he's been doing it for longer than I've been alive.)

I've written mammoth before, in the novel *Them Bones,* where I have one of the last ones (in an alternate mound-builder present) pretty much straight out of Cornelius Mathews' *Behemoth: a Novel of the Mound-Builders* (1838), and in "The Lions Are Asleep This Night" in which I have one of the Pilgrim Fathers out turkey-hunting come face-to-trunk with one (again, not *our* 1620).

But I've never written so pure and unadulteratedly about mammoths as here, and it was a joy to imagine a world where they once again shared the earth with us, like they did 10,000 years ago, before we learned to poke a hole in the ground and put in a seed, rather than poking a hole in *them*. When we got agriculture, we got government and the military…

Not that this one wasn't hard to do—it was, but the mammoth scenes wrote themselves.

It was the people-stuff that got in the way.

Maybe Leslie What was on to something…

The Other Real World

SUNDAY
Stranger on the Shore

Bobby sat in the small beachside park watching the waves come in from Japan.

It was a park put up by the WPA twenty-five years before, probably nice once, that had been allowed to run down. There were a few picnic tables, some missing slats from the tops, three firepits and a poured concrete bench overlooking the ocean.

An old lady there once told him that it had once been quite popular with families just after the war. Then bodybuilders had started using it, and the kinds of crowds *they* attracted, she'd said, arching her eyebrows, and then the Colored had moved into the area, and *now* look at it.

Now, looking at it, he saw a couple of surfer guys paddling around out there, and their girlfriends lying on towels on the beach, even though it was October, and a guy walking a dog back and forth, eyeballing the girls' butts.

Bobby came here because he usually wasn't bothered. There were two orders of French-fries from the In-and-Out Burger a mile away beside him.

He heard a car pull into the parking lot, a door slam, and the sound of a tinny transistor radio playing "Fly Me to the Moon (Bossa Nova)" getting closer.

"You gonna eat all those fries?"

"No, I was hoping some dork grad-school physicist would come along and want some."

"Hello, Bobby. Swell mood."

"Hello, Stewart. Plenty to make me this way. Sorry. What's up?"

"Went by the place, you weren't there, you weren't at the pool hall, figured you were here."

"Turn that thing down."

Stewart fiddled with his shirt pocket, turned off the brown and silver radio, took his Chesterfields out of the other pocket and lit one up.

Bobby moved away from him on the bench, coughing. "What's up?"

"Saw Gadge at your apartments," he said. "Pomphret's busting his chops again at j.c. Making him think and stuff. The bastard."

"He was making everybody think when we were there; why should he quit now?"

"Yeah, but you know how Gadge is. He says when he first saw the prof, six or seven years ago, he was a science reporter named Johnson; now he's at the junior college teaching English and his name is Pomphret."

"Maybe he's got a half-twin brother or something? Anyway, what's on Gadge's mind?"

"You know, since he discovered girls, he wants to be called Brian?"

"Yeah, yeah."

"Well, he said he talked to Dobie, and Dobie's worried about his dad again."

"From what I hear," said Bobby, "his dad ain't been the same since he had to go up into the hills and identify his brother Joe's body in the swimming pool at that crazy old bat's house. That was before my time, though."

"Well, there's that. There's also trouble with Dobie's uncles. His dad's a triplet, you know; Joe was a younger brother. Anyway, there's him, Herbert T., then there's his brother Norbert E. who used to be *the* taxi service in some podunk town, and then there's Elbert P., who everybody used to call Pinky and worked in a male psycho ward in New York."

"Okay. Triplets. What's the deal?"

"Well, Pinky—that's Elbert P.—got to looking through some state records and ran across their birth certificates. Pinky was always told he was born last. But the records say that was Norbert E. He can't be Pinky—he's Herbert T. or he's Norbert E. but he can't be Elbert P. So Norbert's Pinky, or Dobie's father is—"

"What does this have to do with anything?"

"Well, now Herbert T. thinks he may be Pinky. And Norbert doesn't know who he is."

"I think Dobie's runnin' his dad crazy, hanging around with beatniks, chasing after girls who only want rich guys when he ain't got two nickels to rub together—"

They were interrupted by singing from below the rise at the edge of the park: "Medea—I just met a girl named—Medea—" off-key, very off-key.

Stewart walked to the edge of the park and looked down. "Go somewhere else, squirts!" he yelled. He walked back.

"It's just that Opie and young Theodore," he said. "Go on."

"I said, Dobie's running his father as crazy as his dad's worrying about which triplet he is. How did we get off on this?"

"You asked me what Gadge said. I'm telling you the truth, Ruth. He's worried about Dobie's—"

"Sorry I asked in the first place. God, I wish life was as simple as wondering whether I'm me!"

"Gal trouble?"

"I don't want to talk about it."

"Suit yourself."

They watched the ocean in silence. Stewart finished his fries. "Well," he said. "I better get back and check on Roger. Want to shoot some pool later?"

Roger was Stewart's little brother, who hadn't spoken in six years.

"Naw. I'd rather brood."

"OK" said Stewart. "You might want to check the news when you get back—you may not have heard out here on Despondence Slough Point, but some big-ass deal's up in Washington, cars coming and going all day, Kennedy flew back from campaign-stumping for senators in the midwest. Not that I give a rat's ass." He paused. "And I wouldn't go selling Dobie's friend too short. Nicholas of Cusa was a Krebs." He got in his Merc and left.

Bobby brooded for an hour or two, then that lost its charm. He went back to the parking lot.

As usual, there were notes stuck under his windshield wipers, two under the left and one under the right. He pulled that one out. It said: "Don't listen to those guys!! I'll top any of their offers by $75. Call Spud," then a phone number.

Bobby's car was a 1946 Ford Super Deluxe wagon: pale green hood and fenders, black top, with light blond wood doors, sides and back, and rear door. It had a green Continental kit and whitewall tires.

Every gremmie and would-be hodad on the Coast was always trying to buy it from him, so they could use it to haul their surfing-boards and beach-bunnies around in it and look cool. He tore up the notes and threw them in the park garbage can.

He got in, made sure the greasy rag was handy on the floorboard, the one that he used when the gears hung between first and second, when he would have to jump out in the street, open the hood, yank the shift-levers even, and start all over again. It was happening more frequently lately.

No matter. He put it in reverse, swung out, shifted and headed for home.

Trouble or not, his rod was not for sale.

MONDAY
I Remember You

Bobby came in from work, took a quick shower, and lay down on his bed, which was three steps from either the door or the shower.

He looked around at his place. What a dump. He had to make some more money, or something, and get out of here.

He looked up at the wall where there was a license-plate holder. Above, it said "DC Cab" and below "Call LAwrence 6 1212." The license plate itself was number H0012. He'd gotten it when he was eleven. He remembered the day he'd gone to the cab company to get it, the day they changed all the license plates for the next year. It hadn't cost him anything: by then everybody seemed to have forgotten everything that had happened.

He'd had it with him ever since, in DC at the boarding house; when he and his mom had moved to California for her new job in '54, when his mom died in '58 and he'd been out on his own.

He also remembered, back in '51, that the first thing he'd done that summer night was to beat the shit out of Sammy, the neighbor kid, for putting the finger on Mr. Carpenter. "They was Army guys!" said Sammy that night as Bobby pounded some more on his snotty nose, "What could I do? Don't hit me!" But Sammy knew he had it coming.

He turned on the radio. "—will make an address in about six more minutes. Meanwhile, here's 'Sea of Heartbreak' by Don Gibson, from way way back last year in 1961—" The music came up.

There was a knock on the door, then Stewart came in. "Hey, turn on the box. Kennedy's gonna blow off his bazoo in a few minutes."

Bobby switched on the TV, fiddled with the rabbit ears and the tinfoil till Channel 9 came in as well as it ever did. Some afternoon game show was wrapping up.

Stewart fired up a Chesterfield with the flamethrower Zippo he used.

"God, those things stink!" said Bobby.

"You don't like smoking, move to another country," said Stewart. He rebreathed his own smoke three or four times.

"That kind of smoking went out in the Stone Age," said Bobby.

"The hell," said Stewart. They heard a motor-scooter buzz up outside.

Gadge, who lived in the same apartments, came in the door with his books under his arms.

"Kennedy talking yet?" he asked, dumping his books all over the floor. "Pomphret's busting our asses again."

"That right? Well—"

The TV had gone to the network logo, and a "Please Stand By—Special Bulletin" card. The announcer said: "We take you now to the White House where the President of the United States will address the nation."

Bobby looked at the clock. Four pm PDT. That would be 7 o'clock on the East Coast.

∞∞∞∞

"—within the last week, unmistakable evidence has established the fact that a series of offensive missile sites is now in preparation on that imprisoned island. The purpose of these bases can be none other than to provide a nuclear strike capability against the Western Hemisphere.

This government, as promised, has maintained the closest surveillance of the Soviet military buildup on the island of Cuba—"

∞∞∞∞

It was weird listening to this. It was coming out of the TV. It was coming out of the radio that Bobby had forgot to turn down. The President was saying it. Nukes in Cuba, a few minutes flight away from DC. Bobby knew all the DEW radars were in Canada, Alaska, Greenland, pointed north, over the Pole, toward Russia. They fired those things off from Cuba, you'd be dead where you sat.

∞∞∞∞

When it was over, and the quarantine—Kennedy's word for blockade—was announced, Gadge said, "Gee Whiz!"

Stewart was quiet.

"Where's the admiral?" asked Bobby.

"He had to go back to the Pentagon last Friday. Some big-cheese reunion of the old code-breakers or something...Hey, wait! I bet it had something to do with *this!*"

Gadge started to laugh.

"What's so funny?"

"Boy!" he said. "I just got a picture of Krushchev and Kennedy waving their dongs at each other, their hair all standing up straight..."

"Krushchev doesn't have any hair," said Stewart.

"He does on his back," said Bobby.

"Yeah, well, it's just a big-dick contest!" said Gadge.

"It's a big-dick contest with H-bombs," said Stewart.

"Hey," said Bobby, looking at him, "you're the one who's usually a card. Why so glum?"

"I better get home," said Stewart. "No telling how Roger's taking this. See you guys later."

"Lemme put this in perspective," said Bobby, stopping him at the door while turning off the TV, and turning back up the radio, which was playing Bert Kaempfert's "Wonderland by Night" from 1960. "Kennedy thinks he's got problems, what with Russians and missiles and Castro in Cuba. Me, I gotta find a shifter gate collar for a '46 Ford."

∞∞∞∞∞

After they had gone, Bobby put on *The First Family* album on his Silvertone record player. He listened and laughed. He liked the way Vaughn Meader, as Kennedy, said "Cuber."

TUESDAY
Wheels

The junkyard was as crummy-looking as most, but it was bigger.

There was a parking strip, and a tiny office you had to go through, attached to a barn-size building with a couple of garage doors through which you could see the entire history of the internal-combustion engine and the transmission stacked up to the ceiling. Beyond that was about two miles of 10-foot-high fence topped with four strands of barbed wire with a sign every fifty feet saying "Patrolled by Vicious Dogs." There was a big wrecker with the junkyard name on it, and a smaller one made out of a pickup, dark blue with a dribble of pink paint on the left fender, that was unmarked. On one side of the garage-part, hoods of cars and trucks were stacked up like rental boats at a lake in the off-season. There were four or five cars out front when Bobby pulled up. He took out some wrenches and screwdrivers and went inside the office.

A fat guy was on the phone. His hands looked like he'd cleaned them last during the third Roosevelt administration. He held up one of them. He finished talking and hung up.

"First thing you do, kid, you go to that stack of pads there and you write your name and address and you sign and date it."

"I thought I was at a *junkyard*," said Bobby.

"Ho-ho. So you are, kid. This is for my insurance company. Something happens to you out there, and you've signed the form, *I don't care.* You don't sign it, you don't get in on your quest for the perfect hot rod."

Bobby stepped over to the pad of mimeographed forms, read it—the standard "own risk" crap, wrote out his name and address, signed and dated it.

"Letting lawyers doing your thinking for you, aren't you?"

The guy sighed. "You got cars, glass and junk, you get insects and worms. You get insects, including bees and wasps, and worms, you get birds and rats. You get birds and rats, you get snakes, many beneficent, but including the coast rattler, the copperhead and the mocassin. You reach for the headlight assembly on an El Dorado and grab a handful of coast rattler, you die.

"I really don't have time for a nature lecture, kid. I just don't want anybody asking me in county court why I let idiots in such a dangerous place. That is the short answer. You through?"

"Yes."

"Happy hunting."

∞∞∞∞

The junkyard rose slowly toward the back of the place, up toward the hills maybe a mile away. Bobby assumed any Ford Super Deluxes they had had been stripped long ago; he'd have to look at any Ford made between '46 and '49, including pickups. He had a tracing of the shifter gate collar, top and side view, he'd made after Kennedy's speech yesterday; he figured while the thing was working at all, he'd better take it off, trace and measure it, and put it back on before he went to the junkyard. He'd had to hand-jerk the gears eight times today, including two blocks before he got to the junkyard. His hands weren't much cleaner than the guy's who ran this place.

∞∞∞

An hour later and no luck. Every early postwar Ford he'd seen was stripped back to the firewalls, most missing the steering columns, even the wheel hubs. He'd found lots of wasp nests, and once thought he heard a snake under a car when he climbed up on the bumper—maybe it was just a lizard or frog or rat.

∞∞∞

He was near the back of the place. Off to one side was a long pen full of the snarliest dogs he'd ever seen, ten or twelve of them. They were barking and bounding off the double-reinforced cattle fence that looked like it had been through a waffle-maker. The dogs' feet never seemed to touch the ground; they floated back and forth closest to anyone out in the salvage yard. Geez.

There was a slow rise at the back of the place, mowed grass on it, a mound. In the middle of the mound was what looked like a bank-vault door. Above the door and to one side was a dark indented slit in the mound.

Bobby jumped down inside the front of a '54 wagon, made, he knew, too late after they changed everything, but he looked anyway.

∞∞∞

Some minutes later a truck pulled up through one of the narrow twisting lanes between the junkers and drove around to the back of the mound. The truck was from the Pure Water people; a guy got out, hooked up some hoses, and let Newton do the work, as Stewart was always saying when gravity was involved.

Bobby walked closer. He saw that the inset slit above the door contained the business end of a submarine periscope.

He knew then that he was looking at a pretty serious fallout shelter. So the junkyard guy was going to bunker-up during WWIII, instead of taking his chances outside with all the radioactive mu-tants. To each his own.

ⓄⓄⓄⓄⓄ

He found what he was looking for on a 1951 Chrysler. They weren't supposed to have parts that would fit Fords. He checked the drawing twice and measured three times. Same adjustable screw sleeves and everything.

He tossed it up in the air and caught it a few times. He walked to the edge of the mowed grass around the fallout shelter. The water truck was long gone. The dogs were going crazy. The sun was heading down in the drink, and they were getting restless. Maybe they lived for each night, hoping just once somebody would be out in the place when they were turned loose. He saw there was a big lift-gate at the front of the pen, and a walkway above it so the gate could be pulled up and the dogs couldn't get to whoever opened it. This was *some* operation.

ⓄⓄⓄⓄⓄ

He went back to the office just as the big back overhead garage doors of the engine and transmission graveyard opened, and a kid with sunstreaked-blond hair jumped back in another wrecker, towing a car that looked like a photograph of a wave on the hook. The car was all blue; *all* the glass had been spiderwebbed, and it was hilled and vallied in six places. It must have spun on the top, or gone under a moving van. Bobby didn't see any blood as it went by him.

"Out in the 34 area," the fat guy was saying to the kid. The kid nodded, looked at Bobby, bounced away.

"You look happy. What you got, kid?"

"Shifter gate collar."

"Shifter gate collar? Well, normally that would be 50¢. But being how the world's gonna end this week, that'll be a quarter. You'll need it to get up in the hills to the people who'll steal and rob and kill you."

"Thanks," said Bobby, handing him two dimes and a nickel. "I see *you're* ready."

"That I am. But don't come around when it happens thinking I'll let the whole world and his uncle in. All my family's ready too, 'ceptin that boy you saw there; he says he'll take his chances."

"Well, he may be right," said Bobby. "Maybe people are more or less good. Maybe they'll help each other if that happens."

"Kid," said the fat guy. "Prepare yourself for one *big* disappointment."

∞∞∞∞∞

There were two more names and phone numbers stuck under his windshield wipers. He crumpled them up, threw them on the seat. He jerked up the hood, undid the top screw from the old shifter gate collar, crawled under, backed the bottom screw out, pulled off the old collar, slipped the new collar over the column till it snapped into place, put in the bottom screw, climbed out from under, pulled the gear rods down, put in the top screw. He wiped his hands on the rag, got in, ran through the gears letting the clutch in and out. Smooth as silk. All that aggravation fixed for a quarter.

He turned on the radio. The DJ was saying, "and now, here's the Republican campaign song for 1964," and Ray Charles came on singing "Hit the Road, Jack."

Then Bobby noticed the fat guy and his sun-blond kid standing on the office porch looking at him.

"Hey, kid," said the guy. "My son wants to know if you want to sell your car?"

Bobby cranked up and put it in reverse.

"Not for all the farms in Cuber," he said, and drove away.

WEDNESDAY
West of the Wall

Roger, who was thirteen, was putting together an Aurora model of the Frankenstein Monster. He had it standing up on its tombstone base, its left arm outstretched and in its shoulder socket, and the two halves of the right arm together and held with rubber bands while the reeking airplane cement dried.

"You okay, kid?" asked Stewart, coming in and putting his papers on the chair nearest his bed in the room they had shared for six years.

Roger shook his head yes.

"School okay?"

Roger shrugged.

"Yeah, I know what you mean. Neat Frankenstein."

Roger pushed the box, with all the parts already broken off the sprues, over toward him. He pointed to the sides, with its pictures of Dracula and the Wolfman, and the slugline "Collect 'Em All!"

"I'll bet you can hardly wait for your next allowance, huh?"

Roger smiled, then went back to gluing.

∞∞∞

The hall phone rang and Miz Jones the housekeeper answered it. She talked a few minutes, then called Sarah, the admiral's sister to the phone.

Sarah was upset when she came into the boys' room. "It's the admiral," she said. "He wants to talk to Roger a minute, then you," she said to Stewart.

Roger ran out into the hall. After a couple of minutes he came back in, pointing over his shoulder with his thumb.

Stewart picked up the receiver.

"You okay, Admiral?" he asked.

"Yeah, yeah, Stewart, I'm fine as could be. Eating good old Navy chow again, working with some of the old gang. Look, Stewart—" he said, then stopped. "I—"

"We'll be fine, Admiral. It's you we're worried about."

"Yeah, well, I was fine for about 40 years before you was born, kid. I want you to know how—uh—"

"Hey! I want you to know how much I—me and Roger—appreciate all you and Sarah and Miz Jones did for us. Especially for Roger, Admiral. We couldn't have been an easy thing—"

"Aw, hell. All I said was give me those kids; they need something like a parent right now, and I don't have time to argue with you."

"Wasn't like ordering around swabbies on a boat, though, was it?" asked Stewart.

"Well, no," said the admiral. "But I got you, didn't I?"

Then he cleared his throat. "Look, Stewart. This thing might get a little hairy. Keep on top of stuff. Get Roger and Miz Jones and Sarah somewhere safe, if it comes to it. You're the man of the house right now."

"Of course I will, Admiral," said Stewart.

"Well, gotta get off the blower here—they're only giving everybody one call. I oughtta know, I signed the order myself. And I'm strict." He laughed.

"Admiral, we—"

"Get back to your books, Stewart. Tell Sarah and Miz Jones I'll be back the minute this little flap is over."

"Sure thing," said Stewart. There was a transcontinental click on the other end of the line.

∞∞∞

Stewart remembered the first few days after the lab explosion that took his mom, dad and that fugitive Nazi scientist whose body was found in the debris with them. Roger of course had never spoken afterwards. Stewart had been in a daze—he'd been doing his math homework one minute; the next the lab across the driveway and half the house were gone. It was two days before his hearing had come back.

The admiral, who'd been working with his parents the week before, and who was on his way back from Washington when it happened (the week after the collapse, then sudden reemergence of the Soviet Union, when it looked like the messages his dad had been getting from Mars were faked by the Nazi from South America) got there in the first few hours while the ruins were filled with firemen, police, FBI and the military.

Aunt Jessica and Uncle Hume had wanted to adopt them, but of course the State of California said "They're *actors*. New York actors, mostly, and they have kids of their own."

So the admiral said "Give them to me. Those boys need me." The State reminded him he wasn't married. "You're right," he said. "I figured if I needed a wife, the Navy would have issued me one. But I've lived in the same house when not on blue-water duty for 21 years, my sister lives with me, and we've had the same housekeeper for twenty of those years, and we don't intend to change now. And I don't want either boy to go into the Navy—assuming the little one starts talking again—they got too many brains for that, I've seen their IQ scores. They'll have to get real jobs when they grow up, like everybody else. I'll give them a good solid home and I'll take care of them till they're ready to leave. Now tell an admiral in the US Navy he hasn't got the onions to be a fit parent."

A week later they'd moved into the admiral's house, and their lives had been swell ever since.

∞∞∞

Stewart watched Roger finish the Frankenstein monster while he fiddled with what was turning out to be some Fibonacci curves. He plugged in some unknowns.

Roger climbed into bed, staring at the monster, which he'd put on the top of the bookcase that was the footboard to his bed. He'd put it there, striding toward him off its graveyard base, arms outstretched for him.

He reached down under his bed, from the ragged pile there, and took out *Famous Monsters of Filmland #12*, which seemed to be his favorite. He went to sleep with his bedlamp on, the magazine across his chest.

Stewart got up, put the magazine back in the pile, pulled the covers up around Roger, and turned off his light.

Then he went downstairs to raid the refrigerator.

THURSDAY
Because They're Young

"Ready to go?" asked Stewart.

"I don't know," said Gadge.

"What do you mean? All this stuff getting you down? I'm the one who's worried the hell about Roger and the admiral. I'm here. I'm ready. I want to see some flicks.

"Look," he went on. "I been zombieing around for three days. I haven't had the fun of fighting over groceries and lugging five gallon cans of gasoline home, or stocking a fallout shelter, or buying shotgun shells. I been moping around and worried about my little brother, who hasn't said a word in six years anyway."

"How is Roger?"

"Who knows! No different than always. Watches the news. Don't change the subject. Are you coming with me to the drive-in or not?"

"Look, Stewart. Everything's pretty spooky right now. I mean, what if there's World War Three while we're there?"

"Listen at you. All the Russian ships slowed down but the one that's 50 miles out ahead of the others. It won't reach the blockade till Saturday. Nothing's gonna happen till then. Besides, what would you do? I mean, supposing you only had an hour to live?"

"That's easy," said Gadge. "Send *both* Veronica and Angela Cartwright to my room. Have Hayley Mills wait outside in case *they* don't kill me..."

"Right! There you go! And where is it you can ever hope to see girls like that?"

"At...at the movies." said Gadge. He sighed. "Let's go."

∞∞∞

There were only a dozen other cars waiting to get into the Luau Drive-In, with its neon Hawaiian party going on on the backside of the screen facing the road. There were red neon flames where the pig cooked; a guy's neon hands plucked on his neon ukelele strings; two hula girls' hips moved back and forth in their neon green grass skirts.

"Look, guys," said the owner who was taking tickets, and who lived in the house that was the screen, with its upper story porthole windows. "Not enough people show up, there won't be movies tonight. We'll announce it and give your money back as you exit."

"Whatta ya mean, no show?"

"Kid, the world might end any time."

"Yeah, well," said Stewart, "if it doesn't you'll regret being out our six bits."

∞∞∞

The sound piped in over the speakers before the show started was the local radio station. The DJ was saying, "and that was Charley Drake with 'My Boomerang Won't Come Back.' And now here's one from way back in 1959 to take us up to the news…" "Quiet Village" with its rainfall and bird noises and tinkling piano came on.

"I'll go get some crap to eat," said Gadge. He got out and headed back toward the concession stand as the flood-lights around the screen came on with the dark.

∞∞∞

He got back in with the big cardboard carrier. There were two big bags of popcorn, two big Cokes, two Clark bars, a big box of Dots and a roll of Necco wafers.

"How much I owe you?" asked Stewart.

"Man, this place is expensive," said Gadge. "It came to a dollar-ten in all. If you don't want any of the Dots, give me 50¢."

∞∞∞

There were previews, then a cartoon (an old Looney Tunes), a newsreel and some more previews, and then the first of the triple feature started to roll.

"I really don't know why I'm here," said Gadge. "Hayley Mills isn't in any of these movies—I'm sure she's not in *Bride of the Gorilla*—when it was made she would have been about two years old."

"Where's your spirit of adventure?" asked Stewart. "Maybe you'll see another girl of your dreams in this. Or *Poor White Trash*. Or *High School Confidential?*"

"Yeah, right. If they were my age when these things were made they'd be about firty by now…"

"Come on. Where's your appreciation of cinema history?"

Raymond Burr, the guy who played Perry Mason on TV, was having trouble in the jungle.

"Seriously," said Gadge, biting into the Clark bar. "How *is* Roger?"

"He seems okay," said Stewart. "Well, no different anyway. He just watches TV more. He's been in study-hall for two days. They sent some of the special ed kids home Tuesday—some of them got too upset. He still answers any yes or no questions you ask him, shakes his head, like he always has. I talked to his shrink last week before all this happened."

"What'd he say?"

"Same stuff as you and me heard growing up. Post-wonder effect. It wears off or it doesn't. Not enough of us around to figure out if *everybody* comes out of it or not. I mean, it's what, a decade or less…Bobby was one of the first and that was *only* eleven years ago."

"It was sure as hell less time for me than since *this* movie was made," said Gadge.

∞∞∞

Stewart awoke with a start. Gadge was snoring away in the passenger seat. Stewart looked at the screen. It was another movie—a guy in a black hat was doing something bad.

He looked at the clock on the dash. Only 9:30—this must be *Poor White Trash*. Yeah, there was Peter Graves.

"Hey," said Stewart. "Wake up."

"Huh, what? Huh?"

"You know the idea I had about going to the movies to forget our troubles?"

"Yeah?"

"Bad idea."

"Bad idea," Gadge repeated. He looked up at the screen. "What happened to the gorilla?"

"Wrong movie," said Stewart. He cranked the motor, put the speaker back out on its hook on the post, and drove toward the exit with his parking lights on.

There were still two cars way out in the back row, their windows steamed up. The lights in the snack bar were already out.

"Wake me up when we get to my place," said Gadge.

Then he was snoring again.

Stewart was thinking about "My Boomerang Won't Come Back." When the song first came out, there was a line in it about practicing till you were black in the face.

Now the song said blue in the face. Go figure. The Aborigines must have a tough union.

FRIDAY
Gzachstahagen

Bobby said "A Raymond Burr gorilla movie?"

"If I'm lyin', I'm dyin'," said Stewart.

They were sitting in Stewart's '53 submarine Merc at the Hi-Spot, eating burgers. Stewart had swung by to pick up Bobby just as he'd swung in from work with his paycheck in his pocket. They went by Bobby's bank, where he cashed his check and put $8.00 in his savings account, and then they'd driven here.

"That guy was always having trouble with gorillas, wasn't he?"

They had the same radio station on in the car as the one piped in over the drive-in's speakers. The song ended and the DJ said, "...and that was Larry Verne with 'Please Mr. Custer' and then Ben Colder's 'Don't Go Near the Eskimoes' and a happy oog-sook-mook-ee-ay to you, too..."

Then the news came on and it was grim. The blockade waited for the Russian ships: the one out ahead of the others, the *Grozny*, was still coming on strong, the others slow behind it. The President and cabinet were meeting in the War Room. Absenteeism in schools and jobs was running 35%, 50% at defense plants on the East Coast and the Midwest. Stores all over the US were out of toilet paper, bulk foods and batteries. There was price-gouging all over; some stations were selling gas for as much as 50¢ a gallon. The weather forecast came on, then the DJ played Jack Scott's "What in the World's Come Over You?"

"And Gadge thought this was a big bluff thing," said Bobby.

"Yeah, well…" Stewart chewed on his fries. "Look. Don't you sometimes wish…I don't know…"

"What?"

"I mean, look at us. You, me, Gadge, especially Roger. All that stuff we went through. It didn't change a goddam thing."

"Well, how do we *know* it didn't change anything?"

"Okay, Mr. Philosophical. Everybody *knows* there's guys from outer space. Well, one, and his big robot enforcer. They went away. We *never* heard from them again. Then everybody thought my and Roger's dad was talking to Mars; things went crazy. The Russian Orthodox Church overthrew the Commies, for god's sakes…"

"For about a day," said Bobby.

"For *about* a day. Then Krushchev and Beria came down on them like a ton of bricks. It was like, you know, a little holiday, and then business back to Commie usual.

"And Gadge—his gramps makes a robot. Then all kinds of spy stuff—where Pomphret comes in: Commie spies. Then it's over. Gramps sends up the robot in a souped-up V2. It's never seen or heard of *again*. 'Cranky Old Man Shoots Robot into Space.' The end. Two years later—Ooops! Sputnik!"

"Your point being?"

"*Nothing* changed. Not one thing. We're right back to Us vs. Them, like *The* World is all there is, like we're *all* that matters…"

"Well," said Bobby. "Most people can't handle the idea we're not alone; that strange and marvelous stuff happens all the time, that—that—"

"But it did happen. *We* saw it; *they* saw it; *they* went crazy, too. But to them, it wasn't *personal*. It was just The News;

then something else took its place. It was just this year's tortilla Jesus."

"We got on with *our* lives. Well, except for Roger," said Bobby. "Why shouldn't people who weren't even *there?*"

"Yeah, but Truman? Eisenhower? Kennedy? Krushchev too. They saw what happened. You don't see any of that influencing foreign policy, or scientific research, or anything. Just business as usual. *Now* look where it's got us!"

"You expecting somebody to drop down from Pluto and straighten this out?"

"No. That would be the easy way out of this mess our world leaders have gotten us into."

"Well, what *do* you want?"

Stewart looked over the steering wheel out into the big plate glass window of the Hi-Spot where the carhops whizzed by on roller skates.

"I want a world *better* than this one," he said. "I want a world with shadows, and wet streets, and neon lights flashing "Hotel," "Hotel" outside my windows. Everything *here* seems to be taking place in a gray flat light. I want to be able to smoke like Robert Mitchum, and drink all day and night like Barton Maclane, and never, ever blow my beets. I want—I want to break someone's heart, or have mine broken, in the rain…"

"Why, why," said Bobby, "…you…you're a…*romantic!* Take me back to my place before I become so filled with cheap sentiment that I can't move."

"*Asshole.*" said Stewart, and flashed his lights for the carhop to come and take the tray.

ⓧⓧⓧⓧⓧ

They pulled up in front of the apartments. Things looked different.

There were two times in his life when Bobby had gone somewhere to do something, and when he got back found the world completely changed.

One had been in 1951. He'd gone off to play baseball in the neighborhood park, and when he got back, he found that his mom and Carpenter had gone off in the cab, and the rooming house was full of cops, FBI men and MP's.

The other was tonight, when he stepped out of Stewart's car and realized his 1946 Ford Super Deluxe wagon was *gone.*

∞∞∞∞

He awoke from a dream of Hayley Mills, in a T-shirt and a pair of shorts, climbing over a high fence.

Gadge got up and took a pee, then got back in bed.

What a week. Teachers on his case. Russians with missiles all over, bad gorilla movies, and now Bobby gets his woodie stolen.

He turned on his radio; the DJ was babbling, it was 2:30 in the morning. Good thing he only had a language lab on Saturdays at noon.

Ral Donner's "The Girl of My Best Friend" came on, a Golden Oldie from way back last year.

He thought of Gramps; he could see him and the robot like it was yesterday. Gramps had been dead four years now; the robot had been gone five. After all that stuff with the Commie spies, Gramps had shot the robot off in the V-2 the Army had given him, a year before Sputnik. They'd lost contact with the robot and the rocket a few minutes after takeoff, and that was that. While he was still little, ten, eleven years old—he held out hope that the robot was *still* up there. He'd watch the night sky for hours at a time for some blink of light, some flashing thing passing overhead. *Nothing.*

When they made that crummy movie based on Gramps, they hoked it all up. There wasn't any telepathy-thing with him and the robot. It was a fairly simple big machine and could perform some simple functions. That didn't mean Gadge hadn't loved it, and Gramps.

And there wasn't a love-interest for his mom, either. They made all that stuff up. His mom had died three years ago. He had enough money left over from Gramps to go to junior college, and live in these swell apartments, and eat and put gas in the Vespa, and that was about it. There was more money coming when he turned 21.

As if the Russkies would ever let that happen, now.

What he mostly remembered about the night he and Gramps went to the planetarium for the supposed lecture (a cheap Commie trick to kidnap them) was that there had been a bunch of teenagers in a circle out in the parking lot; in the middle two of them were having a knife-fight. He'd watched from the back seat, between the two big Commie refrigerators with bad haircuts, as they pulled away. One of the juvies was throwing down his knife.

Then the Russkies had put the sack over his head and thrown him down on the floorboards, and one kept his feet on him the whole trip out to the Last Chance Garage.

Orphans. We're all orphans in one way or another, Gadge thought. His dad was killed in Korea; his mom, Gramps and the robot in the last five years. Bobby's dad had bought it at Anzio, and his mom got cancer five years ago; Stewart and Roger's mom and dad were blown up in a lab fifty feet from them, five years ago.

The Cold War sure was rough on kids.

Now the radio was playing Neil Sedaka's "Happy Birthday, Sweet Sixteen." Yeah right, thought Gadge. Welcome to the future, kid. Fifty megatons, right up your butt. Like the posters people printed, of the toothless old man in the jet helmet—"Sleep Tight Tonight. Your Air National Guard Is on the Job!"

He turned off the radio and went back to sleep.

At some point in the night, Hayley Mills climbed down the other side of the fence, real slow.

SATURDAY
Midnight in Moscow

Things began to happen pretty fast that morning.

Bobby was staring at the empty space where his car had been in front of the apartments.

The guy in the house across the street, who had talked to the cops the night before—he told them the wrecker had been "black or blue" and that "it had a big hook on it"—walked over to him.

"I just remembered something. You know, in the excitement and all. I had been watching TV when I saw the cops over here, after I'd seen the tow truck pull your car off. The TV was showing pictures of little Caroline Kennedy playing with her pony Macaroni at the White House. They were near that tree house JFK had built for her, out in the back yard. You could—"

"What was it you remembered," asked Bobby. It would probably be something like, "The tow truck had wheels on it."

"—oh yeah. That wrecker had some pink or lavender paint on the front fender. You think that's enough we should call the cops back? You think it'll help get your car back?"

"Thanks," said Bobby. "I don't think we should call the cops about it. But I think it'll help get my car back."

The guy looked at him funny, then scratched his head. "Well, okay," he said.

∞∞∞∞

From the field up on the side of the hill—a failed subdivision, a few houses further up, roads paved, then gravel, then dirt, then nothing, going nowhere—Bobby could look down over most of the junkyard. Up here, at the back, closest to him was the fence, the bunker, and the dog pens, then nothing but acres of cars; far away the office and the garage.

All three tow trucks were outside. He looked through Gadge's 80x300 binoculars he'd borrowed before Gadge had to go off to his language lab.

The back garage doors, facing him, were open. His wagon wasn't there. And for a Saturday, the junkyard was pretty empty.

He was listening to his transistor radio. The news was that all the Russian ships had stopped except the *Grozny*, which came on toward the American quarantine line.

It was hailed.

It didn't stop.

A Navy destroyer escort fired a shot across its bow.

The *Grozny* steamed on toward Cuba.

The Navy shot off its rudder.

The news got out about 27 minutes after it happened.

∞∞∞∞

Things really started happening down at the junkyard then.

People moved around at the office. A few minutes later a couple of cars pulled in, and women and kids got out of the cars that drove into the garage and came out back. They carried boxes and blankets and dolls, and after awhile they came out of the mazes between the cars and went into the bunker.

The fat guy closed the place up and came back toward the fallout shelter in a '59 Ford pickup. The back end was full of shotguns, rifles and ammo boxes. He and some other guys carried the stuff inside.

Then nothing happened in the junkyard for two hours.

ooooo

Not much happened anyplace. The teletype between Washington and Moscow must have been red-hot. The radio said the *Grozny* was boarded, and it was full of wheat, tractors and medical supplies. This left the Americans with red faces, and a ship they'd disabled dead in international waters.

Some Cuban tugs were sent out.

Meanwhile the rest of the Russian freighters got up good heads of steam and plowed toward that imprisoned isle.

ooooo

Bobby's back was killing him. Nothing moved in the junkyard. A couple of cars pulled up out front, saw the place was closed, drove away. The dogs in their big pen figure-eighted back and forth: they knew something was up.

Then the bleached-blond kid and the fat guy came out of the bunker. They talked. The fat guy handed his son some money. The kid walked out through the junkyard, through the office, got in the big wrecker and left.

Then for a while nothing happened but the radio. One of the songs it played was "Asia Minor" by Kokomo, and Bobby Darin's "Beyond the Sea," a song Bobby had always liked.

∞∞∞

A half-hour later the big wrecker came back, pulling Bobby's wagon. The kid opened the doors and pulled it into the big garage, closed and locked the front garage doors, and walked back out to the bunker. The fat guy met him. The kid handed him a pink slip and some money back. Nice touch.

The junkyard owner went back inside the fallout shelter. The kid went up on the catwalk—the dogs were banging themselves against the side of the pens and gate. The kid opened the lift-gate like a sluice. Dogs squirted out like water from Grand Coulee Dam.

The kid jumped down on the outside of the fence—dogs slamming against it and barking and growling all along it. They seemed a little confused being out in the daytime, and the kid walked along the fence to the front of the place and got in one of the cars and drove away.

The radio said a disc jockey in Cleveland had just been fired on-air for dedicating a record to Nikita Krushchev, and then playing the Cuf-Links' "Guided Missile (Aimed at My Heart)."

∞∞∞

Bobby was on the pay phone three blocks over to Stewart.

"Yeah, well. Get on over here—we gotta work fast."

"Everbody here's upset," said Stewart. "Sarah's flut-tering around like ZaSu Pitts. It looks like it's even getting to Roger."

"What if I sent Gadge over?"

"I thought he had class?"

"They cancelled it. He was already home when I called him by mistake trying to call you. They're all shook up out at the college, too."

"You think this is a good idea? I mean, this is looking like *it*."

"And if the world doesn't end, I've lost my wagon for good. Soon it'll be purple and pink and the wood'll be dark teak. And legal-like, too."

"Hang tight, then. I'll be over as soon as Gadge gets here."

Bobby called Gadge back. Gadge didn't want to go, with everything looking serious and all.

"Look," said Bobby. "What if WWIII happens? Can you see yourself riding away from the Apocalypse on a Vespa? Come on, Gadge—"

"Call me Brian. I told you that a thousand times."

"Ga—Brian. There's three or four cars at Stewart's place. Something happens, you all jump in two or three and take off."

"I wanna go with you guys, if I'm going anywhere. I *know* something's up."

"Look, G—Brian. I do not know how long this is gonna take. Stewart's worried about everybody there. Roger likes you; you'll calm him down; he'll calm Sarah and Miz Jones down; everybody will be calm, including you."

"Roger gives me the creeps sometimes."

"Yeah, well, remember what he went through and what you went through. I'm pretty sure everything gives Roger the creeps. Look. Just do it. I'll give you—I don't know—money."

"Never mind that," said Gadge. "I'll do it. What you said about A-Bombs and motor-scooters made sense."

"You're a pal," said Bobby.

"Yeah, right."

OOOOO

Stewart showed up with food and blankets. He looked the place over. He was formulating a plan. But first he said, "You should call the cops. *There's* your wagon. There *they* are."

"Nah. The kid's gone. There's dogs all over the place. The cops'll get their asses eaten getting in there, or they'll have to shoot all the dogs. What if, say, it's *not* mine? I know it is, you know it is. They gotta get a judge to sign a warrant. And the fat guy didn't do it. It's the *kid.*"

"Call the cops," said Stewart. "No matter how much trouble it is, no matter how many fallout shelters they gotta look in to get a judge."

"No," said Bobby.

"Why not?"

"Because *now* it's personal."

"I *knew* you were going to say that," said Stewart.

OOOOO

"Look at the setup," said Stewart. "How do you think they get the dogs back in the pens in the mornings?"

"Uh..."

"You climb up on that catwalk there, from outside the fence. You throw food in the pens. You open the gate. They come in. You close the gate. That'll be my job."

"What's mine?"

"While I'm doing that, you open the front garage door and you drive your wagon out. You pick me up, two blocks over that way. Or, things still being quiet, I walk back to my car up on the hill and drive myself home. We go to the nearest cops and you tell them you found your car. Someday, when no one's looking, you backshoot the kid."

"There's things that can go wrong with your plan, as I see it…" said Bobby.

"Yeah. I can fall in the pens and get eaten up. Or the people in the bunker see what they think is someone stealing a car they think is legally theirs, and they shoot you full of big holes. Other than that, what's there to worry about?"

Stewart got up.

"Where you going?"

"You think food for the dogs is gonna walk down here? And how are the front garage doors locked?"

"Slaymakers as big as toolboxes," said Bobby. "Oh."

"Oh is right. Stick tight."

"What if the kid comes back and starts doing stuff to the car?"

"The kid ain't coming back today or tonight unless bombs start dropping; if they do, he ain't gonna be thinkin' about chopping and channeling your rod. If he were coming back, he wouldn't have let the dogs out, because then he's gotta put 'em back in again. He'll be back tomorrow when they *usually* put the dogs back in. Ever read any Pavlov? I thought not."

"Well—"

"Worst comes to worst, Bob," said Stewart, "You can *always* call the cops."

He left. While he was gone, Bobby doodled in the sand with his finger the symbols: ♂ ♀ ✳ † ∞ .

ＯＯＯＯＯ

It was dark. They lay wrapped in their blankets. The lump of ten pounds of raw meat—$2.00 worth—lay over to one side, double wrapped in three yards of cellophane. Hopefully the dogs couldn't smell it up here. Occasionally a shape moved in the junkyard: one of the dogs looking for something to kill. Sometimes there was a dogfight.

"Guy in the store said raw meat was the one thing that wasn't selling. Nobody wants to take fresh meat down in a fallout shelter. Gave me a big-guy discount."

The bolt cutters lay between them, the size of a small lawnmower. Stewart got them from a tool rental place a mile away.

"See," said Stewart. "We could be home. We could be playing Scrabble. We could set our alarm clocks and get out here tomorrow at dawn. But no. You gotta play like Tom and Huck rescuing Jim, when Jim's *just fine.*"

"Shut up," said Bobby. "I'm just as cold as you are."

"Ah, yes," said Stewart, "but the difference is, you want to be cold, not me."

ＯＯＯＯＯ

At some point in the night Bobby woke up. Stewart was mumbling in his sleep.

Bobby turned on his radio. It was 4 a.m., Pacific time. Some minutes before, daylight already out over the Atlantic, over central Cuba, either the Russians or the Cubans had shot down an American U-2 spyplane.

"Wake up!" said Bobby.

"Huh?" asked Stewart, sitting up.

"We're in deep kimchee. The timetable's been moved up."

SUNDAY
Monster Mash

Just dawn.

ooooo

They'd put the blankets and stuff in Stewart's car up on the hill. Then Bobby'd taken the long way around, and stepped out of the weeds and watched till Stewart climbed out on the catwalk. He heard and watched as the dogs made a beeline for the pens.

He cut the bolt of the lock on the right-hand door. It popped apart like cheap swing-chain. These things must have about 6 million tons of torque, he thought, admiring the bolt cutters. He lifted the garage door—what a racket—then closed it in case anyone was driving by.

His car was still up on the wrecker hooks. He threw the bolt cutters inside.

He went to the wrecker, cranked it up, tried to figure out which gears and levers did what. He pulled one. Nothing happened. Then another. His car moved an inch.

He thought he heard yelling. He killed the motor. He heard yelling.

A blur of a dog shot through the back garage doors and bounced off the wrecker.

About that time, the front garage door opened. There stood the bleached-blond kid with a pistol in his hand; beyond him a car with its lights on idled.

The dog went over the kid's head and lit out for San Pedro.

The kid fell on his back and started emptying the pistol into the ceiling.

Bobby cranked up, gunned the wrecker motor and roared out of the garage, missing the kid by a foot with the fishtailing Ford wagon.

"Geez!" said Stewart, when Bobby roared to a stop for him two blocks away. "Now we're the thieves! Head for my place. We'll call the cops from there!"

"What happened?" asked Bobby, grinding the gears.

"The dogs didn't all come in. Then they must have seen me from the bunker, 'cause I saw guys with guns. About then I saw the kid pull up out front. I yelled as much as I could running as fast as I could. I think they shot at me—I heard shots anyway. I don't think I got the gate all the way down, either. The place is probably full of mutts. Geez!"

They swung out on the road. They didn't hear any sirens; no one was chasing them yet.

"Hey!" said Bobby. "This thing doesn't have a radio!" Stewart turned on his pocket transistor. He had to hold it up against the door handle to get better reception.

Groovy Ray Poovey was running down the Top Ten of the week: "That was #5, Frank Ifeild's 'I Remember You,' now here's #4!" and the Crystal's "He's Not a Rebel" came on.

"Great driving music," said Stewart.

They turned a corner a couple of miles from Stewart's house. "That was #3 this week," said the DJ, "The Contours' 'Do You Love Me?' Here's the #2 record for the week of October 28, 1962, the Four Seasons with 'Sherry'."

Bobby and Stewart wailed along with the falsetto Frankie Valli, nodding their heads back and forth. Stewart looked out the back, over the Ford. No one chasing them still.

Bobby downshifted, ground the gears. The wrecker rolled to a stop.

"Damn!" He found first again.

"Now," said Groovy Ray Poovey, before we find out what that #1 song is, we'll play an—" his voice went into echo-chamber bass "—Old One from-m-m-m the-th-th Vault-ault-ault-ault" And out came the piano notes of Floyd Cramer's "Last Date" from 1960.

∞∞∞

"Swing over on Lattner," said Stewart. "It's downhill. Geez, were doing fine for awhile. What happened?"

"I must have been running on adrenaline. Hey—what's this?" He was down in some kind of compound grandma gear. He started over. The rig started moving more than half a mile an hour again.

"And now," said the DJ, "the number one tune of the week, and you know what it is—"

There was the sound of a creaking door, bubbles, a dragging chain...

And the mellifluous voice of Bobby "Boris" Pickett doing "Monster Mash."

It stopped. There was dead air. Then a weird high warbling tone came over the radio as they got in sight of Stewart's house.

"Video portum," said Stewart, his face ashen.

∞∞∞

The Conelrad warning came on the radio. Sirens started up all over the city.

Bobby slammed the wrecker to a stop. He fiddled with the levers. His Ford dropped to the ground.

Gadge, Miz Jones, Sarah and Roger ran out of the house carrying blankets and food. Bobby undid the hooks, fished around for his keys, cranked the wagon.

Gadge and Miz Jones jumped in the car with him. Stewart and Sarah got in the admiral's sedan. All over the neighborhood people were running around like crazy.

"Get in, Roger!" yelled Stewart.

Roger stood facing north, looking far up into the sky.

He turned back and looked over his shoulder at the two waiting cars.

He did a little clumsy dance.

"Oh boy, oh boy!" he said. "Now you're really gonna see something!"

∞∞∞

Over the Conelrad warble, over the sirens and crashes and car horns, over the Pole, the missiles came down, passing some going the other way.

For Bill Warren, Joe Dante, David J. Skal and William Schallert: keep watching the skies, guys. And for Aunt Ethel Simpson, 1914-2000.

Explication and Glossary

1.   "Stranger On The Shore"—by Mr. Acker Bilk. The first pre-Beatle British record to make #1 in America, the week of May 26, 1962. It was used in the film *The Flamingo Kid*, which was set in 1962. If you're an alto sax or B-flat clarinet player, and can play this, you'll have all the girls (or boys) you *want* hanging around the bandstand...

2.   In-and-Out Burger: for real and true.

3.   "Fly Me to the Moon (Bossa Nova)": just making its way onto the charts.

4.   Bobby (Benson): see *The Day the Earth Stood Still* (1951). Hereafter *DTESS*.

5.   Stewart (Cronyn): see *Red Planet Mars* (1952). Hereafter *RPM*.

6.   Gadge: Brian "Gadge" Roberts. See *Tobor the Great* (1954). Hereafter *TTG*.

7.   Pomphret (Also spelled Pomfrett, Pomfritt): English teacher, at first, in high school, then Peter Piper Junior College (j.c.). See the television series *The Many Loves of Dobie Gillis* (1959-1963). Played by William Schallert, one of the dedicatees of this story.

8.   Johnson: see *TTG*. Played by Schallert, too. See also some of the many books around on the CIA's use of

journalists, teachers, etc. as "covers" during the 50s through the 70s.

9. Dobie: Dobie Gillis, of the novel by Max Schulman and the TV series. Played by Dwayne Hickman. Blond the first season, brunette afterwards.

10. Dad: Herbert T. Gillis. Played by Frank Faylen.

11. brother Joe's body: see *Sunset Boulevard* (1950).

12. Norbert E.: taxi driver from Bedford Falls. See *It's a Wonderful Life* (1946). Bert and Ernie are the taxi driver and cop there. Since *neither I nor anyone else* remembers which is which, I made up the name Norbert E. so it could stand for *either* Bert or Ernie. (You have to watch me every minute.) Played of course by Frank Faylen. (Yes, Bert and Ernie on *Sesame Street* are named for the pair.)

13. Elbert P., "Pinky": see *Lost Weekend* (1945). Played of course by Frank Faylen.

14. "Medea": a standard kids' goof-off version of "Maria" from *West Side Story.*

15. Opie and young Theodore: either it's Opie Taylor (played by Ron Howard) of *The Andy Griffith Show* and Theodore Cleaver (played by Jerry Mathers) of *Leave It to Beaver,* or Stewart is just using his Eddy-Haskell-type (Ken Osmond) sarcastic voice (as *LITB* would have it "to give some squirt the business") about a couple of nondescripts.

16. running his father crazy: the Frank Faylen catchline on *TMLODG* was "I gotta kill that boy! I just gotta!"

17. Roger was Stewart's brother: see *RPM*. The six years started where *RPM* ends.

18. Krebs: Maynard G. The first beatnik on television. Played by Bob Denver, later Gilligan (no first or middle name) on *Gilligan's Island*.

19. Bobby's car: it's a woodie, a wood-panelled station wagon, as described. Surfing was just starting big. Woodies were status symbols, and utilitarian, for carrying (as then called) surfing-boards to and from the beach.

20. Gremmie: short for gremlin. Ho-dad wannabees. They had everything they needed for surfing except a board and a car...

21. Ho-dad: hotshot surfers who knew how to hang ten, shoot the pier, run a pipe, etc.

22. "I Remember You" by Frank Ifeild: the second British song to bust the top 5, at #3 in the fall of 1962.

23. LAwrence 6-1212: the number Helen Benson and Mr. Carpenter must have called to get a cab. See *DTESS*.

24. H0012: the license plate of the cab Helen and Carpenter took. See *DTESS*.

25. When he was eleven: okay—we've go to do this sooner or later. The chronology: *DTESS* is the only one of the

three movies that takes place the year it was made, i.e. 1951. *TTG,* made in 1954, is set in 1957 or 1958, as Gadge's dad was "killed in Korea seven years ago." Unless he was killed in a peacetime accident in 1947, he died sometime after June 25, 1950, which puts the movie in 1957, at the earliest. *RPM* was made in 1952, but takes place "at the next closest opposition of Mars," which would have been in 1956. This is why everybody is the ages they are in the story...

26. Sammy: Sammy blabbed about the cab to the Army and FBI men at the boarding house. Most people forget Bobby is never seen in the movie again after the scene where his tennis shoes are wet from the dew at the Mall.

27. "Sea of Heartbreak:" as it says (#21, 1961).

28. rabbit ears and the tinfoil: remember *broadcast* television?

29. the admiral: Admiral William "Bill" Carey. Played by Walter Sande, an actor you instantly believed in any role. See *RPM.*

30. "Wonderland By Night:" as it says (#1, 1960).

31. *The First Family:* Album of the Year Grammy. Comedy record by Kennedy imitator Vaughn Meader. Events made this album sound very strange in later years.

32. "Wheels:" instrumental by the String-A-Longs (#3, 1961).

33. date it: once you could go to *any* junkyard in America and pry off anything you wanted and pay something for it and take it home. As in so many things, California led the nation in fear-of-lawsuit.

34. time for the nature lecture: He just gave one. This junkyard owner in 1962 understood ecology better than most people still do.

35. mu-tants: as it was pronounced in so many 1950s sf films, including *The Day The World Ended* (1955).

36. steal and rob and kill you: see *Panic in Year Zero* (1963).

37. "Hit the Road, Jack" (#1, 1961): I heard this, from a DJ, in 1961, over the air.

38. "West of the Wall:" Miss Toni Fisher (#37, 1962). About lovers separated by the Berlin Wall, which went up in 1961. August, to be precise.

39. model of the Frankenstein monster: hot off the mold in 1962.

40. Miz Jones, Sarah: *I* made them up. This is fiction, and you have to do *some* of that, you know?

41. after the lab explosion: for this paragraph, see *RPM*.

42. Aunt Jessica and Uncle Hume: Jessica Tandy, Hume Cronyn.

43. I figured if I needed a wife…: old Navy/Marine saying.

44. *Famous Monsters of Filmland #12:* there are three movies (now four, but *13 Days* doesn't count and I don't include *Missiles of October* which was made for TV) set during the Cuban Missile Crisis: *The Steagle* (1971), Joe Dante's (another dedicatee) *Matinee* (1992), both set in the US; and *The Butcher Boy* (1995), set in Ireland, Kennedy's spiritual homeland. It was David J. Skal (another dedicatee) who pointed out that 1962 was the height of monster-worship, in his book *The Monster Show* (1993).

45. "Because They're Young:" Duane Eddy instrumental (#4, 1960). Theme music to the movie of the same name, starring Dick Clark.

46. fighting over groceries: this is in *Matinee*. This is also for real, too. People stayed home from work, got in their fallout shelters, etc. Leigh Kennedy wrote about it in her novel, *Saint Hiroshima*.

47. All the Russian ships: the news stuff I give for the bulk of the story is accurate. Up to a point...

48. Veronica and Angela Cartwright; hubba-hubba 12- and 13-year-old sister actresses *(Make Room for Daddy, The Birds)* in 1962 and hubba-hubba actress sisters now, too.

49. Hayley Mills: daughter of Sir John, sister of Juliet. Hubba-hubba at 12 in 1962, even more so now. Started with Disney. Tore a hole in the screen.

50. Six bits: that's 75¢ to you young whippersnappers. That was on a regular night. On "carload nights," usually

Monday and Tuesday, as many people as you could cram in or on a car got in for 50¢ for the whole load.

51. "My Boomerang Won't Come Back:" as it says (#21, 1962).

52. "Quiet Village:" instrumental by Martin Denny (#4, 1959).

53. give me 50¢: about what half this stuff would cost in 1962, without the box of Dots.

54. *Bride of the Gorilla* (1951), *Poor White Trash* (1957), *High School Confidential* (1958): this is a pretty spavined lineup even for a 1962 triple feature at a drive-in.

55. guy in a black hat: this is from *The Big Chill* (1983).

56. Peter Graves: Graves played Chris Cronyn, Stewart's dad, in *RPM*. (You have to watch me every minute.)

57. "Gazachstahagen:" instrumental by the Wild-Cats (#57, 1959).

58. always having trouble with gorillas: *Bride of the Gorilla* (1951); *Gorilla At Large* (3-D, 1953).

59. Larry Verne, "Please Mr. Custer (I Don't Wanna Go):" (#1, 1960).

60. Ben Colder, "Don't Go Near the Eskimoes" (#62, 1962). Ben Colder was Sheb Wooley, who had a hit in 1958 with "Purple People Eater" (#1). He was *supposed* to record "Don't Go Near the Indians," which became

a hit for Rex Allen (#17). *This* song was a parody of the one he should have recorded. Sheb Wooley's the second person you see in *High Noon* (1952) after Jack Elam. He's Frank Miller's brother, Ben.

61. oog-sook-mook: phonetic equivalent of the Eskimo chorus in this song.

62. 50¢ a gallon: gasoline was 22.9¢ a gallon in 1962.

63. "What in the World's Come Over You?": as it says (#5, 1960).

64. Okay, Mr. Philosophical: see *DTESS*, *RPM*, *TTG* for details.

65. roller skates: it was true. Also in *American Graffiti* (1973).

66. "The Girl of My Best Friend:" Ral Donner (#19, 1961).

67. He thought of Gramps: see *TTG*.

68. a bunch of teenagers in a circle: that would be Jim and Buzz with the knives. See *Rebel without a Cause* (1955). The Griffith Planetarium is used again at the climax of that movie; in *TTG* (1954), *Phantom from Space* (1953), *Invaders from Mars* (3-D, 1953); *War of the Colossal Beast* (1958), and is the nightclub in *Earth Girls Are Easy* (1989).

69. "Happy Birthday Sweet Sixteen:" as it says (#6, 1961).

70. "Midnight in Moscow:" instrumental, Kenny Ball and his Jazzmen (#2, 1962). An even better version was by the Village Stompers in 1965.

71. Macaroni: I'm not making this up. Millions of people were worried about what would happen to this horsie if WWIII started.

72. "Asia Minor" by Kokomo (#8, 1961): rock version of Grieg's Piano Concerto in A (get it?) Minor.

73. "Beyond the Sea" by Bobby Darin (#6, 1960): this is Darin's version of Charles Trenet's "La Mer" in 1945.

74. "Guided Missile (Aimed at My Heart):" 1961.

75. ♂♀✳†∞: The symbols drawn on the blackboard at the opening of every episode of *Ben Casey*. "Man. Woman. Birth, Death. Infinity." would intone Dr. Zorba, head of neurosurgery. Dr. Zorba was played by Sam Jaffe. Jaffe also played Professor Barnhardt in *DTESS*. (You have to watch me every minute.)

76. kim-chee: only Koreans, or people in California, would know what kim-chee was in 1962.

77. "Monster Mash:" Bobby "Boris" Pickett, #1 the week of the Cuban Missile Crisis. See Skal's *The Monster Show*.

78. "I Remember You:" as it says.

79. "He's Not a Rebel:" as it says. We're doing the top 5 of the Cuban Missile Crisis Week 1962. Also next two songs.

80. "Last Date:" instrumental, Floyd Cramer (#2, 1960).

81. *video portum:* "I see the port/home."

Helpful in the writing of this story: *That Old Time Rock and Roll: the chronicle of an era 1954-1963* by Richard Aquilla (1989); *The Billboard Book of #1 Hits* by Fred Bronson (1985 edn.); *The Golden Age of Novelty Songs* by Steve Otfinoski (1999). And of course dedicatee Bill Warren's *Keep Watching the Skies: American Science Fiction Movies of the 1950s:* Vol. one: 1950-1957 (1982) & Vol. two: 1958-1962 (1986).

Afterword to "The Other Real World"

As far as I know (I haven't finished the original for this book yet, so I *may* be wrong) this was the hardest story I've written in more than 20 years. ("The Ugly Chickens" was *no picnic,* let me tell you…)

And again, it was written for Eileen Gunn at InfiniteMatrix.com but ended up with Ellen Datlow at Scifi.com. That wasn't the hard part, that's just what happened.

⁂

I started making notes for this on Washington's Birthday, 2000 AD, and didn't complete the first draft till December 4, and finished the rewrites on Pearl Harbor Day. That's too long.

⁂

The old cliche question you get asked is: Where do your ideas come from? And your answer, after 35 years of writing is still, *I don't know.* Sometimes you can point to a piece of research, or someone's chance phrase, or just a feeling you get one day walking down a street.

Usually, your mind's working on a story while you're not, and it just starts swimming up to the front part of the brain from the lizard level, or wherever it's been. Then you can do something about it, like *think* about writing it, and you start looking in the right places for what you need.

One day I asked myself: "What happened to all those kids from 50s SF movies, afterwards?"

This is not an astonishingly original idea. I knew that David Thomson, the film guy, wrote two novels, *Suspects* and *Silver Light,* one dealing with lots of film characters after their movies (I hear Ilsa Lund from *Casablanca* died in the plane crash that killed Dag Hammerschöld, etc.); the other with characters from classic Western movies (Cherry Valance from *Red River* is the father of Liberty Valance from *that* movie…). He wrote those in the late 80s, I think.

More specifically, the idea came to me in the form of: What happened to those movie kids during the Cuban Missile Crisis?

I absolutely knew Gadge would be in it—that's because of Bill Warren telling, in his great, definitive 2-volume *Keep Watching the Skies!,* which is about all the SF films of the 1950s, of someone stealing the original Tobor the Great from out in front of the salvage shop where a guy had bought it (unseen) at an auction—Warren asked what if some kid who'd fallen in love with the movie just couldn't resist the temptation, and had it somewhere still? (One of the places the story started from was a caper involving stealing Tobor back for Gadge…)

I was thinking about this. I was sitting on a rock in the Sauk River, changing flies, and David E. Myers was out in the water up to his ass, releasing another damn 15-lb. coho or something, and I asked him who his favorite kid from 50s SF movies was.

"Bobby Benson," he said, "from *The Day the Earth Stood Still.*" Then he grunted and set the hook and started playing a ten-pound Dolly Varden or something that had bit his Green Butt Black Bear.

That made two. About an hour later the third (set) came to me: the two brothers from *Red Planet Mars* (1952), a truly awful movie.

I knew it would be in California, that there'd be woodies and surfing, and like in Joe Dante's *Matinee,* copies of *Famous Monsters of Filmland,* and the Aurora plastic model monster kits, the first three of which had just hit the shelves in the fall of 1962.

I knew also there'd be music, and that the song titles would be the section titles, and would have something to do with what was going on at the time, just like in *American Graffiti*, which was set six weeks before the Missile Crisis.

∞∞∞∞

For those of you who weren't born at the time: you can't imagine what the Cuban Missile Crisis was like. See *Matinee* for a start—it's *all* there, the runs on the grocery stores, fallout shelter paranoia, the feeling that it would All Be Over that week. Or the made-for-TV version of *The Missiles of October.* Or read Leigh Kennedy's *Saint Hiroshima* which has a harrowing fall-out-shelter sequence. Or talk to some oldster who was there....

And I'd read David J. Skal's *The Monster Show* where it was he who pointed out that the #1 song the week of the Missile Crisis was Bobby "Boris" Pickett's "Monster Mash."

Things started to fall into place. And at some point you sit down in front of the TV and grind the still/pause button on the VCR to mush, picking up stuff from the films. And fun though all this is, at some point you have to sit down in the chair and write the goddam thing...

I sent this, as I said, to Eileen Gunn at InfiniteMatrix.com, who loved it, but for complex and uninteresting reasons, couldn't give me a contract or pay me, because some of the backers were flip-flopping, or *something,* I never knew what. ("That's why they're called backers, Eileen," I said. "They back out.") I would have let her hang on to it longer, but after three months, she felt bad and sent it back, because at the time, *nothing* was happening. (I think it's okay *now.*) I sent it to Ellen Datlow at Scifi.com, who bought it of course immediately. She also wanted The Explicated "The Other Real World" to put up with it, to answer anybody's questions ahead of time, so I got to do that to show how much work went into it. (As I said before: "I suffered for *my* art. Now it's *your* turn.") It went up on the site July 18, 2001.

This one came hard. I think it was worth it.

ᴏᴏᴏᴏᴏ

Life's little ironies: While I was writing this, "The Other Real World," my friend Steven Utley, unbeknownst-like, was writing a story called "The Real World." We told each other *that* in letters that crossed each other, the same week. Coincidence, or what?

$\mathbb{D} = \mathbb{R} \times \mathbb{T}$

1, 2, Buckle My Shoe

There were two clubhouses behind the abandoned gas station, under the sign that said G.M.H.-M.R.C., which stood for the Greater Mayfield He-Man Racing Club.

One clubhouse was a 10 x 12 thing, the usual shed-roofed cube, made of 1 x 2s, 2 x 4s, pieces of plywood and old Ralston-Purina feed signs. The whole thing was colored red-orange. The paint had been kyped from the county equipment yard the year before.

Outside the door was usually parked three pedal-cars—a Big Dump Truck from Sears, painted blue with a black bed; a Sears Sleek Sports Car, blue and white with silver trim; and a Gendron Speed Boat, with a yacht watch-bell and a 48-star flag, stained cedar on the wood, with silver aluminum trim. On the outside of the bright orange clubhouse had been lettered the words NO GIRLƧ ALLOWED, just like in the *Little Lulu Comics*.

Thirty feet away, across the driveway, twelve feet up in a big oak tree was the other clubhouse, 8 x 10 with a big doorway facing west and a slider window on the east side. The treehouse was painted dark brown. Parked under the tree usually was a Garton 1949 Mercury Wagon with wooden sides, light green hood and chrome bumpers. There was a 3-piece collapsible ladder leading up from the ground that could be swung up over the doorway when someone was inside. Lettered across the side of the treehouse were the words *SOME* GIRLS ALLOWED.

∞∞∞

The Big Dump Truck belonged to Croupie, a short kid with a burr haircut who wheezed like a steam engine when he played hard or got excited, and usually had a fit of low coughs that echoed like he was in a silo, only he wasn't.

The Gendron Speedboat was Beanpole's. He had turned nine years old on April Fool's Day, 1953, and he was already five feet seven and a half inches tall and weighed sixty-four pounds. He hadn't grown an inch or added a pound since he was seven. He had the Speedboat because the front was open, and his knees, up around his ears when he pedalled, didn't bang into the sides of the thing, like with all the other pedal-cars he'd tried.

The Sears Sleek Sports Car, a long low thing, more than 42 inches front to back, was Sankandank's. That wasn't his real name, but the closest his little brother could come to Henry Franklin when he started to talk.

For that matter none of their names were their real ones, but nobody but teachers and their mom's and dad's friends called them by their real names.

The fourth kid's real name was Osbert Sitwell Forbes but everybody knew him as Sticks. He'd had polio when he was five, and had been retrained to walk with braces and two aluminum crutches like some kind of clattering metal spider, and he could do it faster than most kids could run. He didn't have a pedal-car; he rode on the back of Croupie's Big Dump Truck and helped by bringing his crutches down in a sort of two-point lever action, rowing, as it were, against the pavement. They could make some real speed even though there were two of them. Sticks had turned himself into a human gorilla from the waist up in the five years since they'd told his parents he would *never* walk again, even with braces and crutches.

The Garton Mercury Wagon belonged to Dave, the leader of the G.M.H.-M.R.C. He had built the treehouse. He was always dressed in a flight jacket and an aviator's brown leather helmet, a T-shirt, blue jeans and boots. The Mercury woodie was his everyday car; he'd saved his quarter weekly allowance for four months to buy it from a kid across town. His real car, which he only took out for races, wasn't a car at all—it was a 1941 Steelcraft Pursuit Plane painted dark green, held back by an uncle from a 1942 scrap-metal drive. It had three wheels—two at the front and one at the rear, and a 4-foot wingspan. When you pedaled it, which Dave did with such ferocity that he was the fastest kid in town, the silver-painted propeller on the nose spun.

∞∞∞

There were two girls in the neighborhood.

Sally was one of the boys, but she couldn't go into the regular clubhouse. "What good is it being one of the boys," she'd asked, "if I can't go in there?"

"Because biology is destiny," said Sticks, who'd read his share of thinkers, somewhat apologetically. "Sorry."

She was their mascot, and an honorary member, and a swell mechanic. She dressed in a pair of cut-down overalls and wore one of those stupid hats with the buttons all over it like Jughead in *Archie's Pals and Gals*, or the Bowery Boys. She kept all the cars in good repair except Dave's Pursuit Plane. He was the only one who worked on it. He kept it in a packing-crate hangar back at his parent's house.

And then there was Therese.

∞∞∞

She was the nine-year-old equivalent of a society dame.

Whereas Sally's hair was mousy-brown, that of Therese was wheat-blond, almost white. What eyebrows she had were so light that she had to draw others above them. (She already used makeup.) Her eyes were as blue as the paint on a real DeSoto convertible. She was really something.

Her parents had come down a little in the world since the War, but they still lived in the biggest house for miles around, and she still had her rich-girl clothes. She was the first in town to have a poodle-skirt and cat-eye sunglasses.

When you fell for Therese, you fell hard, and they all did. All except Dave followed her around like baby ducks when she walked through the neighborhood or rode her English Racer bike, the first seen in Mayfield. Dave watched from a distance, but he watched.

∞∞∞

Sometimes Dave and Sally went up into the treehouse and pulled the ladder up behind them. Croupie, Beanpole, Sankandank and Sticks imagined all sorts of things going on, from their place over in the other clubhouse.

Sometimes Dave and Sally fooled around a little bit; sometimes they kissed till they got bored with it. Mostly they lay around on the cushions and pillows and read *Monster of Frankenstein* and *Airboy* and *Vault of Horror* comic books, or old *Popular Mechanics*. They just used it as a place to get away from everything.

And there always came a time, late in the day, just before everyone left or was called away to supper, when Dave stood in the doorway, silhouetted by the setting sun, with the evening wind in his hair, and holding his leather helmet in his hand, and he would take out a Lucky Stripe candy cigarette and put it in his mouth, and enjoy the last one of the day. He would think on the lost days of his youth, and stub the cigarette out till it broke with a crack, and toss it out onto the pile in the driveway. Then he would unfold the ladder, and help Sally down if she were there, or let himself down, and pedal his way home, if he knew his father wasn't drunk, or go over to Sankandank's house if he knew he was, and either stay there all night, or go home when his mom sent word that his dad was already passed out.

3, 4, Close the Door

Into every idyll a little *merde* must fall.

∞∞∞

It was summer and it was hot. The days were long and filled with as much ennui as anyone could handle. Any kid with sense and money was down at the movies where it was 3° cooler inside, watching *Phantom from Space* or *The Beast from 20,000 Fathoms*, or best of all, the pee-inducing *Invad-*

ers from Mars, the one with the sand opening up at your feet and the big furry green Martians grabbing you from below.

The swimming pools were all closed because of another polio scare.

If you were lucky you had TV (only Beanpole's folks did, and it was a used Dumont with an 11" screen, and Beanpole's dad was always watching *Roller Derby* or *Wrestling from the Jamaica Arena* and stuff.)

What they had at the clubhouse were two radios, one in the regular clubhouse, and via a long cord buried under the driveway and up the back of the tree, another radio up in the treehouse. (They'd found the electricity to the old garage had never been cut off, and they'd run cords from one of the plugs inside to the regular clubhouse.)

Well, music sucked, except when they played something old, like "Sing, Sing, Sing!" by Benny Goodman, or "Big Noise from Winnetka." What was on the radio these days was Patti Page, or Guy Mitchell (who *tried*, anyway), stuff like that. Over on the end of the dial was the whiny honky-tonk hillbilly noise.

One morning while Dave was up in the treehouse, he heard sounds like he'd never heard before. He leaned out. "What's *that?*" he yelled.

Croupie stuck his head out the clubhouse window. "Wow!" he said. "870 on the AM dial! Listen to *that!*"

Since the radio in the treehouse only got AM, Dave twisted the Bakelite knob over. It was scratchy, far away, from one of the big cities. There were four or five voices in it, a bass, two or three middles, a high one. The music came in and out on a wave of static, and then a voice—a Negro voice—told him that had been Billy Ward and the Dominoes singing "Sixty-Minute Man." Then they played a whole other song called "Lightning Hit the Poorhouse."

Dave climbed down the ladder and pedalled away in the Mercury woodie wagon. He came back ten minutes later with a hundred foot roll of 8 gauge wire, and made antennae for both radios, so the static came in much clearer at first, and *then* the station. It was their favorite radio station in the whole world. Sankandank had a strong desire to break off the tuning knob once they had the music coming in strong.

That was *all* that happened the first half of the summer of 1953.

∞∞∞∞∞

One day Croupie, Beanpole and Sankandank were going down Paradise Street—Sankandank first in the Sleek Sports Car, Beanpole in his Speedboat and Croupie in the Big Dump Truck—when something went by with a flash and whir and the zizz of sprockets and made an inertialess turn at the next alley.

5, 6, Pick Up Sticks

"There's a New Blur in town," said Sankandank, "Geez!"

"It gleams in the sun," said Croupie. "It's *fast!*"

"It's got a chain drive," said Beanpole.

"Chain drives are for wusses." said Dave, putting out his Lucky Stripe on the back of his hand and tossing it away. "Guys come, guys go. Fast, not so fast."

"But, Dave," said Sankandank. "He's, I mean, *fast!*"

"There's good and fast," said Dave, "and then there's fast and *stupid.* We'll see."

ooooo

Sally was walking up a sloping street with Sticks, who was clattering and pinging his way along in sort of a loose slow-motion fall uphill. They were on their way to the clubhouse. Usually Croupie always came by to get Sticks earlier, but he hadn't been by this morning.

"You doing all right?" asked Sally.

"Whatever do you mean?" asked Sticks.

"Never mind."

And out of nowhere, in the bright sunny morning, there was a flash and streak, and the skidding sound of brakes locking, and a vision strobed to a stop in front of them.

They stood looking at him, and while they did a B-36 flew over, headed for the North Pole. Aside from its faraway drone, there was no sound at all.

Sally saw that the machine he was on was a Murray Ohio Custom Atomic Missile—it sold for $28.95 in the Western Auto catalog; the newest and most expensive pedal-car made. It was three-wheeled; unlike Dave's Pursuit Plane, on this, the wings and two wheels were in the back. The nose was streamlined like an F-80 Shooting Star, and it had a high tailfin over the back wings. There were jet nacelles on the outer tips of the wings. The nose above the front wheel was tilted upward, the steering wheel was a single molded piece of black plastic, and the pedals and cranks went into a smooth molded casing; there was probably a 6 to 1 chain drive. It was sky-blue and red; it said Supersonic, with a lightning bolt through it on the nose, and on the tailfin was the Atomic Symbol.

The guy wore a Captain Video fishbowl space helmet, with the inflatable collar and the open lower third. Inside the helmet, over his eyes, were a pair of *Bwana Devil* 3-D glasses. He wore an outfit that could only be described as Early Buck Rogers.

"Call me Rocket Boy," he said.

And was gone. Just like that, although he must have taken *some* small space of time to do it.

Sticks just sat down in the middle of the sidewalk. Sally sat down beside him.

They didn't say anything for a while. The world had changed, as if the Lady of Fatima had come to them, or King Kong had leaned around a building to look at them...

Then they got up and went on to the clubhouse.

∞∞∞∞

They didn't have long to wait. The next afternoon around 2 pm, Dave was in the treehouse listening to the rhythm and blues station. There was a skidding sound and the radio went off.

He went to the doorway and looked down, throwing his *Walt Disney's Comics and Stories* back on the pile. Croupie, Sticks and Sankandank were leaning out the clubhouse window.

The guy was there. Dave couldn't see his face for the reflection off the globe of the helmet. The machine was as beautiful and overpowering as the others had said.

Rocket Boy looked up at Dave.

"Thrill Hill," he said. "Noon Thursday."

And he took off, leaving a cloud of dust in the air. They heard his chain-drive over on the next block.

Croupie came out and reconnected the extension cord to the clubhouse where Rocket Boy had unplugged it. The radio came on behind Dave. Muddy Waters was singing "Another Mule Been Kickin' in Your Stall."

Beanpole pedalled into the drive before the dust settled.

"Did I miss anything?" he asked.

"You missed Rocket Boy," said Sankandank.

"When?"

"A minute ago."

"How can that be?" asked Beanpole. "I was gonna tell you guys I just saw him at the store, talking to Therese."

"When?"

"Just now, the time it takes to get back here."

"Are there *two* of him," asked Sticks, "or is he really just that *fast?*"

They all looked up at Dave.

7, 8, You're Too Late

Rocket Boy must be out of his crawfishing mind.

Thrill Hill was where they held the Soap Box Derby every year, and it was a killer, even with the traffic blocked off, and the padded barricades. Guys fifteen and sixteen years old couldn't make it up that hill on their ten-speed English Racers without standing up on the pedals. Cars had to come in low gear all the way up. There was no need for the 20 mph sign on *that* side of the road.

On the left side looking down, you had vacant lots, except halfway down there was Mean Old Man Rebers' house. He didn't even like kids walking on that side of the street. On the other you had ten or twelve houses. The hill had three plateaus—one each at Fleagle, Susquehana and Niagara Streets. The hill looked like the top third of the State Fair roller coaster. If you came up on the intersection of Romeo Street—which the hill was on—and Juliette

Blvd.—at the top—and looked down too fast you'd get vertigo and the world would swing and sway.

At the bottom was the yellow and black octagonal stop-sign where Romeo Street dead-ended onto Highway 4, with traffic going by at 50 mph. Across the highway was a pit full of water where they'd dug the gravel to pave Highway 4.

"Put out the word," said Dave. "This is going to take some planning." The G.M.H.-M.R.C. took off in four directions, Sally taking his woodie wagon, while he walked home to go get his 1941 Steelcraft Pursuit Plane and bring it back to the clubhouse.

ထထထ

Since his dad was out of work and home all time, Dave had to be quiet.

He unlocked the big generator-crate hangar and opened the double-doors back wide. His pedal-plane gleamed in the bright sunlight as he rolled it out. Once it had been the shiniest, best-looking pedal-craft in town, and the fastest.

Now it seemed a little duller-looking, and he wasn't so sure about the fast part, either.

When he'd first got it, three years ago when his uncle had given it to him (his cousin had died the year before *that*), he'd restored it to a like-new 1941 condition, and he'd kept it in that shape since. When something went wrong, he'd gone to the White's Auto Store (they still handled Steelcraft though that had been bought by another company) and got the part on order. (So far that had been one front wheel hubcap that took a whole week to get there.)

His Pursuit Plane had one big disadvantage. In most pedal-cars the pedals were connected to the rear wheels by rods; the pedals went back and forth on cranks connected by the rods to cranks on the rear axles. In Dave's plane, the two front wheels did the work; the pedals were directly on the two big offset-cranks of the front axle, one down, one up, on slip-fastenings. You needed a lot of knee-room, and you had to pedal straight up-and-down, and it was slower to get moving from a standing start.

Rocket Boy, with his chain drive, would get a lead on him before they got to Fleagle St. and the first flat plateau, where Dave could gain some. But he didn't know if he could gain enough. If Rocket Boy were still ahead at Susquehana, it was all over.

Dave let out a sigh, and pushed the Steelcraft Pursuit out beside the house and for more than a block before he got in it and rode, the propeller a soft wavering blur in front of him, to the clubhouse.

∞∞∞

"The way I see it," said Sticks, helping Dave stack up bricks and then putting old horse blankets over them, and lifting the front end of the plane, crutches braced against his armpits, while Dave took the back and lifted, and they put it on top of the bricks and blankets so it wouldn't get scratched, "is that you're the Alan Ladd of the piece. This Rocket Boy guy is Jack Palance. Or—you're Gary Cooper—Marshal Kane, and he's Frank Miller—*hey, loss*—" Sticks was a bigger movie fan even than Dave. "I mean—you're minding your own business, and he comes along..."

"I can see the fargin' allegory," said Dave. "Please hand me the oil can and the emery cloth."

∞∞∞

Two hours later, he pushed the pedals back and forth like a maniac and had Sankandank time it once he let go. It was one minute and 17 seconds before the wheels came to a stop.

"Wow!" said Sankandank.

"Not wow enough," said Dave. Then he started working on the rear wheel.

∞∞∞

Wednesday evening. Dave had done all he could. Word had been coming in all day—Rocket Boy seen here, Rocket Boy seen there. Somebody said he'd been down at the Rocket to the Moon Ride at the Piggly-Wiggly, with a handful of nickels, training, which Sticks thought was hooey, and so did Croupie.

Somebody else said he'd been seen riding very slowly, talking to Therese as she walked along Paradise Street. Dave didn't think that was hooey.

The sun was going down; everybody else had gone home for supper. It was cooler, but that was no satisfaction. The store had been out of Lucky Stripes so he'd had to settle for a Pink Owl Bubblegum Cigar. This one had lost all its flavor; he stubbed it out on his overall leg and threw it onto the chalky pile of broken Luckys.

Earlier today he'd walked down, then up, Thrill Hill. The way he figured it, he'd be 15 missile-lengths back when they crossed Highway 4. Things were too grim.

He wished, like in *The Day the Earth Stood Still*, there were some words, some phrase that would stop everything, make it right again, put it all back like it was before. He wanted to stand in front of Rocket Boy, hold up his hand, and say magic words that would make everything *status quo ante*.

He turned in the direction of Thrill Hill, a mile away.

He said *"Klaatu barada nikto."*

The earth kept turning. Night came on. It was still going to happen.

ooooo

Dawn on Thursday.

He was oiling everything for the twentieth time when he heard the slow squeak of wheels he didn't know out on the street.

Sally came around the corner of the garage, pulling her little brother's Western Flyer wagon. It was full of window sash-weights, sheet tin, a blowtorch and dark goggles.

She pulled it up next to the Pursuit up on the blocks.

She handed him a pack of Lucky Stripes.

"Where'd you get these?" he asked.

"Havemeyers," she said.

That was all the way across town.

"Thanks," he said, and had the first one of the day.

She didn't say anything.

"What am I supposed to do with *this* stuff?" he asked.

She looked at him.

"You know I've kept the Pursuit like-new," he said. "You know I've never altered anything on it. Me, it and the world. I won't start *now*."

She put her hands on his shoulders.

"This isn't a movie. This isn't a race, even," she said. "This is murder, plain and simple."

He looked at her a minute, then put on the dark goggles and lit the blowtorch. "Hand me some tin." he said.

9, 10, The Big Fat Hen

The news of what was going to happen had gone through the kids like a hurricane through the Sargasso-summer doldrums.

They were milling around up and down Thrill Hill, but in lumps of five and ten; more were at the top and bottom.

Officer Handy drove by and knew something was up. He stopped near a bunch on the left side of the road just past the Rebers place.

"What's up, kids?" he asked. "And don't lie to me."

"We're looking for four-leaf clovers!" said a girl named Paula. "Ricky Lee found one here this morning!" All the kids immediately got down on their hands and knees and started crawling around.

"Yeah, right." said Officer Handy. "Make sure you stay out of the road." He drove off.

This was reported up the hill, where Dave and Rocket Boy were out of sight.

"We're ready," said Beanpole, listening to the war-surplus walkie-talkie. Sticks was down at the bottom with the other one.

Dave ran his Pursuit out from the left, Rocket Boy from the right. Standing at the top of the hill was Therese, a red silk kerchief in her hand.

Dave could see, way down at the bottom, kids running around putting plywood over the curbs across from the intersection on the highway. Cars were still turning out from Fleagle and Susquehana and going downhill. The kids were still off to the sides of the streets.

"Any time you gentlemen are ready," said Beanpole.

"Let's do her," said Dave.

They lined up even with each other, ten feet apart. Therese was just a little downhill, between the two. She lifted the red scarf.

Dave could see kids running everywhere, to stand across the three side streets, down at the highway brakes squealed. He couldn't see what was going on. He pulled his goggles down.

Rocket Boy leaned his helmet toward him. "Eat my protons," he said.

Therese dropped the scarf.

They went by her. Then a lot of stuff happened at once, but it started out in very slow motion.

It was like pedaling in molasses the first few feet, there was so much weight in the Pursuit. Rocket Boy moved like a bullet, getting smaller. Then Dave's pedals caught up, began to feel right. But the Pursuit felt wrong, most of the weight was in the middle and back; there wasn't that much in the front as that was taken up by the pedal-throw and the propeller gearing. The plane pulled to the right.

Rocket Boy's feet blurred on the pedals and he moved further ahead, nearing the Fleagle intersection, where kids had linked their arms all the way across the sidestreet.

Rocket Boy's Atomic Missile hit the flat and rose, like a champ he came down with his pedals still flying.

Dave's Pursuit had started to really begin to move, as fast as he was usually going about fifty feet into a race, and he was already a third of the way down.

He hit Fleagle, rose, came down on the far edge of the flat, still in control of his pedals. The propeller was whining like a banshee.

Rocket Boy was forty feet ahead; Dave could see the kids from Fleagle running into the middle of Romeo behind them to watch.

The whine of the propeller rose higher; it was strobing in the noon sun.

Rocket Boy moved further away.

And then Dave noticed the whine was getting nearer. He turned his head quickly to the left. Officer Handy was coming down the hill behind them, sirens on, red bubblegum machine lights on top whirling away, flashing red and white. He was waving them over.

Dave pedaled faster than he ever had.

Rocket Boy bent forward and hit Susquehana, only his nose wheel touching the pavement.

The intersection came up and lifted Dave and the Pursuit over it; it was all he could do to keep his feet on the pedals.

He heard Handy brake, take the hump, and speed up behind and to his left.

The Atomic Missile was shuddering ahead, just before Niagara; it moved left and right and pulled ahead again, taking the intersection two feet off the ground.

The Pursuit was running like a whale sideways to a typhoon, trying to go right from the weight. Niagara came and went; so did the propeller—with a ping it was gone somewhere to the left.

He heard a big pop, and the squeal of Handy's brakes, a slide and a soft bump.

Then he was even with Rocket Boy, whose legs were a round blur, and he saw the instant Rocket Boy lost his pedals—he'd lifted his feet off them to keep his ankles from getting beaten up. As Dave shot past Rocket Boy he heard the awful sound of a chain leaving a sprocket and getting ground up around the rear axle.

Dave broke the finish line string they were holding at the highway—it was like a cobweb—and shot across the highway, hit the plywood, rose, came down on grass and weeds, broke a wing, turned sideways and shuddered to a stop.

Just in time to see Rocket Boy go by upside down, three feet in the air, moving away from the upside-down Atomic Missile and go over the lip of the quarry, to make two Edgerton-slow splashes, like twin Royal Crowns of England.

And then people were picking him up, and the Pursuit, and someone was fishing Rocket Boy and his water-filled globe helmet out of the water, and kids were running in every direction but up.

And from Dave's upside-down view he saw an upside-down tiny Officer Handy jumping down-and-up in the middle of the Niagara Street sky, shaking his tiny fists at them all as they disappeared into the bushes and trees.

ꙨꙨꙨ

Rocket Boy, after being left coughing at Third and Main, was never seen again. Somebody said he'd only been visiting his grandmother for the week anyway.

The Atomic Missile was way at the bottom of the quarry, and stayed there.

Therese came to the clubhouse and invited Dave to her birthday party.

He said, "Maybe."

Then he handed Sally a bucket of orange-red enamel and a brush.

She walked over and painted out the NO GIRLꙄ AL-LOWED letters.

Afterword to "D = R × T"

I asked myself a few months ago: could I write an existential pedal-car story?

I think so.

∞∞∞

It started out way long ago as an entirely different story: a Fitzgeraldian thing about reward and loss, that is, Earth after the aliens have Come. And Gone, leaving us just another backwater tourist-trap of a middling planet around a so-so star.

You know, middle-period Silverberg-land. But Bob had been there before—"Passengers," "Schwartz among the Galaxies," "When We Went to See the End of the World." All great, all done 30 years ago and about as well as they could be, by a human being, anyway.

My instincts told me *not* to go *there*.

Like with "The Other Real World," the starting image I'd had was a guy on the beach, only then I knew it was the Pacific, and the guy was Bobby Benson. This one was a guy on the beach, only it was some Atlantic City/Coney Island-type place, near a waterfront amusement park, now old and ratty, only on the boardwalk were upright squids, 4-eyed mutants, things like that. (If you write this stuff long enough, these are the kinds of images that come to you *all the time*. Trust me.)

Well, I didn't write *that* story.

∞∞∞

Howard Waldrop

I've used pedal-cars in stories before; in this collection's "US"—see the Call Me Chucky section, and in the early '90s story "Why Did?"—the fabled Little Moron story—where an inmate who thinks he's Otto Soglow's Little King pedals his way from the (true) Funny Farm to the psychiatrist's downtown office to deliver the rebus. (The story's in my last collection, *Going Home Again*.)

Pedal-cars started being made as soon as real ones were, the early *last* '00s. At first they looked like soap-box racers—a hoodlike thing, a seat, a steering wheel and some pedals (but then, the Model T Ford looked pretty much like *that*, too.) It wasn't until cars started being styled that pedal-cars were, too. And, as with real auto manufacturers, at first nearly every toy and bike-maker turned out some kind of pedal-car—some were generic, some licensed by actual automakers. By the end—the 1960s—there were only a couple of companies still making them. (Now, they're battery-powered jeeps and Hummers and Barbie play-cars that require *no* pedaling at all.)

The heyday was from the 20s to the 50s, and they took astounding forms: every kind of car, truck, tractor, fire truck and ambulance ever made. After Lindbergh's flight: planes (there were many *Spirit of St. Louis*-looking ones), bombers, fighters, *zeppelins*. There were locomotives, boats and submarines. Beginning in the late 1940s: jets, missiles and spaceships. You couldn't walk down a sidewalk without getting your knees knocked off by some 3-foot-high pedaling demon—kids were as car, plane and speed-obsessed as their parents were.

∞∞∞∞∞

If you have pedal-cars you need kids, and this is where the existential part comes in, leftover from the Fitzgerald-type story I'd originally meant to write.

272

The reason film short (and comic-book) kid stories *still* work is that (except for the wartime MGM ones) things like The Little Rascals (Our Gang) series were set in a no-time kind of place—their concerns were local and kid-specific. The bullies (Butch and Woim) are always with us; mean old men still run orphanages; mean old men still build future slums on the Gang's vacant ballfield; Petey still ends up in doggie Auschwitz with no money to bail him out; somebody's always wishing their little brother Cotton was a monkey; kids are *always* searching for pirate treasure…

Or, in *Little Lulu Comics,* the gang—Tubby (when he's not it his guise as The Spider), Alvin and Iggy stay in their clubhouse trying to thwart the nonexistent designs of Little Lulu to co-ed up the place (a lot like the Augusta Golf Club—I'm waiting for someone to paint NO GIRL2 ALLOWED on it). Or, as in one episode, they set out to play a trick on Lulu, and, in John Stanley's totally logical, and with step-by-step complication they end up 1) in diapers 2) in the middle of the intersection of First and Main 3) at high noon 4) in a little red wagon covered with a sheet 5) in front of a cop who pulls the sheet off in front of 6) 3/4 the adult population of the town. Trust me.

These are kid-things. They could have happened in 1912; they could happen *tomorrow* (though not without some semiotic and metafictional connotations…).

∞∞∞

I knew I had to have a period-specific story, because certain pedal-cars weren't built before a certain time. I wanted *a lot* of cultural baggage. I wanted a *Shane*-like confrontation (Jack Palance is Alan Ladd turned inside out, Shane gone over to the Dark Side of the Force), only this time The Cool Guy meets The Coolest. You might say this was a prefiguration of the Beach Boys' "Don't Worry, Baby" ten years before Brian Wilson wrote the song.

Howard Waldrop

Before I started this, I thought "The Other Real World" was the hardest story I'd done in decades. On this one, I hit The Wall, so I'm not so sure anymore.

Besides, I needed to use those wasted kid hours *trying to get up,* and then, *trying to stop coming down* Pantego Hill, on a 3-speed English Racer stuck in high gear, with no brakes so I had to stop it by jamming my tennis shoe sole onto the back tire. Try *that* at 74 kph….

Acknowledgments